Jo's smile faded . . .

"I'm warning you, Gray. I haven't changed my mind about rodeo sports, and if you're getting my boy involved in something like that and he gets hurt, I want you to know that I'll never forgive you. Never."

"Joanna McLean," Gray murmured, his voice suddenly husky, "if you were to get mad at me and never forgive me, I don't know if I could stand it."

Jo gazed up at him, stunned and almost frightened by the look of hunger that flared in his face and the depth of longing in his darkly lashed eyes. "Gray," she murmured in protest as he tugged her gently toward him and drew her into the shadow cast by the open door of his pick-up. Then his lips were on hers, and her words were stilled, drowned in a wave of yearning that swept over her and left her numb and weak. . . .

The Bookstore
5065 Forest Hill Ave.
Richmond, Va. 23225
Paperback Book Exchange
Over 55,000 Books

ABOUT THE AUTHOR

"Oh, it's beautiful here," says Margot Dalton when asked about her new home in British Columbia. "Our house sits up on a bench of land, and we have a view of low, rounded mountains that look all blue in the distance. And, of course, spring comes a month earlier here.... But still, sometimes I find myself yearning for the prairies, for the flatness and the space and the scent of sagebrush. I grew up on the prairies and lived there all my life until now, so I guess I'll always miss them, and I'll visit them often—at least in my books."

Books by Margot Dalton

HARLEQUIN SUPERROMANCE
401–UNDER PRAIRIE SKIES

Don't miss any of our special offers. Write to us at the following address for information on our newest releases.

Harlequin Reader Service
901 Fuhrmann Blvd., P.O. Box 1397, Buffalo, NY 14240
Canadian address: P.O. Box 603,
Fort Erie, Ont. L2A 5X3

Sagebrush and Sunshine

MARGOT DALTON

Harlequin Books

TORONTO • NEW YORK • LONDON
AMSTERDAM • PARIS • SYDNEY • HAMBURG
STOCKHOLM • ATHENS • TOKYO • MILAN

Published October 1990

ISBN 0-373-70425-9

Copyright © 1990 by Margot Dalton. All rights reserved.
Except for use in any review, the reproduction or utilization
of this work in whole or in part in any form by any electronic,
mechanical or other means, now known or hereafter invented,
including xerography, photocopying and recording,
or in any information storage or retrieval system, is forbidden without
the permission of the publisher, Harlequin Enterprises Limited,
225 Duncan Mill Road, Don Mills, Ontario, Canada M3B 3K9.

All the characters in this book have no existence outside the
imagination of the author and have no relation whatsoever to
anyone bearing the same name or names. They are not even
distantly inspired by any individual known or unknown to the
author, and all incidents are pure invention.

® are Trademarks registered in the United States Patent and
Trademark Office and in other countries.

Printed in U.S.A.

CHAPTER ONE

THE SKY WAS GRAY and brooding, and a threatening bank of clouds along the western horizon obscured the setting sun. The wind, biting cold and increasing steadily, howled and whistled across the bleakness of the prairie, driving tumbleweeds that rolled and massed against the barbed wire fences. The temperature plummeted, and snow, driven by the wind, began to fall in tiny flakes as sharp and stinging as bits of ice.

On the open range cattle moved out, drifting with their tails to the wind, seeking shelter from the coming storm. It was early April, and many of the cows already had calves at foot. They paused frequently to allow the small ones to nurse, knowing the calves would need their bellies full of milk if they were to survive the bitter night to come.

Darkness rolled in, covering the vastness of the land with a chilly blanket, and lights began to flicker on in isolated farmhouses and small towns along the highway. The graveled road leading out of one of these towns was starred with lights, like a necklace of rhinestones, as long lines of vehicles moved slowly out of the village. Most were pickup trucks, battered and dusty from covering too many miles in too little time, and most pulled double horse trailers behind them.

The town was Black Diamond, south of Calgary, and its annual spring rodeo, held indoors in the town's hockey arena, was just concluding. The long lines of vehicles belonged to the rodeo contestants, who had ridden their stock, pocketed their winnings—or absorbed their losses—loaded their horses and were now setting out for the next rodeo on the endless circuit.

One of the trucks paused briefly at the intersection leading out of town. It was a big dark blue Ford with a small camper fitted into the truck box and hay bales attached to the fenders of the horse trailer. Three men sat in the cab of the truck, all of them large, muscular and wearing broad-brimmed Stetsons. They were talking and arguing amiably as the truck pulled carefully out onto the main highway, allowing the horses in the trailer time to adjust to the turn, and then started off down the highway and into the gathering storm.

A fourth man was inside the truck camper, and feeling quite smug about it; riding in the camper was a privilege given to the man who'd won the most money at the rodeo. Graham Lyndon—known as "Gray" to his many friends—had won almost six hundred dollars, winning both the calf roping and the team roping. He was extremely pleased with the day behind him and with his present position.

I'll just turn this little heater up, he thought, and then I can take off these dirty clothes, climb into bed and sleep nice and cozy all the way home, while those poor guys are crowded into the front of the truck, listening to ol' Burt explain fifty times how he could've ridden that bull if he'd just tied his rope differently....

Gray chuckled, picturing the conversation, and stripped rapidly out of his dusty jeans and shirt, standing in his stockinged feet on the dirty linoleum floor of the tiny camper. Naked except for his shorts and socks, he paused to look down at his hairy, muscular body with brief approval.

Not bad for an old guy, he told himself. No big belly on this cowboy.

He peeled off his socks, as well, and crawled hastily into the bed of the camper, wincing at the coldness of the stale, musty sheets. But soon his body warmth and the little heater had warmed the small, enclosed space, and he felt himself growing deliciously comfortable, even a little drowsy. He lay on his back, hands behind his curly black head of hair that was frosted with silver at the temples. He grinned suddenly, his white teeth flashing in his tanned face, his gray eyes sparkling in crinkled lines as he lay smiling up at the ceiling, his big body adjusting easily to the soothing motion of the moving camper.

There was a big stain on the ceiling where rain had leaked in around the light fixture. Gray studied it, trying to see animals and birds in the ragged shape, just as he often did when watching the massed clouds in the prairie sky. The wind howled and shrieked around the corrugated metal edges of the camper, and as he listened to it, Gray's sense of well-being began to ebb away, leaving him a little melancholy.

Actually, he admitted to himself, things didn't seem to be as much fun anymore. This experience right now, for instance, riding in the cozy camper, with the good feeling of having won a lot of money at the rodeo—it would feel a lot better if he had someone to share it with.

Not, he realized, that he didn't have opportunities. These days women didn't make any secret of their feelings, and during the fifteen years he'd been a widower there had been no shortage of women who'd indicated they were entirely willing to share his life and work . . . and his bed.

Gray stirred restlessly. He remembered that the twins, Margaret and Elizabeth, had been just three years old when their mother had died, hardly able to understand what was happening. Gray had raised them, all alone, and it hadn't always been easy.

He grinned, thinking about Peggy and Libby. They were gone now, attending their first year of university at Calgary, and the ranch seemed desolate without them.

His grin faded, and he frowned a little, flexing his long legs restlessly. The truth, he admitted finally to himself, was that these days he was feeling a little lonely. He knew how much this would surprise anyone who knew him, especially his male friends, because he lived the kind of carefree life that all of them longed for. They saw him constantly surrounded by a laughing, happy crowd.

But sometimes, at moments like this one, Gray felt himself growing a little tired of everything. He wanted to stay home more, spend time in quiet pursuits, have somebody waiting for him when he got home, and sitting quietly by his fireside talking with him in the evening.

What Gray wanted, in fact, was a wife.

But at forty-two, wily and cautious after being pursued so much and wary after seeing the miserable marriages of so many of his friends, he wondered where he could ever find the right woman.

Not that he didn't know what he wanted. He knew exactly what kind of woman he was looking for. He had just given up hope that she existed. Gray wanted a woman he could confide in, someone he could tell all about the secret things inside him, and know that she wouldn't laugh at him or, worse, look at him as if he were crazy.

Gray's secrets weren't anything earth-shattering or damaging. They were just things that mattered to him, and he would like to meet a woman who cared enough to listen to them. His first wife hadn't, he realized. They'd had a good partnership and had gotten along pretty well, but there were things about himself that Gray had never told another living soul.

Like, for instance, that he was so terrified of spiders that he felt paralyzed with fear if he even suspected there might be a spider somewhere in the room. Try telling *that* to a cute girl you've just met at the bar!

Or babies. There was something about babies that made Gray feel all weak and shaky with tenderness. Looking at a little baby asleep in its crib with its teddy bear cuddled up beside its face was enough to reduce him almost to tears.

And then there were his fantasies...like riding on a camel. Gray had never told another single person how he'd always longed to ride a camel across a desert, feeling the gentle, easy rocking of the majestic beast under him, and seeing the acres of sand shimmering under a blazing sun...

He smiled drowsily, thinking partly about himself, riding the camel, and partly about the faceless woman, somewhere, who would love him enough to care about his wistful fancies....

Outside, the storm increased and snow began to fall in earnest, whipped and driven in front of the howling wind. The spring blizzard snarled around the edges of the little camper, making Gray feel cozy and secure in his tiny cocoon of warmth. Lulled by the easy swaying motion and tired by the day of activity behind him, he burrowed into the pillows and fell into a sound sleep.

He was awakened presently by a change in the rhythm of the vehicle—a sudden cessation of motion. He rolled over, sat up and pulled the curtain aside to peer out the little window. Burt was out on the side of the road, collar turned up and shoulders hunched against the wind, checking his tires.

Gray chuckled aloud. Burt, everybody knew, checked his tires every hundred miles or so. It was a standard joke around the rodeo circuit. Often he went so far as to take out his little pressure gauge and test the air pressure in all the tires, but Gray doubted that he would be so thorough now, not in a storm like this one. Likely he would content himself with kicking all the tires to assure himself there were no leaks and then continue.

The wind howled and shrieked outside, and Gray frowned in the warmth of the bed. Ranchers on the Alberta prairies all dreaded these vicious spring blizzards when the temperature could drop without warning to thirty below and four feet of snow could suddenly be dumped from a sky that had been warm and balmy just a day earlier. Especially damaging were the storms that came in April after the cows had calved and the calves were still tiny and vulnerable.

I hope it's going to blow through, he thought. The last thing we need is another three feet of snow just when the grass is turning green....

Still worried, he levered his long body out of the bed, stepped gingerly across the cold floor in his bare feet and opened the camper door. The wind caught the door, wrenched it from his hands and flung it against the back of the camper. With a soft curse Gray stepped carefully down onto the trailer hitch and reached up to grasp the doorknob, shivering in the bitter chill.

God, it's cold, he thought. Must have dropped twenty or thirty degrees in the past hour. I'd better get back in there before I— But, just as his hand closed on the knob, the truck started with a lurch that flung him off balance, and he leaped wildly from the hitch, narrowly avoiding being run over by the horse trailer.

He hesitated, stunned and speechless, watching as the truck pulled off the shoulder and out onto the highway. All at once he came to his senses and began to run behind the trailer.

"Hey!" he shouted. "Hey, stop! I'm out here!"

His voice was drowned out by the howling wind and the roar of the truck's engine. Aghast, he watched as the wind caught the camper door and blew it shut. A truck window on the passenger side opened briefly, and the glowing arc of a lighted cigarette butt flew out onto the snowy roadway.

Then the vehicle, trailer and all, vanished, swallowed up in a swirling gust of snow.

Gray huddled on the shoulder of the highway, hugging himself to preserve some body warmth. Slowly the full enormity of his situation began to dawn on him.

Jeez, he thought. Here I am out in a blizzard with nothing on but my damn shorts. And they're not going to know I'm gone till they get to my place and look in the camper.

He peered into the wind-driven snow, trying to calculate his position. There was almost no visibility now, but instinct, born of a lifetime on the prairie, told him that he was on a stretch of highway about twenty miles from his own ranch.

Might as well be twenty thousand miles, he reflected bitterly.

For one thing, this was an isolated piece of road. Nobody lived on it but him and one other rancher. The chances of anyone coming along were remote. And, in this storm, the men in the truck were driving slowly; it could be an hour or more before they got to his place, discovered he was missing and came back to find him.

Dispassionately he considered his plight. This could be it, he thought. I could die tonight. He shivered and hugged his body tighter with his big, muscular arms, dancing up and down on the frozen highway.

Well, he thought, if this is the way I have to go, I guess I've had a pretty good life. But damn it, he thought rebelliously, I hate the idea of being found dead in a snowdrift, wearing nothing by my goddamn *shorts*!

Knowing that it was essential to keep moving, to keep his blood circulating, he turned in the direction of his home and began to run into the biting clouds of snow. Small stones along the shoulder of the road bruised his bare feet, and the bitter wind chilled his body. Fighting down a choking, nauseating fear, he ran steadily with a slow, easy lope, his arms

swinging, his hairy, bare legs pumping, his breath coming
in noisy, ragged gasps.

"KEITH, QUIT CRACKING THAT GUM!" Joanna pleaded. "I
just can't stand it anymore. *Please* quit."

She gripped the steering wheel and peered ahead into the
dark swirl of gusting snow, her delicate face contracted in a
frown of tension.

"Why?" her son asked from the back seat where he was
lounging comfortably in a nest of suitcases, reading a paperback western, with his stockinged feet resting against one
of the rear windows.

Jo turned her head slightly and met his gaze in the rear-
view mirror, feeling a little shock of surprise, as she always
did when she unexpectedly encountered her own small,
chiseled features reproduced in this young masculine face.

It was a mystery, she often reflected, how Keith could
look so much like her and yet be so definitely boyish, while,
in appearance at least, she was a dainty and feminine
woman....

"Why what?" she asked absently, struggling to hold her
little car in the driving lane as wind-driven gusts of snow
buffeted its sides.

"Why should I quit cracking my gum?" Keith asked reasonably.

"Because I said so. And I mean it."

"Or what?"

"Or else," Joanna said darkly.

"No, really, Mom. I'm curious. What would you do to
me if I didn't quit?"

Joanna looked at him blankly in the mirror. His face, like
hers, had a golden dusting of freckles across a small, straight
nose. His dark chestnut hair was as fine and shining as her
own, but hers was brushed into a glowing mass of bur-
nished curls, cropped boyishly short, while Keith's lay across

his forehead and around his ears in soft, flowing waves. His eyes, darkly lashed and a deep blue-green in color, like a mountain lake, were also identical to hers; they regarded her now with cheerful interest.

Startled, she considered his question.

Or else what?

What, in reality, could she do to control a fourteen-year-old boy who was already taller than she was and whose thin, wiry strength was at least equal to her own? If he deliberately chose to disobey, what on earth could she do about it?

She frowned and bit her lip, gazing blindly ahead into the snowstorm.

"Or else I'll scream," she said in despair. "If I have to listen to you crack that gum one more time, I think I'll just pull over to the shoulder, put my head down on the wheel and scream right out loud."

The boy's face twisted in concern. "Aw, Mom," he said, instantly contrite. "I'm sorry. I was just kidding you. You know that. Look, I'll even throw it away." Suiting actions to words, he rolled down the window and tossed his wad of gum out into the hissing snow.

"Oh, Keith..." Jo began. "Keith, you didn't have to do that. I'm sorry, son. You know I'm not one of those women who get their own way by going into hysterics. I don't know what's gotten into me. I'm just so tired."

"Poor Mom. I know. How much farther is it, anyhow?"

"You're the navigator."

"Okay." Keith took a folded sheet of paper out of his book, opened out the road map and held both of them up near his little battery-operated reading light, frowning in concentration. "Now let's see. We had supper in Calgary, right?"

"Right," his mother said.

"And we've been driving southeast for... what do you think, Mom? About an hour?"

Joanna checked her watch and nodded. "About that."

"Well, we should be almost there, then. He says in the letter that it's about fifty miles southeast of Calgary."

"But, Keith, we haven't been driving anywhere near the speed limit, you know. I just can't make any time at all in this snow. Especially now that it's gotten so dark. Why is it snowing, anyhow?" Jo said in despair. "It's *April*, for God's sake! What kind of country *is* this?"

"Poor Mom," Keith said again, reaching over the back seat to pat her shoulder. "You look so tired. Why don't you let me drive for a while?"

"You!" She flung her head around to stare at her son. "What do you mean?"

"Hey, Mom, watch the road!"

Joanna stared through the dark windshield, trying to control her trembling, and gripped the wheel until her knuckles were white.

"What did you mean," she repeated tensely, "about you driving? Have you driven somebody else's car?"

"Jeez, Mom, relax. I was kidding you. I just wish I could learn, that's all. Lots of the guys are learning to drive already."

"Not you," Jo said, her face firm and determined.

"That's for sure," Keith agreed gloomily. "Not me. I'll probably still be riding a bike when I'm thirty, if you have *your* way."

"Keith," she began, "please don't start—"

But the words died in her throat, and she clutched the wheel in sudden panic as the headlights glimmered on something large and white in the driving lane ahead of her. She slammed on the brakes, sending the car into a wild spin. The engine died, and the power steering immediately seized up so that Joanna had to fight to hold the car on the road. Finally they came to rest, safe but precariously near the edge of the ditch, and Joanna dropped her forehead against the wheel to rest for a moment and regain her composure.

It must have been a horse or a deer or something, she thought. I'll have to be more careful out here in the middle of nowhere.

Taking a deep breath, she looked up and then screamed aloud in sheer terror. Something white ran past her window and leaped briefly into view in the snowy gleam of the headlights. The creature, whatever it was, seemed huge and was covered with hair and it was running upright, waving its arms.

My God, Joanna thought, her brain dulled with horror. This is a nightmare. I must be asleep. It has to be a bad dream.

But she knew this was no dream. She was wide awake on a lonely, stormy highway with her son in a stalled car, and some terrible, hairy creature was pounding on the front fender. Disjointed images and fragments of memory lurched through her mind: Bigfoot, Sasquatch, the legendary man-ape that supposedly roamed the Alberta mountains and foothills. . . .

"Lock the doors!" she screamed.

Keith stared at her blankly, his eyes wide with alarm and confusion. Finally he recovered and hastily locked the rear doors. Then, at the same time as his mother, he lunged across to lock the front passenger door.

But they were too late. Even as they reached for it the door was flung open, admitting a swirling cloud of fine, icy snow and a freezing gust of night air. The two in the car cowered in their seats, staring fearfully as a manlike creature, hairy and enormous, bellowing over the roar of the storm, pulled the door shut after him and slid into the seat next to Joanna.

Joanna, after what seemed like hours, though it could only have been a few seconds, was the first to recover her senses. She still gripped the wheel and gazed straight ahead into the darkness, trembling with shock and alarm. But out of the corner of her eye she could see the big, hairy, hard-muscled body that filled the whole front seat of her car. And she knew that this was no legendary apelike creature.

This was a naked, human male.

Her nauseating terror ebbed away to be replaced by a new fear—urgent, personal and sexual. Rapidly, with all the protective maternal instincts that were so natural to her, she calculated her position and her resources.

Keith was her first concern, of course. Keith must be protected at all costs, regardless of any danger to herself. But how? Tire irons, tools—anything that might serve as a weapon was locked away in the trunk. And they were on an empty stretch of highway in a blizzard, miles from anywhere.

Her scurrying, disjointed thoughts were interrupted by a deep voice; the man, she realized, was saying something. She clenched her hands tightly into fists to stop their trembling and tried to listen, to concentrate on what he said, to bring her racing thoughts under control and be cool and rational.

"God, I'm so sorry," the man was saying. "Look at you. You're just scared to death, aren't you? No wonder."

Jo was still too shaken to take in what he was saying, but something in his voice, a sort of basic warmth and courtesy, penetrated her terrified brain. Cautiously she glanced over at him, and he smiled back at her, a rueful, embarrassed grin that made his eyes crinkle and showed a flash of even white teeth.

His face, Jo realized, wasn't all that terrifying, either. Actually, it was quite a nice face, tanned and strong, with clear gray eyes, regular features and warm lines obviously etched by a lifetime of outdoor work and good humor. His eyes were set in generous dark lashes beneath arching black eyebrows, and he had curly dark hair, graying at the temples.

And everywhere else, too....

Jo shifted uneasily in the seat, trying not to look at the big male body that was so close to her. He appeared to be well over six feet tall, broad and strong, and completely naked except for a skimpy pair of navy blue jockey shorts. He held his large hands awkwardly in his lap in an attempt to cover himself, and all of him, from his wide chest and heavily muscled arms to his long, steel-hard thighs and calves, was dusted with springing, curly, gray-black hair.

"Hey, kid," the man said, turning to look over the seat at Keith, "toss me one of those jackets, could you?"

Keith, who was still gaping, nodded and responded instantly, picking up a soft woolen jacket of his mother's and passing it across to the front seat. The man clutched the jacket and draped it over the front of his shivering body while Joanna kept her eyes averted, staring out the window beside her.

"That sure feels better," he murmured when he was partially covered. "Look, ma'am," he said earnestly, "I really am sorry about this. I hate to scare you like this when you two are...on your own like this. But there's not a lot of traffic on this road, you see, and I'm damn lucky you came by. It's getting real cold out there," he added with his charmingly boyish, abashed grin.

Jo looked over at him, still bewildered, her blue eyes wide and shadowed with fatigue and fright. "How...?" she began, and faltered. "How did...what happened to you? Where did you come from? Who are you?"

"Well, it's sort of a complicated story." He stretched his long legs, holding his big feet up near the floor heater and sighing with bliss as the warm air flooded over them. "Ah...that feels so good. You see, I was at an indoor rodeo over at Black Diamond, and we were on our way home—''

"A rodeo!" Keith interrupted from the back seat. "Are you a rodeo cowboy?"

The man turned and rested his arm along the seat, smiling over at the excited boy. Jo shifted behind the wheel, uncomfortably aware of the expanse of broad, muscular chest presented to her when he turned. He was so big and so close to her that she could almost feel the springing texture of his mat of graying, curly chest hair.

I'd forgotten, she thought. It's been such a long time since I've been this close to a man's body.... I'd almost forgotten how good it looks.

"But not anymore," the man was saying to Keith. "Bull riding, that's a young man's sport. When a man turns forty, like me, he's got to smarten up and leave those things behind or he's going to get hurt. So now I stay home and run the ranch and just go to a few rodeos close to home to do a little calf roping and team roping."

"Do you win a lot of money?" Keith asked eagerly.

"Some. I've got a great horse, and that helps."

"Wow!" Keith breathed. "A real rodeo cowboy."

Jo glanced back at her son, troubled by the look of hero worship on his face. She knew that the boy still suffered from his father's absence, though he never said anything. The last she'd heard, Roddy had been working on an offshore oil rig in the North Sea, but he hadn't come around to visit the children for more than five years.

Joanna had sent him a letter after Mandy was killed, but he had never answered. At the sudden memory of her daughter's death, the old chill gripped Jo, and the familiar blackness washed over her again. She fought against it, took herself firmly in hand, squared her shoulders and looked at the stranger in her car.

"Please," she said in a small, shaking voice, "could you stop talking about rodeo for a minute and tell me what happened to you?"

He sobered instantly and turned away from his conversation with Keith. "Hey, are you okay?" he asked. "You look as white as a sheet."

"I'm just...I don't know," Jo said, floundering, moved in spite of herself by the warmth of his voice and the concern in his dark gray eyes. "I mean, this is so awful. You were out in a *blizzard* with no protection at all. You could have died, couldn't you have? At first I was terrified, just seeing you like...like that, and not knowing why you were...but now I guess a reaction's setting in and I keep thinking what could have happened to you...."

"You poor girl," he said gently. "You really *are* just about at the end of your rope, aren't you?"

"I've been driving for twelve hours," Jo said, feeling, absurdly, almost on the verge of tears, "and this storm hasn't helped any. I just want to know...what happened to you?"

"Yeah," he agreed, still looking at her with concern. "I guess I'm not helping the situation much, either, am I? My name's Graham Lyndon," he went on briskly, "but everybody calls me Gray. I have a ranch a few miles east of here and I was on the way home, as I said, with some friends from a rodeo. I was sleeping in the camper and I'd taken my clothes off because they were so dirty and dusty. The driver stopped to check the tires, and I opened the door to see what the storm was doing, and then it blew out of my hands. I stepped out to catch the knob, and they drove off just then and left me behind."

He looked over at Jo, his face a little sheepish. She stared back at him, wide-eyed with shock.

"Does this sound pretty stupid?" he asked.

She shook her head, her tired face tragic with horror and sympathy. "It sounds . . . just terrible," she said, her voice faltering. "You really *could* have died out there. How could they just drive off and leave you?"

"Well, I guess in that storm they didn't realize I'd gotten out of the camper, and they didn't hear me yell when they started up again. They just drove off and left me there, stranded in the middle of the highway with nothing on but my shorts."

Keith chuckled suddenly, and Gray turned to grin at the boy, his eyes crinkling with humor. "Sure, kid, go ahead. Laugh all you want. But let me tell you, it's no fun to be facing the prospect of a prairie blizzard with just your shorts on."

"How long were you out there?" Keith asked with lively interest.

"About fifteen minutes, I guess. I started running down the highway, trying to keep warm and keep my circulation going, hoping somebody would come along, but I knew the chances were pretty slim. Nobody lives out along this stretch of highway but me and Mac."

"Mac?" Keith asked. "Is that Malcolm Burman?"

"That's right." Gray looked at Joanna. "You know Mac?"

She nodded. "He's my uncle. That's where we're going, actually. I'm Joanna McLean," she added, "and this is my son, Keith."

"That's it!" he exclaimed, slapping one hand against his bare leg. "*Now* I remember!"

She looked at him, puzzled. "What do you remember?"

"Where I've seen you before. Mac's got a big picture of you on the mantel over his fireplace. I always thought the girl in that picture was just so pretty. I used to imagine what you were like and how nice you must be."

Joanna laughed awkwardly, taken aback by his easy, boyish frankness. "I'm not all that nice, Mr. Lyndon. I yell at people and everything. Just ask Keith. And besides," she added, "that has to be a very old picture. I think it was taken almost twenty years ago when I graduated from high school."

"I know," he said, grinning. "That picture used to keep me awake nights, back in the days when I was young and hot-blooded."

"Well," Jo said, her voice safely under control and firm once again, "we're all a lot older now. And these days my face could hardly launch a thousand ships. In fact, the way I feel right now, I doubt it could even launch a rowboat. So if you'll just give me some directions, I'll—"

"Are you just visiting Mac?" he interrupted, looking at the pile of suitcases wedged around Keith in the back seat and the tarpaulin-covered luggage rack on the back of the car.

Joanna fiddled with the key in the ignition, but didn't answer.

"We're moving in," Keith announced from the back seat. "Uncle Mac invited us, and Mom thinks it's a safer place for me to grow up than Vancouver, where we used to live. Mom's real big on safety," he added gloomily.

Gray looked from the boy's rebellious young face to Jo's determined profile, with its sweetly curving mouth and the golden dusting of freckles that sprinkled the bridge of her delicate nose. "I see," he said quietly. "And what do you think about living out here, Keith?"

"I dunno," Keith said. "I can't see anything but snow. Are there any kids around here?" he asked hopefully. "Do you have kids, Mr. Lyndon?"

"Call me Gray. Everybody does. Yes," he added, chuckling, "I have kids. Sometimes it feels like I have fifty of them, but there's actually just two. They're twins, Margaret and Elizabeth. But they're away at university in Calgary, so I'm all alone at the ranch these days."

"Where's your wife?" Keith asked with the easy curiosity of youth.

"Keith," Jo began, "I don't think—"

"It's all right," Gray said. "She died a long time ago, Keith, when the girls were just three years old."

"My sister died, too," Keith said. "Last fall, just before Christmas. She was killed in a car accident. She was ten."

The boy volunteered this information in a carefully casual voice, but his face was pale, and his lips trembled a little as he spoke. He looked at the big man almost pleadingly, his face suddenly very young and vulnerable.

Gray returned his gaze quietly for a moment and then turned to Jo. She sat tense and erect, gripping the wheel, her face tight with anguish, her whole body locked in a miserable stillness.

He dropped his hand gently on her shoulder and let it rest there. "I'm sorry," he said with quiet sincerity. "It must be terribly painful to lose a child that age."

Jo looked up at him, her eyes empty and dark with despair. This is crazy, she thought. It *must* be a nightmare. How can I possibly be sitting here in a blizzard with a naked stranger and talking about Mandy?

"Look," she whispered finally, unable to bear any more. "Can we just *go*? Please?"

"Sure," he said, removing his hand and drawing the coat up around his chest. "Just straight ahead a few miles, and my place is to your left, right off the highway. You can drop me off at my place, and then Mac's just a couple of miles farther. Or would you rather have me drive?"

"I'll drive," Joanna said wearily.

There was silence in the little car as she shifted into gear and pulled cautiously out into the snowy driving lane.

CHAPTER TWO

"WELL, HE SEEMS comfortable enough down there," Malcolm Burman said, coming up the basement stairs and smiling shyly at Jo, who sat at the kitchen table with a mug of coffee.

Jo smiled back at him. "He certainly should be. It's a beautiful room, Mac. You've done such a nice job of finishing that basement, and I think Keith's got more space in his closet down there than he had in his whole room back in our apartment in Vancouver."

"I guess rent's pretty high out there, isn't it?" Mac said, crossing the room to pour himself a mug of coffee from the pot on the counter. "And it couldn't have been easy for you all on your own like that." He took a sip of coffee and grinned. "Keith says the room needs a little brightening up, though. Says he can't wait to get all his posters unpacked in the morning."

Jo shuddered. "Wait till you see them. There's no way I'm letting him put those awful posters on the walls of that nice room. Besides, we don't even know how long we're going to be here, Mac."

"You're going to be here a long time," her uncle said firmly, "and Keith can hang as many posters as he likes. Boys need things like that just to irritate their mothers."

Jo smiled lovingly at the older man. Malcolm Burman, her mother's eldest brother, was a tall, thin, diffident man with a shiny balding head, a gaunt, awkward frame and a craggy face of ineffable sweetness. Jilted in his youth by the only girl he had ever mustered the courage to court, Malcolm had withdrawn into a gentle solitude, living alone on the family ranch after his parents' death and passing his time pleasantly with outdoor work, carpentry, reading, painting and music. At these last two pursuits he was surprisingly accomplished; some of his delicate watercolors hung in galleries in the city—though he always hated to sell them—and he was a regular finalist in the old-time fiddling championship held annually at the Calgary Stampede.

Joanna had always adored him, and her childhood visits to Uncle Mac's ranch in the years when her mother had still been alive had been the highlight of her life. But she had lost contact with Mac after she married and moved to Vancouver, and later, during the difficult years when she was divorced and alone with two small children, articling for her chartered accountant's license and preparing income tax forms in the evening to earn enough to keep food on the table.

Things hadn't changed much, either, after her career was established; it became almost impossible to get away, and even when she could it was so hard to make the long drive from Vancouver to Calgary with two small children in the car. Eventually, to her sorrow, her relationship with her beloved uncle had dwindled to little more than a brief exchange of letters at Christmas and birthdays.

And then, incredibly, one rainy evening in February Jo had answered the door and found her uncle standing in the entryway of her Vancouver apartment. She could still remember how he had looked, so shy and awkward and so out of place in that huge city, with rain dripping from the shoulders of his old-fashioned gabardine topcoat.

But his eyes, in that craggy, weathered face, had been warmly loving, full of shy, gentle compassion and understanding. Joanna had run into his arms like a child, and for

the first time in the two dreadful, lonely, nightmare months
since Amanda's death, she had finally been able to cry.

They had talked far into the night after she recovered her
composure, and Malcolm had left the very next day to return to Alberta. But now, two months later, as a result of
that conversation, Joanna had left her job, given up the
apartment, sold all her furniture and moved out here to the
prairie with her son.

The decision to move had been a momentous one, even
frightening, but as she watched her uncle cross the kitchen
with his coffee mug and seat himself awkwardly across the
table from her, Jo was certain she hadn't made a mistake.

"Everything's so clean," she marveled, looking around
at the gleaming kitchen. "You're a better housekeeper than
I am, Mac."

"I like to look after things," he said with his gentle, self-
deprecating smile. "It's a pity," he added, his smile fading,
"that I can't keep my finances in the same kind of shape."

Jo reached over and covered his hand with her own.
"Don't talk that way, Mac. It's not your fault. These are
terrible times for prairie ranchers, with the drought and the
drop in beef prices. I'm sure you're not the only one having
problems."

He was silent, stirring sugar into his coffee and staring
gloomily into its swirling brown depths.

"Besides," Jo said with forced brightness, "that's why
I'm here, remember? That's part of our deal. Cash flow is
my business, you know. Once I get into those books and
have a chance to find out what's happening, I'm sure we'll
find that things aren't as bad as you think they are. I'm certain of it, Mac."

He gave her a wan smile. "Well, Joey, you've always been
a smart girl, and I guess you know your job. But if you can
pull me out of the mess I'm in, you'll be a miracle worker.
I'd never be able to find a way to thank you."

She leaned over and put her arm around his bony shoulders, hugging him warmly. "You've done so much for me already, Mac. I'm so glad to be here. I really think I would have gone out of my mind if I'd stayed out there in that apartment, just thinking and remembering..." Her voice broke, and she looked down at the table.

Malcolm patted her shoulder gently.

"Besides," Jo went on, "I think this is going to be a lot better for Keith, too. If we should decide to stay here for a couple of years, I mean. It's so dangerous for a boy his age, living in the city. There's drugs and liquor and kids in cars...so many ways they can get hurt."

Malcolm watched her for a moment in thoughtful silence. "It's dangerous everywhere, Jo," he said finally, his voice gentle. "Life is dangerous. And kids have to be allowed to grow up, you know. You can't protect them from everything."

"I know that," Jo said. "How could I have protected Amanda? She was with a reliable, responsible adult...four little girls, just having fun at their friend's birthday party. Nothing sinister at all, Mac. And everybody else walked away from the accident, but Mandy was killed." She stared out the window at the whirling gusts of snow, her face bleak with memory.

"That's what I mean," Mac said. "It was fate or whatever you want to call it. You couldn't have stopped it from happening, no matter what you did."

"But it happens all the time in the city!" Jo said. "Tragedies all the time, every time you pick up a newspaper. At least out here Keith will be safer. He won't be in the middle of...all that. I can't stand the thought of him driving and partying and riding in cars with kids who've been drinking or taking drugs."

"They're hard, frightening years for parents," Malcolm agreed. "But most kids do get through them safely, you know. And Keith's a sensible boy. He's not likely to come to any harm."

"Not if I can help it," Jo said quietly.

They were silent for a moment, sipping their coffee and listening to the prairie wind as it howled around the corners and under the eaves of the snug ranch house.

"So," Mac said finally, "I understand you've seen my neighbor, Gray Lyndon."

"Yes, I have," Jo said, and then looked up, her wan, tired face sparkling suddenly. "Actually," she added with a grin, "I've seen quite a *lot* of him."

Mac laughed. "Keith was saying something about that, but in all the confusion of unpacking the car and getting him settled downstairs, I kind of missed it. What was Gray doing exactly? How did he come to be running around in a blizzard with no clothes on?"

Joanna got up to fetch a package of doughnuts from the counter, opened them and set them on the table. "Well," she said slowly, "it all seemed so terrifying to me. Apparently he was coming home from a rodeo with some other cowboys in a truck and he took his clothes off and fell asleep in the camper. And then when they stopped to check the tires, he got out for some reason without them being aware of it, and they drove off without him."

Mac roared with laughter, and Joanna watched him, smiling, pleased to see him relax for once and lose the tense, worried expression he seemed to wear habitually these days.

Finally he sobered, rubbing his streaming eyes with the back of his hand. He swallowed a chuckle and reached over to select a doughnut.

"Poor Gray," he said. "It's easy for me to laugh, but it couldn't have been much fun out there in the snow and wind, wondering if he'd freeze before he got home. It's a lucky thing you happened along."

"I suppose so. But he didn't seem...you know... particularly upset or embarrassed about any of it. He was just...kind of casual. If it'd been me, I don't know what would have been worse—terror over the blizzard or humiliation at being caught in such a state."

"Well," Malcolm said thoughtfully, pausing to sip his coffee, "nothing upsets Gray all that much. It takes a lot to shake that man. Sometimes I think he's made of steel. But he's really a warm, generous fellow, you know. Best neighbor a man could ever have."

Joanna was silent, remembering the man's commanding physical presence, his beautiful, virile body and his finely shaped head and those clear, penetrating, dark gray eyes. Something about him troubled her, she realized. There was a blunt, cutting edge to him, a presence that was disturbing, even threatening.

Not in a physical sense, of course, she thought. You could tell just by looking at him that he'd never do you any physical harm. But still, she had a definite feeling that Gray Lyndon was a man who could hurt them badly and cause a terrible upset in their lives if he was allowed to get too close.

And I really didn't like the way Keith reacted to him, she thought as she looked up to find her uncle's quiet, faded blue eyes resting on her thoughtfully.

"You seem upset, Jo," he said. "Any particular reason?"

"No, of course not." She smiled automatically. "I was just thinking about this neighbor of yours. Something about him seemed...I don't know..."

Mac rolled a doughnut thoughtfully through the sugar bowl and waited for her to continue.

"I guess I just...didn't like the way he talked to Keith."

"Why?" Mac asked in surprise. "I can't imagine him saying anything out of line to Keith. Gray loves kids. And they always seem to love him, too."

"That's just it!" Jo said helplessly. "It was like he was in the car for all of two minutes, you know, and he and Keith were already best friends, chatting a mile a minute about that horrible rodeo. By the time we got to his place, if you can believe it, he was even offering to take Keith *with* him next time he goes! I just didn't like it, Mac."

"Jo...Keith could use a little of that, you know. Man talk, I mean, and some friends besides you and a chance to be involved in something that interests him. He's been awful close to you, I think, ever since...since it's been just the two of you."

Joanna was silent, toying with the doughnut crumbs on her plate, lining them up in neat parallel rows. Finally she looked up. "I know all that, Mac. It's just...hard right now. And he's still so young. If he's going to be getting involved with...other people, you know, and activities...well, I'd like to have some say in it. I don't appreciate having a stranger, like Gray Lyndon, just come breezing into our lives and have Keith start falling all over him—"

"Oh, come on, Jo, I hardly think—"

"Besides," she said rebelliously, "why does he have to involve *Keith* in his life? He's got children of his own, doesn't he?"

Malcolm's face creased in a slow, fond smile. "He sure does. The twins. He told you about them?"

"A little. He just mentioned their names and that they're away at university now."

"They'll be coming home for the summer," Mac said, "in just a couple of weeks. It's sure been lonely around here this winter without Peggy and Libby."

Jo looked at him in surprise. "Really? Do you see a lot of them?"

Malcolm chuckled. "As soon as they were old enough to ride their fat little Shetland ponies, those two little hellions started tearing down the road to visit their Uncle Mac, and they've been coming ever since. I can even tell them apart, most of the time, and that's more than other people can say."

"My goodness," Jo said. "They must really be identical if they're still hard to tell apart when they're eighteen."

"Oh, well, they play it up, too, the little devils. They like to play those twin games, you know, and fool people just for the fun of it. But they can't fool me. Did you see pictures of them? Did Gray ask you into the house at all?"

"Of course not. Why would we want to go into his house?" Jo said. "Besides, his friends were already there in a truck with a big horse trailer behind. They'd just unloaded the horses and discovered he wasn't in the camper, and they were all in a panic, wondering what to do about it. I just dropped him off and got out of there."

She paused, smiling in spite of herself. "When we drove out the gate," she added, "he'd obviously been telling them what happened, and nobody seemed too alarmed. You could hear them laughing all the way across the ranch yard."

Mac nodded, his eyes twinkling, and then he sobered. "It's not a real gentle society out here, Jo. Things around here are pretty rough and ready. That sort of thing might be a disaster or an embarrassment where you come from, but out here on the prairie, everybody's just going to think it's a terrific joke."

"Even though he could actually have frozen to death?"

"You bet. The story of Gray Lyndon on the highway in his undershorts in a blizzard—that's going to be repeated in every auction yard and general store and hotel bar for a hundred miles around. It'll become a legend."

"How awful. Will he mind?"

"Not Gray. He's the sort of man who doesn't care what people think of him. He does what he pleases and goes where he wants to, and he's not concerned about other people's opinions."

Jo shivered a little. "That sounds to me like a dangerous man."

"Dangerous?" Mac asked in surprise. "Gray Lyndon?" He frowned thoughtfully, considering. "I suppose," he said slowly, "that Gray could be a bad enemy. I mean, if somebody were to hurt one of his daughters, for instance, I wouldn't want to be in their shoes when Gray caught up with them. But, as far as I'm concerned, Gray Lyndon is the best friend I've ever had. I'd trust him with my life."

"Well," Jo said crisply, "that may be, but I still have no intention of trusting him with my *son's* life. And now," she added, softening her voice and smiling at her uncle, "I'd better get to bed before I drop. Maybe after a good sleep I won't be so hard to get along with."

"Joey, honey, I'm afraid that after you've had a look at those books, you'll just pack up and leave again."

Jo smiled, getting to her feet and giving her uncle a loving pat on his shiny bald head. "I'm no quitter, Mac. You won't get rid of me that easily. Those books are just going to be a challenge, that's all."

"I hope you're right," he said gloomily, returning to his coffee. "I sure do hope you're right."

JO WOKE TO SUNLIGHT streaming through the bedroom window, rolled over sleepily and lay in her bed, smiling.

I wonder, she mused, whatever happened to all that deep silence there's supposed to be out in the country. This is noisier than Vancouver.

Cattle were bawling outside the window, an engine roared nearby, accelerating and stopping at irregular intervals, and a radio was playing loudly somewhere in the house.

She turned her head on the pillow to look at the bedside clock and realized in amazement that it was nearly ten o'clock. Horrified, she crawled out from beneath the covers and sat on the edge of the bed, raking her fingers through her tousled hair.

I must have been really tired, she thought, to sleep so long, especially through all this uproar. Come to think of it, I guess I've been tired for months. Maybe years...

She climbed out of bed and padded across the room to look out the window. The source of most of the noise was immediately evident; it was feeding time, and a tractor moved slowly through a densely packed herd of cattle in a field near the house, hauling a wagon loaded high with dull green hay bales. Jo recognized her uncle's craggy face beneath a comical furry cap with ear flaps; Mac was driving the tractor, stopping regularly and turning on the seat to look back at the hay wagon.

There was somebody on the sledge, standing amid the hay bales, breaking them open and tossing bundles of hay out to the hungry, waiting cattle. Jo peered at the slim, active figure in jeans, parka and woolen toque and realized with a little shock of alarm that it was her son.

She stared at him, watching fearfully as his slight body balanced against the jerky movements of the wagon while the masses of cattle pressed so close to him, some of them with sharp, curving horns....

Her fingers gripped the windowsill, and she struggled against an urge to fling the window open and shout to him. Just then he turned in her direction, calling something to Mac, and Jo looked in amazement at his vivid, laughing face. Keith had seemed so silent and listless this past winter; she had attributed his lassitude to the shock of his sister's death, and the growth spurt his body was experiencing.

But on this crisp, snowy spring morning he was flushed with cold and exertion and his wiry body seemed vibrant with joyous energy. As Jo watched, her son pulled off the woolen toque and shook out his thick, waving hair. Mac called something to him, and the boy threw his head back, laughing, and then tugged the toque back down over his ears and bent to his task once more.

The tractor started with a jerk, and Keith almost lost his footing. He staggered briefly on the deck of the wagon, clutched at the remaining hay bales to regain his balance and then, still laughing, waved to his uncle to continue.

Jo's heart pounded wildly. She pleated the curtain edge tensely between her fingers, biting her lip, and then forced herself to look away from the slender, fragile, precious body of her only child.

Instead, she studied the vast, snowy landscape that lay beyond her window. The morning after that vicious and surprising spring blizzard was incredibly beautiful. The wind was still, all the clouds had vanished, and the prairie sky soared from horizon to infinity in a lovely, breathtaking sweep of pure, rich sapphire. The sun shone warmly over sculpted, blue-shadowed drifts, sparkling and glittering on the soft powdery surface. Snow blanketed the rolling prairie in an undulating, feathery blanket and wrapped around the corrals and outbuildings, carved into graceful shapes by the howling wind the night before.

As Joanna watched in amazement a pair of shy mule deer trotted around the corner of one of the paddocks, approached the herd of bawling cattle and lifted their noses warily for a moment. Then, satisfied that no danger threatened, they bent their heads and began to pick daintily at the wisps of hay left behind by the foraging cattle.

She saw Keith on the wagon as he noticed the deer and began to jump up and down in excitement, pointing and calling to draw Mac's attention to them. Mac stopped the tractor and said something to the boy, who nodded eagerly, pausing to gaze at the deer again.

Then, suddenly distracted, he turned his head and looked off beyond the house, staring at something with concentrated attention. Jo followed his gaze and saw a truck drive into the yard. The vehicle was a big dark blue four-wheel drive, clearly a work truck, smeared with mud and packed snow and loaded with bulging burlap sacks.

As Jo watched, the truck stopped near the corrals, and a big, broad-shouldered man got out and strolled over to the fence bordering the feeding pen. He wore jeans, boots, a wide-brimmed Stetson and a heavy sheepskin coat. He moved with a lithe, easy stride, climbing up onto the rail fence and calling out a greeting to the two in the field.

There was something about the man that seemed vaguely familiar. Jo, still in her sunny yellow pajamas and bare feet, drew back behind the curtain and studied him intently. When he climbed off the fence again and turned toward the house, she instantly recognized the broad, square jaw and curly graying hair beneath the wide-brimmed hat.

The visitor was Gray Lyndon, and he was coming toward the house.

In sudden panic Jo grabbed her dressing gown and overnight case and sprinted down the hallway to the bathroom. While she was brushing her teeth she heard, faintly, the opening of the back door, followed by a heavy tread in the kitchen and the sound of cupboard doors opening and closing. Soon, drifting down the hallway, she heard a cheerful male voice raised in song.

Cautiously she edged the bathroom door open a fraction of an inch and listened. It was apparently Gray singing, and he had a surprisingly rich, sweet tenor voice. Even more surprising to her was the song itself, which she recognized as one of her lifelong favorites, a hauntingly beautiful old ballad that her Scottish grandmother had often sung to her as a child. Jo forgot herself and listened, lost in pleasure and memory, to the lovely, ageless words.

"When I'm lonely, dear white heart,
  Black the night or wild the sea;
  By love's light my foot finds
  The old pathway to thee...."

His voice trailed off into an indistinct, muffled rhythm. He must be burrowing in a cabinet, Jo realized.

She smiled and eased the door shut again. She was relieved that the man seemed so obviously at home in her uncle's house; at least she wasn't expected to play hostess. With any luck at all she might be able to avoid him altogether. She could just dawdle over getting dressed and putting on her makeup, and Mac would come in, have coffee with him and see him off.

But then, she thought, hesitating with her hairbrush poised in midair, Keith would be alone with the two men, and she wouldn't be around to know what Gray Lyndon was saying to her son. She felt a quick twinge of anxiety and hurriedly finished brushing her hair, then rushed through the application of her few sparse touches of makeup.

Despite her concern, she couldn't help noticing the sparkling neatness of the bathroom. Her uncle, like many elderly bachelors, was an immaculate housekeeper, and every corner and cupboard in the small tiled room was a model of tidy cleanliness. But what Jo found most touching was the clear evidence that Mac had anticipated and prepared for her arrival. Every single article of male toiletries and furnishings had been removed from the upstairs bathroom; it was obviously Mac's intention to share the basement bathroom with Keith and leave this one for Jo's use alone.

Sympathetic, grateful tears gathered in her eyes as she saw the things her uncle had bought in a touching, awkward attempt to make her feel at home: bath salts and scented soaps, soft pastel towels and a pale blue shower curtain, so new that the fold lines were still clearly visible on its surface.

Oh, Mac, she thought, you're such a sweet, silly old dear. You didn't have to do all this.

Still smiling mistily, Jo went back down the hall to her room. As she opened the bedroom door, she heard a gust of laughter and loud voices from the direction of the kitchen, and realized that her uncle and son had entered the small ranch bungalow. She paused in the doorway to her room and bent her head, eavesdropping shamelessly.

"Good morning, boys," Gray Lyndon said heartily. "Got the chores all done?"

"Not even close," her uncle said. "But we got cold, and wanted a break. You got the coffee on?"

"Well, sure," Gray said. "And I got the doughnuts out and some buns to put in the microwave here. Say, what's going on, Mac? I thought you had a woman living here now to look after all this domestic stuff. Where is she, anyhow?"

Mac murmured something inaudible, and Gray laughed aloud, a hearty, masculine sound in the quiet house. Jo's cheeks flamed with indignation.

"I saw you up on the hay wagon, Keith," Gray was saying cheerfully amid a distant clatter of cups and plates. "If you're going to be staying long, you'd better get this lazy old guy to let you drive the tractor. It's the easiest job."

"Hey, neat!" Keith said with enthusiasm. "Can I, Mac? Can you teach me to drive the tractor tomorrow?"

Stunned, Jo marched into her room, closing the door emphatically behind her. She leaned against it for a moment, breathing hard, her delicate cheeks flushed with anger and her dark blue-green eyes blazing.

He's got some nerve! Keith, driving the tractor! That man just thinks he can say whatever he likes, do whatever he wants, when it's none of *his* business at all.

Almost breathless with outrage she dressed quickly, zipping her jeans and buttoning her denim shirt with trembling fingers, tugging on warm woolen socks and soft moccasins. Then, pausing for a moment to square her shoulders and compose herself, she went slowly down the hallway and into the kitchen.

The three of them were seated casually around the table, and all of them looked up at her approach, wearing cheerful smiles. While Jo was still searching for a dignified opening line, Gray Lyndon leaped to his feet and held a chair out for her.

"Mrs. McLean," he said with a teasing smile and small, courtly bow. "Pray, allow me. Welcome to the land of the living."

Jo declined with icy politeness, moving over to the counter and getting out a coffee mug for herself. Gray sat down again, smiling at her warmly. Jo ignored the smile, giving him a level, appraising glance.

He was, she acknowledged reluctantly, an unusually attractive man, and under different circumstances she would probably find him enormously appealing. He had just the sort of strong, sun-browned, clean-cut features that she liked. And there were other things: the fullness of his lower lip, his direct gray eyes, the frosting of silver at his temples, the size and breadth of his body and the lithe, easy way that he carried himself. Everything about him hinted at virility and masculinity, at quiet, controlled power and reserves of great strength.

More than *hinted*, she thought, remembering that she had, in fact, seen most of the power and beauty of that body—of the broad, hard-muscled, hairy frame beneath the faded jeans and casual flannel work shirt.

He continued to regard her over his coffee mug, his rugged face sparkling with a teasing grin, his gray, darkly lashed eyes dancing wickedly as he waited for her reaction.

"Good morning, Mr. Lyndon," Jo said casually, taking two slices of bread and popping them into the toaster. "I hardly recognized you with your clothes on. I must say, it's certainly an improvement."

The three at the table greeted this sally with more laughter, and then Gray sobered and looked at her as she stood leaning against the counter, waiting for her toast.

"I shouldn't laugh," he said earnestly. "The only reason *I'm* still in the land of the living is because of you, Joanna. You saved my life, and I know it. I'm thankful to you. I was just teasing about you sleeping late. Anybody who put in the kind of day you did yesterday deserves to sleep all day if they like." He hesitated. "I really want to thank you, Joanna."

There was no doubting his sincerity. Jo's face softened a little, and she turned aside quickly to butter her toast.

"Mom's usually up before anybody else," Keith volunteered loyally. "She's always been that way. She likes to get up about five in the morning and catch up on her work while the house is all quiet."

"Ah, early rising. An admirable quality in a woman," Gray said, his voice teasing once again, "and one I've tried to instill in my daughters."

Mac grinned. "Nobody instills *anything* in those two without their permission," he observed fondly. "When are they coming home, Gray?"

"Actually, Peggy was planning to stay in the city," Gray said, pausing to sip his coffee. "She was going to take a summer job as receptionist at a car dealership to earn some money for next year's tuition."

"Oh," Mac said with a distinct lack of enthusiasm. "That's nice."

"Not really," Gray said with a chuckle. "Libby called last night just after I got home and said Peggy went to the interview, and the guy who owned the dealership made a pass at her, so she decked him."

"No kidding," Keith said, wide-eyed. "Really?"

"Yeah," Gray said. "Really. Gave him a fat lip and loosened one of his teeth and scraped her knuckles some, too."

"Did she get the job?" Keith asked, fascinated.

Gray shook his head, laughing. "I think she probably told him what he could do with his job. Anyway, they're both coming home for the summer, the weekend after next."

"They're lucky," Keith said gloomily. "*Their* summer holiday starts already."

Gray patted the boy's thin shoulder. "What about you, Keith? When do you start back to school?"

"Next week, right after the holidays end," Keith said. "That's why Mom wanted to move now so that I wouldn't get to miss even one single day of school."

Gray turned in his chair to look over at Jo. "He'll just go into town on the bus, will he?"

Jo nodded dubiously and rummaged in the fridge for the jam. "I guess so. Mac was going to look into it, but we haven't had time to talk about it yet...."

"It's all set," Mac said placidly. "He's registered already, and the bus stops by here next Monday morning."

"Oh, great," Keith muttered.

Gray smiled at the boy and punched him lightly on the shoulder. "Hey, come on, kid! It's only a ten-minute bus ride, and they've got a great school in that little town. Their basketball team won the divisional championship last fall, and they put out a terrific school newspaper, and," he added modestly, "they have a world-class chess club coached by me."

"You?" Keith asked in amazement. "*You* coach the school *chess* club?"

"None other," Gray said placidly. "Every Wednesday night. You see before you the best chess player between the Great Lakes and the Pacific Ocean. Absolutely."

"Well-l-l..." Keith said, grinning broadly. "Maybe not, eh, Mom?" He gave Joanna a significant glance and a meaningful grin. "Tell him, Mom," he prodded.

"Keith," Jo said warningly, "I don't think you should—"

"My mom's the best chess player around," Keith said proudly. "She enters tournaments and wins trophies and everything."

Gray's eyes lighted with surprise and sudden lively interest. He swiveled in his chair to stare directly at Jo. "Tournaments?" he asked slowly. "Trophies?"

"Well, yes, but..." Jo began, flushing a little. "Keith shouldn't have...I mean, I don't claim to be..."

Gray was still gazing at her, his eyes alight with speculation and a distinctly combative gleam. "Tell me, Joanna," he inquired solemnly, "would you happen to be free this afternoon?"

"I'm afraid not," Jo said with dignity. "Mac and I are going to get some bookwork done this afternoon. That's one of the main reasons I'm here, and I intend to earn my keep."

"Jo's a chartered accountant," Mac explained to his neighbor. "She's going to help me out with my cash flow problems."

"My God!" Gray exclaimed, clapping his hand to his curly head and collapsing in his chair in mock amazement, long legs extended. "Is there no *end* to the surprises in this one small woman? Looks like a movie star, plays chess like a Russian genius, solves financial problems with a wave of her magic pencil, leaps tall buildings with a single bound—"

"All right, all right!" Jo said tartly, and then, seeing the hopelessness of it, joined in the general merriment and laughed along with them. "Actually," she said, seating herself at the table with her toast and coffee, "I'm an entirely ordinary person. Just a quiet, dull homebody. Right, Keith?''

"Yeah. And strict, too," Keith said somberly.

Gray smiled at the boy. "It's not easy being fourteen," the big man said cheerfully. "You know, Keith," he added as an afterthought, "they have a rodeo club at that school, too. You might be interested in getting into that. What do you think?"

Keith sat suddenly erect, his cheek bulging comically with the fistful of doughnut he had just stuffed into his mouth, and stared at Gray. "A *rodeo* club?" he asked in an indistinct, muffled voice while his mother glared at him.

The boy chewed frantically, flapping his hands, swallowed and continued. "You mean, out here they have *rodeo* clubs in the schools, just like debating clubs or something? What do they do? Can anyone join?"

Gray laughed, lifting his hand to stem the eager flood of questions. "Sure, they have rodeo clubs. And you join just the same as any other club. And then, here in the western provinces and down into the States, a lot of schools put on junior rodeos, and other school clubs travel around to compete, just like other teams. Each member earns points in his own event, and the school with the most points wins the trophy."

"Wow," Keith breathed. "What a neat idea!"

Joanna opened her mouth to speak and then thought better of it.

I'll talk to Keith later, in private, she decided. This is just so ridiculous....

"How do you know all about the club, Mr. Lyndon?" Keith asked.

"Call me Gray, kid," the big man said cheerfully. "I think you and I are going to be good friends."

He smiled at Keith, and the boy smiled back with an eager, almost worshipful look that Jo found intensely irritating.

"Peggy and Libby were in the rodeo club for three years," Gray went on, "and I hauled them all over the country to school rodeos, pulling a two-horse trailer. And now that they're gone, I still help out some, teaching the kids and going to their practices—that sort of thing."

Keith was still pondering this astounding information. "Girls, too?" he asked. "What can girls do at a rodeo?"

"Mostly barrel racing," Mac contributed. "Barrel racing, that's always been the ladies' event at rodeos. That's where they put three barrels in the arena in a cloverleaf pattern, you know, and the girls race their horses around them and back to a starting point, and the fastest time wins."

Keith nodded. "I think I've seen that."

"Libby did that," Gray said. "Barrel racing was always her event, and she wasn't anxious to get into anything else. She had a real good horse, and she practiced until she could win at least something, almost everywhere we went."

"But not Margaret," Mac said with a fond, reminiscent grin.

Gray chuckled. "No, not Peggy. She tried it all. Calf roping, bareback horses, bull riding—there's nothing that girl wouldn't tackle, I think."

Keith was staring from one man to the other, wide-eyed, his face pale and tense with excitement. "What would be the best event for me, do you think? What would I be good at? Where should I start?"

"Well, let's see," Gray began thoughtfully, considering. "I think a kid like you would be best to start off with—"

Joanna, however, could stand it no longer. "Look, all of you," she interrupted, keeping her voice low and tightly controlled so that she wouldn't start shouting. "I really think this conversation has gone on long enough. Keith just got here yesterday, and he knows nothing at all about this...this 'sport,' as you call it. But I happen to know enough to be aware that it's senseless and dangerous and that people are maimed and even killed all the time. And I would no more consider allowing him to get involved in it than I'd let him take up...bullfighting or hang gliding, or any other stupid, senseless thing." She stopped, out of breath, and gave Gray a level, challenging look.

Keith, meanwhile, muttered an exclamation of bitter disappointment, pushed his chair back and got up from the table. His shoulders slumped, and his body drooped with the old, listless slouch as he wandered off toward the basement stairs and clattered miserably down to his room.

Gray watched the boy disappear around the stairwell and then turned in his chair, returning Jo's glare with a direct, appraising look that made her shift uneasily. "So," he said quietly, "that's the way you want it to be, is it, Joanna?"

She flushed rebelliously. "I just can't understand this...this stupid male obsession with risk and danger," she said. "Why is it that something can't be fun unless there's a possibility you'll get killed doing it? Keith's a bright, sensitive boy. There are so many things he could be doing that would be educational and rewarding and wouldn't involve him risking his—" Words failed her, and she paused, glaring, her blue eyes flashing with anger.

Gray got to his feet, reached for his hat, shrugged into his sheepskin coat and went into the porch to tug his boots on. Then he paused in the doorway and turned to look at Jo, his handsome, sun-browned face quiet and thoughtful. "We've just met, Joanna," he said, "and we haven't even had a chance to get properly acquainted. But we seem to have started off on the wrong foot, and that's too bad, because I really think we could be friends, you and I. The problem, you see, is that I'm in an awkward position here because I also happen to think that's a good kid down there, and I think you're making a big mistake."

"Well," Jo said coldly, "that's my business, isn't it? As you pointed out yourself, you've barely met us, and he's been *my* son for fourteen years. I think I'm the best judge of what's right for him, don't you?"

"I don't know," Gray said honestly. "I know you're a smart lady, and I tend to think you're probably also a person with a lot of rare, fine qualities, but in this particular case I think you should spend some time thinking about it and decide who you're *really* concerned about . . . Keith, or yourself."

He turned to Mac with a brief nod and a quiet thanks for the coffee, and then he closed the door behind him and strode off into the dazzling, sun-bright morning.

CHAPTER THREE

AFTER GRAY'S DEPARTURE, Joanna sat silently at the table, her heart pounding in her chest, her cheeks flushed with helpless anger. Mac gazed across the table at her, and his faded blue eyes were gentle with awkward concern.

"Jo..." he began.

Jo waved her hand abruptly. "No, Mac, don't talk about it. I'll just hurry up and get these dishes done, okay? And then I think I'd like to bundle up and go out for a walk. It looks like such a beautiful morning."

But her uncle refused to be diverted. "I think we should talk about it, Jo," he said quietly.

"About what?"

"Come on, Jo. About Gray and what he was saying just now."

"I think," she said with forced lightness, getting to her feet and gathering plates and cutlery together with quick, abrupt gestures, "that your neighbor has more absolute, unmitigated *gall* than anyone I've ever met! Can you imagine such rudeness? I mean, we've hardly been properly introduced, and he's presuming to tell me his opinion of me and my life and how I should be raising my son. I think it's monstrous."

"Sit down for a minute, Jo," the older man said, still gently. But his voice was compelling in its quiet authority.

Jo sank back into her chair and met his gaze with a combination of stubborn anger and mute, desperate appeal.

"Now, Jo, you've always been a smart girl, and you've always had a solid, sensible way of looking at life. It's one of the things I loved best about you ever since you were just a little bit of a girl." He smiled at her tenderly and patted her hand as if to soften the impact of what he was about to say, but he continued doggedly. "Don't you think," he said, "that there might have been a tiny little bit of truth in what Gray was telling you? Don't you think you might tend to be just a bit too protective of the boy?"

Jo avoided his eyes and toyed with the pieces of cutlery on the table, moving a knife and fork to form a careful V-shape.

"Jo?" he persisted.

Silently she positioned the cutlery into an L and then moved the knife to form a T. Finally she set them both aside and looked up at her uncle.

"I don't know, Mac," she said slowly. "I lie awake nights, thinking about it, and I don't know if it's possible to be *too* protective. I mean, the world is such a dangerous place and so many terrible things can happen. Where does a parent's responsibility end? Can we just wash our hands of our kids and send them out to play in the traffic and think that if they're meant to survive, they'll make it, so we won't worry?"

"Of course not," Mac said. "There's a sensible middle ground to everything, Jo. Can we wrap them in cotton wool and never allow them to leave the house because there are so many dangers lurking out there? Is that the answer?"

She shook her head, close to tears. "I know what you're saying, Mac. I'm not stupid. But I just can't..."

She took a deep breath and paused while her uncle watched her silently, waiting. "I think," she said finally, her voice trembling with emotion, "that a person would have to go through what I did, losing a child in an accident like that, to understand what it's like for me. Mac, I've gone over it a thousand times, thinking it through, wondering if I'd just done something differently...if I hadn't let her go to the party or if I'd gone myself to pick her up or if I'd insisted that she be home an hour earlier before it got dark.''

"Joey, sweetheart, you have to get over that kind of thinking. An accident is exactly that—an accident. Something that nobody foresees and nobody could prevent. It's just a terrible, tragic chain of circumstances.''

"Of course it could have been prevented,'' Jo argued. "If Mandy hadn't gone to that party, she wouldn't have been killed that night. And,'' she added passionately, "if Keith never goes to a rodeo, he can never be hurt by some horrible, half-crazed animal kicking him in the head or stepping on his stomach!''

"Sure, maybe he can't,'' Mac said mildly. "But maybe trying so hard to keep him from danger will do a different kind of damage.''

"Damage? What do you mean?''

"Oh, I don't know. Maybe in the way he feels about himself or about his position as a young man, taking his place in the world.''

Jo shook her head stubbornly. "Not if you'd all just leave him alone and if he doesn't have to deal constantly with ridiculous, childish, chauvinist males like Gray Lyndon, who make a boy feel he can't be a man unless he's out damaging his body and risking his life!''

She paused, breathing hard, her cheeks flushed with emotion. Mac regarded her in troubled, thoughtful silence and sipped at his forgotten cup of tepid coffee.

"Mac...'' Jo began in a softer voice. She looked up and met her uncle's gaze, her deep blue eyes pain-filled and misted with tears. "Mac,'' she whispered, "you just don't know what it's like. You don't know the nightmares I have night after night. Even when I'm awake, sometimes, I start worrying about Keith, if he's late or away from me somewhere, and then I get a mental flash of his body, all crushed and bleeding, and he's in terrible pain and I can't help him...."

Her voice broke, and she paused, trembling, while Mac held her hand, his weathered face wretched with sympathy.

"I had to go down to...to identify Mandy," she said tonelessly. "Apparently it's the law. Somebody has to, and there was nobody I could call. And she was...oh, Mac!"

She stopped abruptly, her voice broken by a quick, stifled sob. Mac reached over awkwardly and put an arm around her, patting her shoulder and murmuring, passing her a table napkin to wipe her streaming eyes.

"I'm sorry, Joey," he murmured. "I didn't know. I mean, when I got that letter from you at Christmas, I had a feeling that things weren't so good with you, and that's why I came to visit you and to see if we could figure out a way to help each other somehow. But I never suspected you were still hurting this much. I wish I could do something for you."

Jo composed herself with an effort and turned aside to mop her face. Then she looked up, trying to smile. "Sorry, Mac. Every time we get together I start crying all over you, it seems. But it's not all that bad. I mean, it's been terrible, but I'm getting better all the time. Really. And coming out here has been wonderful for me. Right after you came to see me, and we made this decision, I started to feel so much more hopeful, like I was actually going to make it. It's just so good to be here with you, Mac."

He smiled at her, his kindly face seamed with tenderness, his bald head gleaming in the overhead light.

"But," Jo went on steadily, "even though I'm starting to get a handle on things and getting a little more control, I'm still not ready for someone like Gray Lyndon interfering in Keith's life and making all these decisions for him. I just happen to believe that what he's proposing to Keith is the wrong thing for him right now, and I want that man to stay away from my son."

"All right," Mac said, patting her shoulder again. "All right, Jo. I'll have a talk with Gray."

"Thanks, Mac." She got to her feet and began to clear the table again, pausing to drop a grateful kiss on her uncle's bald head.

He smiled up at her, and they both turned to look at Keith, who was struggling into the kitchen, hauling a heavy packing crate that had been hacked open on one side.

"Keith," Jo asked, "what on earth's that?"

"It's for Mrs. Brown," he panted. "Mac says she's pregnant, and he said I could get a box ready for her."

"Mrs. Brown?" Jo asked blankly.

"You know," Mac said. "The collie."

"The fat one that wanders in and out of here all the time?"

"She's not fat," Keith said patiently. "She's pregnant."

"But why is she called Mrs. Brown?" Jo asked.

Mac grinned, a little abashed. "She looks just like the wife of a hired man I used to have," he said. "You know, that long, narrow face and big, soulful eyes just a shade too close together?"

Jo nodded, chuckling.

"But she made great scalloped potatoes, Mrs. Brown did," he added wistfully.

"The dog or the housekeeper?" Keith asked, grinning.

"Watch it, kid," Mac said, and went over to inspect the box with a critical eye. "This looks great, Keith. She'll be real happy in here. If you go down to the chop house," he added, "you'll find a bunch of clean burlap sacks that you can line it with, and that'll make it nice and cozy. She can have the puppies out in the porch, where you can keep an eye on them."

"Okay," Keith said eagerly, his boyish face alive with enthusiasm. "Where's the chop house?"

"Remember where we parked the tractor and feed wagon?"

The boy nodded, shrugging into his parka and pulling on his toque.

"Well, that's the Quonset. And the chop house is the little building just to the right of it, with the red roof."

Keith was barely listening, already halfway out the door, bursting with excitement.

"Pick the cleanest sacks," Mac called after him, "and don't forget to latch the door behind you!"

But Keith was already gone.

Jo stood at the window, holding the curtain aside with one hand and watching as her son ran off across the snowy ranch yard, thin legs pumping, arms swinging.

She turned back to the older man with a fond, dreamy smile and began to stack dishes in the sink, turning the faucet to run hot water over the glasses and cutlery.

"This is so wonderful, Mac," she said softly. "Keith loves this, you know. He's always been crazy about animals. He used to beg for a puppy until I thought my heart would break, but our apartment didn't allow pets. Not even a kitten. I got him an aquarium, and every time a fish died he'd be in tears over it for the rest of the day."

"He's a good kid," her uncle agreed. "He's got a real tender heart, that boy."

Jo nodded. "Maybe even a little *too* tender. I worry about that sometimes. I think the realities of life in the country are going to be good for him. Springtime and harvest, birth and death—it's all just part of a cycle, isn't it?" She was silent for a moment, watching the bubbles of detergent mount beneath the jet of hot water. "It's going to be good for me, too," she added softly. "This feels like such a healing kind of place, Mac."

He looked at her directly, his face shadowed with worry and concern. "Jo, I hate to remind you of unpleasant realities, but unless we can do something about the financial mess I'm in, this place won't even see another harvest. Or at least I won't be the owner of it when it does."

Jo reached for the dishcloth and wrung it out with a brisk, decisive gesture. "Oh, yes, you will. I'll just finish up these dishes and then we'll look at the books and develop our strategy. It's going to be fine, Mac. You'll see."

She gave her uncle a quick, reassuring smile and then turned back to the sinkful of dishes, wishing that she felt as confident as she sounded.

GRAY DROVE HOME SLOWLY, his handsome, normally cheerful features contracted in a thoughtful frown.

Well, Gray, old boy, he mused, you really blew it this time, didn't you?

He gripped the wheel tightly in his strong brown hands and tensed, remembering Joanna's angry, bitter response to him and his suggestions about Keith.

Probably, he thought, I picked the one thing in the world guaranteed to antagonize her the most. She's really concerned about that kid.

He pictured the way she had looked when he left. Her pale, delicate face had been pink with indignation, her blue-green eyes blazing. Even her curly dark hair, he thought with a brief grin, had seemed to stand out like a halo, emitting little electric sparks of anger. He remembered her slim, rounded body, taut with emotion, and he could even recall that she'd been holding a half-eaten slice of toast in her hand. Gray was certain that she'd forgotten all about it.

She was, he realized with a small shock of surprise, just about the most attractive woman he'd ever met.

Not flashy or showy, he thought. Quiet and reserved, but pure gold, all the same. A woman who doesn't talk a lot but who gives you the impression that when she does, she's worth listening to.

That was what he really liked about her. She had a sort of thoughtfulness, an attentive, intelligent stillness that indicated a deep thinker and a good listener. She was a woman you wanted to talk to...to probe her mind and ask her opinions and learn how she felt about things.

And you wanted, Gray realized, to make her laugh.

When she laughed, though it happened seldom, the tense, strained look eased from her face, like clouds drifting away from the sun. And then her eyes sparkled, and her lips curved softly and warm little crinkled lines appeared around her eyes, showing that once, in the past, she used to smile and laugh a lot more than she did now.

Poor girl, he thought with sympathy.

He recalled, vaguely, things that Mac had said about her over the years. Mac loved to talk about his favorite niece, and Gray wished now that he had paid more attention to all the stories about Joanna. She'd been on her own for years, he knew, looking after her children; Mac had said something about a handsome, carefree husband who had just grown weary of the responsibility and opted out, running off and leaving her alone.

Gray shook his curly head as he turned off the highway and into his own ranch yard.

Hard to figure, he thought. Good women aren't easy to find. How could a man leave a woman like that? If it was me now...

But it wasn't him, and it wasn't likely to be, either, not the way she'd looked at him when he left Mac's kitchen.

Gray knew, of course, that he could fix things up if he wanted. And he had a reasonable confidence, based on the successes of a lifetime, that there wasn't a woman on earth that Gray Lyndon couldn't charm if he really chose to pour it on. But this was a different matter. To win Joanna's approval he would have to apologize, to admit that he was meddling where he didn't have any right and promise not to influence Keith in any way in the future.

And, if they were going to be living right there on the next ranch, that was a promise Gray wasn't at all sure he would be able to keep.

Because, when you came right down to it, there was another reality in this situation. There was more to it than Joanna's sweet, sensitive face and the thoughtful depth of her eyes.

There was the boy, as well.

Gray parked by the Quonset and got out of the truck, strolling around to lift the heavy bags of feed from the back with effortless ease and toss them one by one inside the building. As he worked, he thought about Keith. Gray spent a lot of time around young people, and he was a pretty good judge of what they were like. And he'd had a fair amount of time to appraise this boy; they'd talked a lot the night before while Joanna was driving him home in the storm. He hefted the bags of feed, visualizing the young boy's bright, eager face, his respectful manner and the honest directness of his gaze, so unlike the shifty, sullen look of a lot of boys that age. And then he remembered the wild excitement in Keith's expression when Gray had told him about the rodeo club.

That's a real good kid, Gray thought warmly. Just the kind of boy I'd have liked to—

He suppressed the thought and hauled the last feed sack out of the truck bed.

This longing for a son was another of Gray's deep secrets, one that he had never confided to anybody. He loved his daughters and took immense pleasure in their lively comings and goings, but sometimes there was an ache in him that went unfulfilled, a deep yearning for somebody to relax and talk man talk with and teach things to and train in manly ways.

I guess I'm just far too old-fashioned, he thought with a private grin, fastening the door of the Quonset. But I can't help it. And if I were to have a son, that boy's just what—

Sternly he reminded himself again that this was all nonsense, that, in fact, he'd only met Joanna and Keith a few hours earlier and that she was absolutely correct in what she said. He had no right at all to involve himself in their lives.

But then, almost against his will, he remembered the bitter disappointment on the boy's face, his muttered exclamation of unhappiness and his listless, slumped shoulders as he'd left the kitchen to wander downstairs.

"Oh, hell!" Gray muttered aloud.

He got back into the truck and sat for a moment, drumming his fingers on the steering wheel as he stared off across the prairie, thinking.

A man doesn't have to be a psychologist, he mused, to understand how she feels. I can imagine that after she's lost one child in an accident, she's going to be pretty paranoid about the safety of the one that's left. Anyone would. But, damn it, there's the boy to think about, too. And a boy that age needs to have a little danger and excitement in his life just to feel like a man. If he can't get it in some wholesome, physical way, like a sport, then he's going to look for it in drugs or shoplifting or something. Can't she *see* that?

He shook his big shoulders wearily, put the truck into gear and drove slowly up toward the house. With sudden firmness he resolved to put the whole matter out of his mind. What he'd do, he decided, was grab a lunch, throw some posts and wire on the truck and drive up west toward Mac's place to spend the afternoon repairing the barbed wire in the west field before he turned his heifers out.

Nothing like a day of fencing, he told himself, to set a man's mind at ease.

He tipped his hat to its customary rakish angle, grinned his quick, flashing smile, just to make himself feel better, and stepped out of the truck in front of his big, empty ranch house.

FORTUNATELY KEITH HAD prepared his small maternity ward just in time. Immediately after lunch, Mrs. Brown began to show definite signs of restlessness, and by two o'clock she was safely established in the big, padded box in the back porch, giving birth to a seemingly endless litter of puppies.

Keith crouched beside the box, watching, rapt and breathless with excitement. At regular intervals he called out progress reports to the two in the kitchen.

"A black one with a white face and white paws!" And later, "Aw, gee, this is so neat! This one's kind of blotchy, like a pinto!"

Mac looked across the table at Jo, trying to smile. "I wonder," he murmured, "who the father was. They don't really sound like purebreds, do they?"

She smiled wanly back at him over the welter of bills, bank statements, record books and income tax forms. "No," she said, feeling wretched. "They sure don't."

They were both silent for a moment.

Finally Mac leaned back in his chair and looked directly at her. "Okay, Jo," he said quietly. "You've been through it all, and we can't put it off any longer. You might as well tell me how bad it is."

She looked up miserably and met his eyes. "It's awful, Mac," she said. "Really awful."

He nodded and got up from his chair, moving awkwardly across to the counter to pour two mugs of coffee. "I knew things were getting really bad," he said, carrying the coffee back to the table. "I guess I've known for a long time. I was just being an ostrich. I figured if I ignored all this—'' he waved his hand at the mountain of paper ''—it might just all go away.''

"It won't go away," Jo said, sipping her coffee. "At this stage it'll just get worse." She looked up at her uncle. "When did it start, Mac? I mean, this has to be recent, I think. You've always been pretty comfortable, until now, haven't you?"

He nodded again, with a troubled, preoccupied look. "Three years ago when the drought started getting really bad and beef prices were falling, I thought I'd take a gamble. I planned to calve out a month early, so I'd have bigger calves to sell in the fall and make a fair profit on them. You understand?"

"Of course. And what happened?"

"What happened," he said with a grim smile, "was that we had a spring blizzard, like the one last night, only twice as cold and three times as long, and I lost two-thirds of my calf crop. Frozen to death in the drifts after the wind quit and the snow started to melt."

"Oh, Mac..."

"But that wasn't all of it," he went on. "Most ranchers can survive one bad setback. I still had some savings and a good line of credit. I borrowed and bought some replacement heifers and feed for the winter. But the next year I got a sickness in the herd. Lost half the calves again and a good portion of my stock cows, too. And since then it's been a downhill slide. I just can't seem to get anywhere but deeper in debt."

She looked at him, her face desperate with sympathy.

"Come on, Jo," he said, smiling at her, his craggy face wrinkling. "It's not the end of the world. I can sell the place and clear the debts and find something else to do."

"Oh, Mac..." Jo looked at him in despair. "Mac, you've lived here all your life. I can't imagine you being anywhere else. What on earth would you do?"

"I'll do something," he repeated. "I could move to town and be a . . . a janitor, or something . . ."

"You could not!" she said with sudden indignation. "That's ridiculous! You've worked hard all your life, and you've never hurt a soul. You deserve to stay right here where you belong and I'm going to make sure that you do!"

He smiled sadly. "Like I said, Jo, you're a smart girl. But you're not a miracle worker. And I need a miracle."

"No, you don't. I just have to think about this and do some research and come up with a plan."

As she spoke, Jo went into the porch and stepped over the recumbent body of her son, who was lying on the floor with his chin resting in his two cupped hands, staring into the box.

"I think she's done," he breathed, looking up at his mother. "She's licking them and everything. There's *seven* of them, Mom."

Joanna smiled down at him, looked briefly at the puppies and pulled on her coat and boots.

"Hey, Mom, where are you going?"

"Just out for a walk," Jo said. "I'll be back in an hour or so," she called out to her uncle. "I just want to get some fresh air and do a little thinking."

"Fine," he called back cheerfully. "Don't be late for supper. I'm making the world's best macaroni casserole."

Jo smiled at him lovingly. "I won't be late."

Outdoors, the afternoon sun was warm and bright, reflecting on the smooth blanket of snow in dazzling prisms of light. Already the snow was beginning to melt, and little rivulets of water trickled down the trails made by the plodding hooves of thousands of cattle. The sagebrush was frosted delicately with a lacy covering of ice that melted and dripped onto the ground with a soft, soothing rhythm. A few horned larks, arriving early from their annual migration, had been caught in the storm and forced to find shel-

ter somewhere. Now they foraged busily on the bits of bare
prairie where the snow had already melted and filled the air
with their lovely, liquid trills of music.

Joanna walked along the fence line, hands in pockets,
looking around her with pleasure. It's been so long, she
thought, since I've walked on the prairie. I'd forgotten how
beautiful it is and how much I love it.

Her uncle *wasn't* going to lose all this, she told herself.
There had to be some way to turn a quick profit and gen-
erate some ready cash flow so that he could at least cover his
interest payments.

Deep in thought, she topped a rise, started down into a
gully along the fence line and stopped abruptly. A truck was
parked at the bottom of the gully, and a man was standing
beside the fence, pounding staples into a post with quick,
sure strokes.

The man, she saw, was Gray Lyndon.

Her first instinct was to flee back up the hill and out of
sight. But that was impossible; he'd already seen her, and
running away would be a childish thing to do. She approached his truck slowly, her hands still in her jacket
pockets.

"Hi, there," he said, smiling, and paused to set his hammer down on the fender of his truck. "Just out for a walk?"

"Yes," Jo said, feeling nervous and uncomfortable. "It's
a lovely day."

"It sure is," he agreed. "I love a day like this, after a
storm, when the sun feels so nice and warm and you can be
fairly certain that spring's finally here to stay."

There was no constraint at all in his voice; it was as if he
had altogether forgotten their angry parting exchange. Jo
relaxed a little and watched while he wound some wire in a
big implement like a curved pipe wrench, wrapped it tightly
around the post and locked the handle of the wrench in po-

sition. As he worked, he chatted about the weather, and Jo responded with automatic politeness, looking at him.

He was, she thought, really a marvelously attractive man. He worked with spare, competent movements, his big body easy and graceful. He had removed his coat in the warm spring sunshine, and she could see the big knotted muscles in his back and arms as he strained at the wire. He had replaced the wide-brimmed hat he'd worn earlier with a dusty tractor cap, and the peak shaded his gray eyes, but as usual, they were still bright with friendly amusement when he looked up at her.

He patted his shirt pocket and frowned, still holding the handle of the wire stretcher.

"Could you hand me some staples, please?" he asked. "I just used my last one."

Jo peered into the battered coffee tin on the fender of the truck. "In here?"

He nodded, and she gave him a handful of staples, then watched as he pounded one of them into the post with three quick strokes of his hammer.

"I'm always so impressed when somebody does that," she confessed. "If I were to try it, I'd take about twenty swings at it and wind up bending it, anyhow."

Gray smiled, and the warm crinkled lines appeared around his eyes. "Nothing to it," he said. "Just pound about a million of them and you'll get real good at it." He hesitated and then looked up at Jo, his eyes troubled beneath the peak of the cap. "Did you have a look at Mac's books yet?" he asked.

She nodded unhappily.

"Pretty bad?" Gray asked sympathetically.

Jo nodded again. "How did you know?" she asked. "Has he talked to you about it?"

"A little. And then I live right next door. I'd have to be blind not to see the run of bad luck he's had. I wish," he added, stooping to test the lower strand of wire, "that I could help out somehow."

"Oh, I don't think that's going to be necessary," Jo said. "I'll think of something."

"Like what? Can you get him another bank loan?"

She shook her head. "It's past that. At a certain point it's not practical to use more credit because any profit you earn just goes to service the debt. What he needs is something small and easy to handle that could show a quick return and not require a large capital outlay." She paused, a little embarrassed under the big man's steady, thoughtful gaze. "I'm going to go into the city and do a little research," she said finally. "Talk to some people and check with some contacts I have there. I'll think of something."

He shook his head in wonder and reached for his wire stretchers again. "You're an amazing woman, Jo McLean. I never met anyone like you."

"Well," she said with a small smile, "you're kind of unique yourself."

He grinned, his white teeth flashing, and then grew thoughtful. His back was turned to her, and he went on speaking as he worked, fitting the wire into the teeth of his wrench.

"Are you just all business, Jo?" he asked without looking at her. "Do you ever think of other things besides cash flow?"

She leaned against the truck and looked at his broad back in puzzled surprise. "Like what?"

"Oh, I don't know," he said casually, reaching behind him for the hammer and taking a few staples from his pocket. "Like dreams or fantasies—things you've always wanted to do. Do you ever dream, Jo?"

"Of course. All the time. Dreams keep me going, when reality's too hard to bear." She was silent for a moment. "How about you?"

He straightened, brushing snow from his knees, and smiled at her. "Yeah," he said, "I'm a real dreamer." He hesitated. "You know," he said almost shyly, "what I've always dreamed of doing?"

"What?"

"Riding a camel. I'd just love to ride a camel. On a real desert. You know...all that sand..."

His voice trailed off lamely, and he turned aside in embarrassment, wondering how he could have been such a fool. What a stupid thing to say and to a woman you've barely met, who doesn't like you, anyway! At least now she's got something to laugh about.

But when he stole a cautious glance at Jo, she wasn't laughing. She was gazing dreamily off at the pink, misty prairie horizon, smiling, with a faraway look in her eyes.

"They call them 'the ships of the desert.' Camels, I mean," she said. "That must be what it feels like, riding on one of them, just rocking and swaying, and all that sand is the ocean.... What a marvelous sensation."

Gray stared at her, astounded by her understanding. Suddenly he was assailed by an urgent longing; he wanted to gather her into his arms, kiss her sweet, curving mouth, bury his face in those shining curls, get as close to this woman as a man could.

He took himself firmly in hand, picked up his hammer and turned away so that she wouldn't see the hunger in his eyes. "What about you, Jo?" he asked casually. "What would you like to do?"

"Sleep on a train," she said without hesitation. "Ever since I was a little girl I've wanted to do that. Once we were playing down by the train station when a passenger train came in, and I saw someone lying down in a roomette, reading, with a little lamp on, and I was so fascinated. I thought what it must be like to be in a cozy little room like that, all warm and comfortable, just lying there reading or sleeping while the miles are passing by.'' She paused, with a little embarrassed laugh, and he smiled up at her.

"You should do it," he said. "Buy a ticket and just go. That's an easier fantasy than mine. Trains are a lot more plentiful than camels . . . at least around here."

"It's not an easy fantasy when you have kids to look after," Jo said. "Holidays aren't easy for single parents."

There was a brief, awkward silence.

"Look, Gray," Jo said finally, "I'm sorry about . . . all the things that have happened. I didn't mean to be rude to you."

"You weren't rude," he said. "Just emphatic," he added with a grin.

She looked down, unable to return his smile. "I was talking to Mac about this just a while ago," she went on, "and he was going to say something to you, but since you're right here . . ."

She hesitated, and he waited, holding the wire stretchers casually in his hand and leaning against the post. Jo looked up at him. "I just don't want Keith getting involved in any of those activities—the rodeo club and all that. I'd like you to promise me that you won't influence him."

He looked down at her steadily, his eyes thoughtful. "I'm sorry, Joanna," he said finally. "I can't promise that."

Color mounted in her cheeks, and her eyes flashed. "Why can't you?" she asked.

"Because," he said quietly, "I don't think it's right. You can't make me promise to do something if I don't believe in it."

"But he's my son!"

"We don't own people, Jo. Not even our own kids. And we're not always the best judge of what's good for them. I'd like to be friends with you. I'd like it a lot. But I can't promise you that I'm not going to influence that boy if I have a chance."

"Well," she said with cold anger, "you won't ever have the chance because my son and I are going to stay just as far away from you as we can. I guarantee it."

She turned on her heel, her body rigid with fury, and walked away without looking back. Gray stood quietly by his truck, watching as her slender figure topped the rise and disappeared into the vastness of the prairie horizon.

CHAPTER FOUR

THE YELLOW SCHOOL BUS pulled up and parked by the entry gate to Mac's ranch yard and gave two quick, cheerful toots of its horn.

"Hey!" Keith shouted, craning to look out the window. "She's early! I gotta go. Bye, Mom. Bye, Mac."

He wolfed down the last of his cereal, grabbed his jacket and gym bag, paused briefly in the porch to greet his family of puppies and then raced off across the yard in the warm spring morning.

Jo stood by the window, coffee mug in hand, and watched him, smiling. She turned to her uncle, who sat at the table in his work clothes, eating breakfast.

"He's really happy here, Mac. This is wonderful, you know. He was so scared about the new school and all, and now, after just a few weeks, it's like he's always been here."

"The kids are nice around here," Mac said, reaching for the butter and returning her smile. "They learn real young in an isolated area like this that you have to treat your neighbors well because you never know when you might need a favor yourself."

"Well, it's all turning out better than I could ever have hoped," Jo said cheerfully, moving over to refill her coffee mug. "More coffee, Mac?"

"Please. For a pretty girl," he added with a grin, "you make an awfully good pot of coffee."

Jo chuckled. "I don't know which is more flattering—to be called pretty or to be praised for my coffee. They're both a novelty for me."

She seated herself at the table again, and their eyes met. Mac looked steadily at his niece, as if searching her face for some kind of reassurance.

Finally he looked down at his plate. "So," he said, "I guess today's the day, is it?"

"I'm afraid it is," Jo said. She reached over gently to pat her uncle's callused, freckled hand. "It won't be so bad, Mac. Wait and see. You'll probably even get to like them after they've been here for a while."

"I'm gradually forcing myself to come to terms with this idea," Mac said gloomily. "But, Joanna, I'm mortally certain that I'll never, never, get to *like* them!"

Jo was silent, refusing to give in to the darkness of his mood. He looked pleadingly at her. "You're absolutely certain there's just no other way? None at all?"

"Mac, we've been through all this before," Jo said patiently. "More than once. You *know* I've spent days and days in Calgary, talking with your bank and with accountants and market analysts and financial planners and reading everything I could find and doing cost projections and market studies of my own. This is your only chance, Mac. It really is."

"If you say so," he said, "then I guess I have to believe you. You're the expert. But *why*," he said tragically, "does it have to be *pigs*?"

The look of comical anguish on his gentle, craggy face was almost too much for Jo, and she turned away quickly, biting her lip to stifle a giggle. "I really don't know," she said when she was sure she had her voice under control again, "why you have this violent prejudice against pigs. From all the research I've done they seem like fairly lovable, intelligent animals."

"Lovable!" he muttered, aghast. *"Pigs?"*

"Well, you just wait," Jo told him. "You may not find them lovable now, but just wait till they're growing and getting fat and making a huge profit and paying all your bills and *then*," she concluded firmly, "see if you aren't beginning to find them a little appealing."

"I can't deny that you make it sound good, Jo. You're a terrific saleswoman. But it's just . . . this ranch has been in our family for over a hundred years, and there's never been a pig on the place. The neighbors," Mac said gloomily, "are just going to think this is so funny. . . . I won't be able to show my face around town ever again. I'll have to become a hermit."

"Oh, for goodness sake," Jo said tartly. "You were just telling me a minute ago how the neighbors here are all so good to each other and stick together and all that."

"That doesn't mean they'll pass up a golden opportunity like this to tease the life out of me."

"Let them tease. It doesn't change the fact that pigs are a marvelous commodity," Jo said. "Low investment, high-profit, rapid turnover, minimal risk—and even though beef prices are depressed right now, the pork market is sky-high. And you have the perfect place for them. That calf pen down there is ideal for weanling pigs. It has a shelter, a ready-made feeding system and everything."

"I know, I know," Mac muttered rebelliously. "But I just wish it didn't have to be *pigs*."

"Well," Jo said, in a voice that brooked no further argument, "I'm afraid it does. Cattle and horses are going to do nothing but drive you further toward bankruptcy. *Pigs*," she added, mimicking her uncle's tone of fastidious horror, "are going to save your neck."

She checked her watch, got up briskly and started to clear the table. "I'd better hurry. I have to leave soon. The sale starts at ten, and it's a half-hour drive, isn't it? And I wanted to get there early to look around at the stock before they start."

Mac watched her quick-moving, slender form. "Just leave the dishes in the sink, Jo. I can do them after my chores." He gazed out the window at the warm sapphire arch of the prairie sky, filled with trailing wisps of pearl-tinted clouds. "I should be coming with you," he said gloomily. "I shouldn't make you do this all by yourself."

"Mac, nobody's *making* me do anything." Jo turned to look over her shoulder at him and ran hot water across the stacked dishes. "We agreed that I'd go to the sale and buy the pigs. It would be such a painful experience for you, whereas nobody's even going to notice me. Besides, I know all the prices and everything. I'm up for this, Mac. I really am."

He nodded reluctantly. "It's great, Joey, and I surely do appreciate all you're doing for me. But especially this. When I think about going to that sale, in front of those people I've known all my life and having to listen to their comments while Mac Burman buys a hundred pigs..." He shuddered and lapsed into silence.

Jo patted him lovingly on the head and hurried to the doorway. "You don't worry about a thing, Mac. All you have to do is get the hotel ready for our little guests. They should be arriving about supper time."

"Everything," Mac said with a distinct lack of enthusiasm, "will be ready."

He sat at the table, sipping his coffee and listening to the sounds of Jo getting ready...the shower, her hair dryer, cabinet doors opening and closing.

She appeared in the kitchen again when he was finishing his third cup, and he smiled at her. "You look beautiful, Jo."

She really did, he thought. There had always been something about this niece of his, ever since she was a little girl, that set her apart and made her special. She wasn't flashy. Quite the opposite. But she had an innate look of class and quality that made her really striking when she was dressed up. And, for this important day, she was wearing beautifully fitted charcoal flannel slacks, a gray tweed blazer and a soft, silvery-gray blouse that brought out the delicate tints of her complexion, her blue-green eyes and curly dark hair. She looked elegant and businesslike, but still gracefully feminine.

"Is it all right?" Jo asked anxiously. "Not too dressy? I want to be taken seriously as a buyer, but not look . . . you know . . ."

Her uncle nodded. "You'll knock 'em dead," he said briefly. "They'll all know you're there, that's for sure."

"Well, I'm off, then. I don't know when I'll be home . . . just whenever I've filled out our order."

"Goodbye, Joey. You have a good day, and thank you for everything."

She paused in the doorway, grinning at him, her eyes sparkling. "Here I am," she said cheerfully, "off to spend thousands of dollars of your money and you're thanking me!"

He smiled back at her. "You know what I mean."

She nodded, gave him a little wave and was gone, hurrying over to the Quonset to back her small car out and head off down the long graveled entry road.

Mac stood at the kitchen, his smile fading, watching the tall plume of dust that followed her car as it vanished toward the endless horizon. Listlessly he let the curtain drop, tidied a few things in the kitchen and then went to the hall closet to get out his violin case. He laid the case on the table, opened it and drew out the shining old violin, handling it with loving care, as if it were something alive and vulnerable. He polished it with an aromatic rag kept in the case, tucked it under his chin and moved into the living room, staring out the big window at the wide sweep of land.

He loved these wild, open vistas, this broad, sun-washed prairie that had been his home all his life. On this shining spring day his love for the land rose up and engulfed him, washing over him in waves of almost unbearable emotion. He thought of the years and seasons he had seen come and go through this window and the ties that bound him to his land—to this place that he would have to leave before another season passed.

Despite Jo's elaborate plans and figures, he had little optimism for the outcome of her scheme. He had managed things badly, gambled and lost, and now he was going to have to cash in his chips. Soon he would have to leave his home, give these shining stretches of land to someone else and go away. And from then on his life would be over, no matter how many more years he lived.

Tears filled his eyes and spilled down his weathered cheeks. He tucked the violin under his chin, still staring blindly out the window and began to play "Danny Boy" with a sobbing, haunting melancholy that sought to express and to ease the anguish of his spirit, but served only to deepen his sorrow.

JO SAT in one of the upper tiers of seats, clutching her clipboard and looking down at the livestock auction ring in rising panic. This experience wasn't at all what she had visualized. She wasn't even sure *what* she had expected, actually, but it wasn't at all like this.

First, she was unprepared for the general appearance of the sales yard and building. From her limited knowledge of livestock sales markets, gained mostly from reading and television, she'd pictured something rather casual and outdoorsy, with people leaning on rail fences in the sunshine,

exchanging pleasantries and casually making bids on passing livestock.

But this was all business, with nothing casual and outdoorsy about it. The livestock ring was arranged just like a
movie theater with a semicircle of comfortable, padded
armchairs rising in tiers above the small oval ring, where the
auctioneer stood high on a little podium, backed by two
hardworking secretaries. The livestock entered singly or in
little groups from a door on one side of the ring, were trotted briskly around a couple of times in front of the buyers
and then scooted efficiently through the door on the opposite side to vanish once more in the welter of pens and corrals outside the enclosure.

Jo wasn't at all sure, either, that she was appropriately
dressed for the occasion; there must be some reason, after
all, why everyone kept staring at her. But it was hard to tell
if she'd dressed right, because there were only two other
women in the entire audience besides the secretaries. One
fairly young woman was wearing a silk dress, high heels and
a fur coat and looked terminally bored. Clearly she was
somebody's wife, forced to wait here for him until they
could leave and go somewhere more entertaining. The other
woman wore filthy bib overalls, work boots caked with mud
and a battered felt hat pulled down over her scraggly graying hair. She was hunched in one of the seats, clutching a
sheaf of order slips, chain-smoking gloomily and was rec-
ognizable as a woman only because she carried a big vinyl
handbag.

There were about fifty men in the crowd of onlookers,
most of them casually dressed in work clothes. A small, select group down at ringside, probably order buyers who had
driven out from the city, wore dress pants and jackets and
wide-brimmed felt hats. They looked prosperous and confident. There was a good deal of boisterous joking and ca-
maraderie among this group and, Jo noticed, they were all

very conscious of her presence. They kept looking up at her and exchanging comments and meaningful grins.

Her cheeks burned, and she concentrated on the numerous sheets of computer information fastened to her clipboard. She had prepared herself carefully for this day, researching all the attributes of a healthy weanling pig. They should be rounded, alert and a good color, with perked ears and tightly curled tails.

But price was as important as condition. The pigs would, possibly, be sold by weight as well as by unit, and she had her calculator ready so that she could estimate immediately what each pig was going to cost and whether it was more than the maximum amount she had figured to allow them a viable profit.

The door opened, the first package of small pigs came scurrying into the sales ring, and Jo took a deep breath.

Okay, she thought. Here goes...

But, to her distress, she soon realized that all her planning hadn't been enough, because there was one thing she hadn't anticipated: she simply could not understand the auctioneer. His patter was so fluid and rapid that she couldn't make out a word he was saying. She hadn't the faintest idea what was being bid on the pigs, and she couldn't even see who was bidding.

Oh, God, she thought. This is awful. What am I going to do?

Frantically she tried to concentrate, looking around intently to see if she could tell who was bidding, but if they were anywhere nearby, she thought, they must be doing it by blinking their eyes.

"Thirty-three!" she heard the auctioneer sing out before he launched once more into his stream of meaningless sound. That was still well within Jo's price range, and these looked like nice, healthy pigs. Awkwardly she waved her hand, and one of the sharp-eyed cowboys down in the sales ring saw her and shouted. Everyone turned to look at her, the auctioneer rattled on, and Jo waved her hand again, more out of desperation than an actual desire to bid again.

The pigs exited the ring, the auctioneer's voice continued to crackle through the loudspeakers, and the audience murmured and chuckled while Jo sat in silent embarrassment, trying to ignore them.

"Hey, lady!" the auctioneer shouted. "You're out! You want these pigs or not?"

Jo wanted to ask what they were selling for, but she knew how stupid that would make her look and how everyone would laugh. Wearily she shook her head, and the auctioneer nodded.

"Sold!" he called. "Millie bought 'em. What pen do you want 'em in, Millie?"

"Put 'em in number seven," the slattern in the bib overalls called gruffly. She wrote something on her buyer's card and then turned to scowl furiously up at Jo before she settled in her seat again and lit another cigarette.

She thinks I'm just fooling around, Jo thought miserably... just bidding her up to have some fun and costing her money by doing it.

She felt lost and lonely, terribly out of place and conspicuous. She was chilly, hungry, tired and uncomfortable. She wanted to forget the whole thing and just go home. But there was no alternative. When she first proposed this idea she'd promised Mac that he wouldn't have to come to the sale and buy the pigs in front of all his neighbors. And, unfortunately, this was the only way to buy them. You couldn't go to some nice, clean pig store somewhere and deal with an understanding clerk. If you wanted to buy weanling pigs you had to buy them here at the sales yard.

Worst of all, though, was that she had suddenly realized that Gray Lyndon was in the building and had been for some time. He was down near the entry doors in the midst of laughing, chatting group of men, clearly the center of attention.

Suddenly Jo felt unaccountably flushed, though it was quite cool in the stands. She felt restless, too, though only a moment before she'd been comfortable enough in the padded seat. "Damn that man," she muttered quietly, then peered down to where he stood, deep in conversation with a spare, elderly rancher, and felt a little shock of surprise at his appearance.

The other times she had seen him he had either been in rough working clothes or in almost nothing at all. She was startled at how he looked today in beautiful polished riding boots, dark brown dress jeans and a creamy cashmere sweater under a soft, expensive leather jacket. He was bareheaded, and his curly graying hair glinted in the harsh overhead lights.

Jo hadn't spoken to him again since their heated exchange the day after she arrived, though she had seen him several times, driving his truck along the road he shared with Mac or, at a distance, checking his cattle and hauling blocks of salt out to the field that adjoined theirs.

Several times, when Jo had returned from a day of study and research in the city, Mac would comment casually, "Gray was here today. He asked about you." And then he would add, even more casually, "Gray sure seems to drop in a lot more often than he used to, for some reason..." But Jo had steadfastly refused to rise to the bait.

Now she watched as Gray moved away from the knot of people by the door and started up the aisle toward the buyers' circle, his big body erect, his stride lithe and easy. As he approached, the auctioneer stopped his lively patter to call out a greeting. "Well, folks, looks like Gray finally managed to drag himself outta bed an' get on down here. Now maybe we can start sellin' a few of them cattle we got out back!"

The crowd laughed, and Gray waved a casual hand. "You just go on, Jim," he called back, "and sell the rest of the pigs and calves. I need a cup of coffee, anyhow, to get myself wide awake before I start trying to buy cattle from this pack of outlaws!" He seated himself in the buyers' ring on another wave of laughter while Jo looked down and fumed.

They didn't stop the sale to give special greetings to anybody else, she thought. I wonder what everyone thinks is so terrific about him, anyhow.

As she watched, the doors opened, and another little group of pigs trotted into the ring. They were nice, healthy pigs, about a dozen of them, and the crowd glanced around to see if she would bid again, but this time she couldn't even tell what the starting price was, let alone the bids. She stared straight ahead, her eyes fixed resolutely on the opposite wall, and tried to ignore the stares of the audience and the look of surly contempt from the gruff woman in overalls.

From the corner of her eye she saw Gray Lyndon leave his seat and stroll out into the vestibule, and she thought, with a strange mix of hope and disappointment, that maybe he was leaving for good. She could stand making a fool of herself again, if she had to, but she hated the thought of having him witness it.

Soon, though, she saw him reappear, carrying a tray with two coffee cups and a plate of doughnuts. He began to mount the stairs toward her, and her heart gave a leap and began to pound almost painfully. She didn't understand this effect he'd begun to have on her. It almost felt like—

"Hi, Jo," he said, smiling and edging into the row of seats beside her. "I thought you might like a cup of coffee. It's cool up here."

Jo looked up at him and smiled, wondering how he always managed—no matter how bitter their most recent exchange had been—to remain calm and friendly the next time he saw her. It was as if their conversations had never been anything but casual and pleasant.

But today she wasn't inclined to be quite so unfriendly. She was, in fact, grateful for his thoughtfulness, and for his show of support in the midst of all these people who were his friends and neighbors, and she even found it hard to remember just exactly what he'd said that had made her so angry. She heard the little buzz of excited speculation as he settled into the seat beside her next to the aisle, and she tried to return his smile.

"Thank you," she murmured, taking a cup from the tray. "I really was dying for some coffee."

"Have a doughnut, too. They're great. Jim's wife makes them right down there in the kitchen."

Jo tasted a warm, sugary doughnut and agreed that it was, indeed, wonderful. Then they sat in awkward silence, watching as two wobbly little Holstein calves were shoved into the sales ring and herded around in front of the buyers. Jo felt warmed and comforted, both by the food and drink, and by the quiet presence of the big, handsome man beside her, sitting easily in the seat with his long legs extended into the aisle.

"So," he began finally, "I guess this is the plan, is it? You figure pigs can solve Mac's financial problems?"

"I'm sure of it," Jo said. She went on to tell him about her research and her profit projections and calculations while he listened, nodding thoughtfully.

"Sounds reasonable," he said when she finished. "How many are you planning to buy for starters?"

"We're going to try for a hundred today and then maybe get more next month if it looks like it's working out."

Gray pursed his lips in a low whistle. "Well, nobody can accuse you of being a coward, that's for sure." He paused. "What does Mac think about it?"

"He hates it," Jo said grimly. "I thought he was just being silly, but when I see the reactions of all these people here, I can understand a little better. Why he's so terribly reluctant, I mean."

Gray nodded. "They don't know you, and they haven't made the connection yet. But when word gets around that poor old Mac's going into pigs, there's going to be lots of teasing, that's for sure."

"But it's so silly!" She turned to look at him, her cheeks pink with indignation. "What does it possibly matter to them whether Mac raises pigs or . . . or elephants if he wants to?"

Gray met her furious dark blue gaze and smiled. "These are cattlemen, Jo. Lots of them, like my family and Mac's, have been here for generations. They're close-knit, but they're hard on each other, too, and they don't like pigs. They don't even associate with people who raise pigs. It's a . . . status thing, I guess. Like, cattlemen are superior to pig farmers."

"But there have to be lots of people around here raising pigs. Look at all the pigs at this sale. They have to come from somewhere nearby, don't they?"

"Sure, there are people raising pigs. But they're mostly newcomers, and they don't mix with the old ranching families. It's a real social distinction, you might say."

"I still think it's just silly," Jo repeated stubbornly. "Stock is stock and money is money. That's all there is to it."

Gray shook his dark head and sipped his coffee. "Not to these people," he said.

"How about you?" Jo asked him. "Are you going to abandon Mac just because he's raising pigs to save himself from bankruptcy?"

Gray looked down at her in amazement. "Well, of course not."

"Why not? You're one of *them*, aren't you? At least you certainly seem to be."

He grinned. "Not really. I mean, they like me, I guess, and I'm accepted in the group and all that. But I've always pretty much followed my own rules, and everybody knows it, so I can get away with whatever I want. But they're not usually so tolerant with other people."

Jo stole a sidelong glance at his square, rugged face and dancing eyes and wasn't surprised that he could get away with anything. She turned aside quickly and took another bite of her doughnut.

"Okay, Jo," he said suddenly as the doors opened and another little batch of pigs trotted in. "Here's a nice bunch. This is the size you're looking for, right?"

She nodded and looked up at him in amazement as he held two fingers in the air. The auctioneer flung his head back in mock amazement, and the crowd roared.

"Well, now, Gray's buyin' these pigs! You figurin' on branchin' out a little, Gray? Costin' too much to put them two pretty girls through college, is it?"

Gray placidly ignored the laughter that rocked the building and talked to Jo in a quiet undertone. "See, he started at thirty. I bid thirty-two just now, and Millie down there went to thirty-two and a half. What's your top dollar?"

"Thirty-four and three-quarters," Jo told him, paying close attention as he explained the bidding procedure.

"Okay. For that you hold up four fingers and bend the finger on your other hand at the tip, like this, so he knows it's three-quarters."

"But," Jo said in despair, "I don't know a word he's saying! I can never even tell what the *starting* bid is!"

"Sure you can. Listen carefully. Now you know he's started at thirty, so he won't say that again, at least not often. He'll just say the second number and the fraction, and you can catch it if you concentrate. See? He's up to thirty-three now.''

Jo frowned, straining to make sense out of the rapid-fire flow of words.

"And a quarter!'' she said suddenly, her face glowing with triumph. "He's at thirty-three and a quarter!''

"Good girl!'' Gray said, beaming at her with approval.

She met his eyes for a moment, warmed by his praise, and then looked down quickly.

"We're out,'' Gray commented. "Do you want back in at this price?''

"Oh, yes. Certainly.''

Gray held up three fingers of his right hand, and the index finger of his left hand, bent at the middle knuckle. The crowd, apparently not yet weary of the joke, roared with merriment once again at the sight of Gray Lyndon buying pigs and exchanged excited whispers and comments.

Jo ignored them, frowning with concentration as she listened to the auctioneer's jargon and clearly heard him accept Gray's bid, then begin asking for another quarter and then for thirty-four.

"Someone bid three-quarters just then,'' she said in confusion. "They had to because he jumped to thirty-four.''

Gray nodded. "Elmer Harms over there in the red plaid jacket by the door. See him?'' Jo nodded, leaning forward to look at the young farmer. "And Millie down there, and Len Beck—they're all bidding on this bunch.''

"How can you tell? I can never see anybody move a muscle.''

Gray held up four fingers, and the auctioneer shouted acknowledgment, increasing the pace of his spiel. Gray turned back to Jo. "See the bid takers down in front of the auctioneer's stand?''

"You mean, the cowboy types who move the stock around the ring?''

"Right. Well, they also take the bids. They know who's bidding, and you can tell by watching them and seeing who they're looking at."

"Oh!" Jo said, excited. "I see! She just bid, and now he's looking to see if . . . I forget his name . . ."

"Elmer," Gray prompted. "He's asking Elmer if he wants to bid again."

"He's shaking his head," Jo reported, leaning past Gray's big body again to peer down at the door.

"So now you know Elmer's out and Len quit bidding a while ago, so it's just you and Millie."

Gray waved his hand once more, and the auctioneer prompted Millie, who shook her shaggy head in disgust.

"Sold!" the auctioneer shouted. "To Gray Lyndon. What pen d'you want them little porkers in, Gray?"

Laughter washed through the building again, and Gray looked around at his neighbors with a cheerful grin. "Mark those sales slips Joanna McLean," he called down firmly to the secretaries scribbling at the back of the auctioneer's stand. "And put her pigs in pen fifty-six. Hank," he added, addressing one of the ring attendants, "you make sure they get there, okay? And keep pen fifty-seven open for Mrs. McLean, too."

At his words the laughter trailed off to be replaced by curious stares, directed at Jo, and a rising, noisy tide of lively speculation. But now that she actually owned some pigs and knew how to buy more, Jo wasn't at all bothered by their reactions.

A seemingly endless parade of Jersey milk cows began to move through the ring, and Jo turned away from the sale proceedings, watching intently as Gray showed her how to fill out her buyer's card and keep track of her stock.

"Those are nice pens," he told her. "They're covered, and warm and they have straw bedding in them, too. But they're pretty small. Keep track, and when you have fifty pigs in the first pen, start asking to have the rest put into fifty-seven.''

Jo nodded and smiled at him gratefully. "Thanks, Gray. I really appreciate this. I think I can manage on my own now," she added.

"Are you sure? You don't want me to hang around and keep an eye on you while you buy a couple of packages yourself?"

She shook her head. "Thanks, but I think I'd be more comfortable if I...didn't have an audience." She smiled awkwardly. "This is...kind of a new experience for me."

He got to his feet and stood gazing down at her thoughtfully. "Joanna McLean," he said in wonder, "you really are just one hell of a woman, you know that?"

Jo flushed under his direct, admiring gaze and looked down in silence at her clipboard, holding it tightly in both hands.

Gray turned and began to descend the steps and then apparently had another thought, because he paused and came back up to stand beside her. "Jo...how are you planning to get these pigs home after you get them all bought?"

"I was...Mac said there are trucks here, and I could just hire one."

"No need for that. I have my big stock trailer with me, and it'll easily hold a hundred little pigs. Let me know when you fill out your order, and then you can just head on home. I'll load your pigs up after the sale and take them to Mac's on my way home."

There was a little smile hovering around his finely shaped, humorous mouth and a merry glint in his gray eyes, and Jo cast him a sudden sharp glance. "Gray Lyndon," she began suspiciously, "you're not planning to tease Mac about this, are you? Because he's sensitive enough about the whole idea without you having fun at his expense. It was all I could do to talk him into it in the first place."

He grinned and didn't answer.

"Promise," Jo said sternly. "Promise me you won't make fun of Mac about these pigs."

"All right," he said with obvious reluctance. "I promise. But it's not fair, you know. If the situation were reversed, he'd sure be teasing *me*. I can guarantee it."

"Well, I don't care," Jo said. "Mac's been through a lot, and he's...pretty fragile these days. I don't want him to suffer over this, not if I can help it. Especially since it's actually my plan, not his."

He looked down at her, instantly contrite. "You're right, Jo. I'll deliver the pigs and I won't say a word about it. Honest."

Jo met his eyes, touched, in spite of herself, by his boyish sincerity. "Thanks, Gray," she said again. "Thanks for everything." She hesitated, about to say something more, and he stood beside her chair, waiting. "I'm...I'm sorry," she began, "for some of the things I said to you the last time we—"

He chuckled. "Don't apologize, Jo. It's just a waste of effort."

"Why?" she asked, looking up at him in surprise.

"Because," he told her with a sudden flashing grin that creased his cheeks and made his eyes dance with laughter, "in no time at all you'll likely be mad at me again and need to tell me off about something else I've done wrong. So why waste time apologizing every time it happens?"

"I had hoped," Jo said a little stiffly, "that none of that was going to be necessary anymore."

"Well," Gray said cheerfully, "you just never can tell, right? I seem to have a rare gift for making you mad, and we never know for sure when it's going to happen again, do we?"

He sobered and looked at her for a moment longer with a searching, intent gaze that made it difficult for her to meet his eyes. "See you, Jo. Let me know when you need those pigs trucked home."

"All right, then. But you'll have to let us pay for it."

"Okay," he said cheerfully. "I know what I want in payment."

She looked up at him, suddenly tense. "And what's that?"

"Well, Joanna," he said with a grin, "you still owe me a chess game, remember? I've been practicing for weeks just to get ready for it."

She nodded, smiling a little in spite of herself, and watched as he bounded down the steps and was gathered into the circle of cattle buyers, all of whom seemed eager to clap him on the back, punch him in the shoulder and ply him eagerly with questions.

But then the last milk cow passed out of the ring and another bunch of little pigs trotted in. Jo leaned forward, tense with excitement as she waited for the auctioneer to begin. She forgot about Gray Lyndon, about the jokes of the auctioneer, about the avid stares and whispers of the crowd—about everything, in fact, but the challenge of acquiring these pigs at the best possible price.

She took a deep breath, waited for her heart to stop racing, and then held up two fingers to make her first bid.

CHAPTER FIVE

RICH, EARLY-MORNING sunlight flooded the sparkling little kitchen, lying in shining rectangles along the countertops and across the floor. Through the open window, a chorus of song from the meadowlarks out in the fields filled the air with sweetness, and a fresh clean scent of grass and damp earth floated on the breeze that lifted the light muslin curtains.

Mrs. Brown lay near the door in a pool of sunlight, watching with weary resignation as her brood of fat puppies played and tumbled on the kitchen floor. One of them trotted over briskly, his little toenails clicking on the polished linoleum, and began to chew on her ear with great energy. She cocked the other ear, gave a small growl deep in her throat and batted at him with a listless paw. Then, apparently defeated, she lowered her shaggy head patiently, enduring the torment in gloomy silence.

Jo chuckled. "Poor thing. She's just about had it. I know exactly how she feels."

Mac smiled across the table at his niece. On this lovely late May morning she wore blue jeans and sneakers and a crisp white shirt, and, to his eyes, she looked as fresh and sweet as one of the shy, dainty bluebells that were now blooming in profusion in the sheltered prairie coulees.

"Well," he said, "she'll soon be getting a rest. Keith says they're all going next week."

"Not *all* of them," Jo said, giving him a severe glance.

Mac grinned. "Well, the poor kid, he worked so hard to find good homes for all of them, and, for some reason he just loves these two ugly little spotted ones. It won't hurt to let him keep just those two, Jo. There's lots of room here for a couple of more dogs."

"You're far too soft with him, Mac," Jo said, shaking her head and returning his smile. "He knows he can get anything out of you."

"He's a good kid. I like him. I just wish—"

Mac lapsed into silence, and his face shadowed with pain. He stared out the window with a brooding expression, and Jo gave him a quick, troubled glance.

"Mac..." she began.

"Ten thousand dollars," he muttered, still gazing at the cloudless blue sky. "Where am I going to get ten thousand dollars, Joey?"

"From the pigs," Jo said patiently. "Look, Mac, it's all right here." She held out the account book she was working on, filled with columns and rows of figures in her neat, precise hand. "See, here's our initial outlay, and our expenses so far have been almost nil, especially with all that feed you had on hand from last winter, and this is my profit projection."

"Jo, you're just playing with numbers. What do we know about pigs, really? Nothing, when you come right down to it. What if your profit projections are way out of line? Those are just numbers on a page. *This*—" he indicated the letter from the bank with a despairing wave of his hand "—is real, Jo. If I can't come up with ten thousand dollars by fall, I'll lose the upper pasture. And it's the only one with good water. And then there's no point in trying to run a ranch anymore."

"I wish you could be a little more optimistic about this, Mac, and not torture yourself so much. Now I admit that it might be a close shave. But with the kind of feed we're giving them, a pig this age doubles in volume and value inside six weeks. And soon we can turn them out into the alfalfa field, and they'll do even better. Now, with some luck . . ." She paused and underlined a couple of figures on the page of accounts. "With some luck we can put through four batches this summer. And if we hit good markets and don't get any sickness or anything, we should realize close to three thousand profit on each group. And that would just make our ten thousand, Mac."

He looked over at her, trying to smile. "I'd like to be as confident as you are. I really would. But I have the feeling that my ranch is already gone, Jo."

Jo opened her mouth to reply but was interrupted by a sudden, furious little uproar coming from the floor near Mac's feet.

"My goodness!" she said, jumping a little. "What on earth is *that*?"

"Just Clarence," Mac said calmly, "doing his thing."

One of Keith's favorites, the black-spotted pup, had launched himself at Mac's pant leg, gripping the hem of the heavy fabric between his tiny teeth and flinging himself furiously from side to side, growling deep in his baby throat.

Chuckling, Mac reached down and tried to detach the puppy, but it dug in firmly, its front paws braced, its little hindquarters lifted high in the air, and growled in defiance.

"Keith!" Mac shouted. "Get in here and rescue me from this monster!"

Keith hurried in from the living room, took in the situation at a glance and laughed. "Come on, Clarence," he said, "quit beating up on Mac."

He knelt down and gently pried the puppy's jaws open, lifting him away from Mac's pant leg and carrying him jauntily under his arm, like a loaf of bread, back into the other room.

Jo watched her son and smiled. They had been on the ranch for less than two months, but she could already see a world of difference in Keith. The changes weren't just physical, although there was no doubt that he was taller and stronger, and his pallor had been replaced by a healthy tan. What pleased Jo more were the less noticeable changes—the new ease and confidence that he displayed, and the gradual disappearance of the moodiness and tension that had plagued him since Mandy's death.

Though she tended to give it less thought, she knew there were changes in herself, as well. She was beginning to be able to think of her daughter without the old crushing, mind-numbing pain and even, occasionally, to look at pictures and treasured little souvenirs without bursting into tears.

Maybe in time we'll both heal . . . if we can just stay here in this wonderful place with Mac.

A couple of cold little shadows flitted across her mind, accompanied by a chill breath of worry, and she frowned. Maybe they wouldn't be able to stay. If she was wrong and Mac was right, then they'd all be leaving, before the snow fell.

And, despite how well everything was going, there were times when she thought that maybe this place wasn't, after all, the best thing for Keith. He seemed happier and more confident, but he was also getting more and more quiet and private, absorbed in his own concerns, and he spent a lot of time away from home, giving only the vaguest of accountings when he returned of where he'd been and what he'd been doing.

"Something wrong, Jo?" Mac was asking, looking at her thoughtful, troubled face.

She shook herself a little and looked up. "Pardon, Mac?"

"You looked concerned just then. Is something bothering you. I mean, besides me loading all my problems on you all the time?"

"No...well, yes, I guess. I was just thinking about Keith."

"Keith? Why are you concerned about him? He's doing great."

"Yes, Mac, but *what* is he doing? All those times he stays after school or says he's over at Gray's place or when he goes off with friends on the weekends—where's he going? What's he *really* doing?"

"Being a kid," Mac said briefly. "Kids need some space and privacy, too, Jo. They shouldn't have to give an accounting for every single move they make. You have to trust them a little that they'll be sensible and use good judgment on their own."

"I guess so." She toyed aimlessly with her pencil, trying to balance it on the rim of her glass. "But when I don't know what he's doing I get...I get so worried, Mac."

She looked up at her uncle, her face puckered with concern, her blue eyes pleading, and he smiled at her gently. "You know what he's doing, Jo. He's learning to ride steers, and he's having a wonderful time."

"Oh, Mac...it scares me so much. He could get so terribly hurt."

"Not likely," Mac said calmly. "Half the kids around here get involved in rodeo and not many of them ever get hurt."

"Not many," Jo repeated gloomily. "That's small comfort, Mac." She hesitated. "Sometimes I get so angry with Gray for encouraging him, you know? It's like he doesn't have a son of his own, so he's taken over mine to make him into a little miniature Gray Lyndon. I just hate it."

Mac shook his head. "You're wrong to feel that way, Jo. I think Keith would have gotten into this on his own as soon as he found out about it. He loves it. Actually, you're lucky Gray takes the time with him to teach him properly. Gray Lyndon's the best there is, Jo. If I had a son, I'd be pleased to have Gray teaching him."

"Well, I'd be more pleased if he'd just leave my son alone. But I can't seem to talk to him about it."

"Well, then, why don't you talk to Keith about how you feel?"

"Oh, Mac," Jo said in despair. "I've *tried* to talk to Keith. But he just gets that set, stubborn look and tunes me out. I'm terrified that I'll lose him altogether if I push too hard. So I just keep quiet about it and worry and worry...."

"I know you worry, Jo. But you have to try not to. You really do." He got up, ambled to the door and took his cap from a hook in the porch. "Tell you what," he said, fitting the cap onto his bald head and turning to smile at her. "You try not to worry so much about that kid, and I'll try not to fret all the time about going bankrupt. Deal?"

"Deal," Jo said, smiling back at him.

"Good. Well," he said in a tone of sudden, deep gloom, "I guess I can't put it off any longer, can I? I have to go out and feed those horrible little things."

"Don't be like that, Mac. They're *nice* pigs. And it's fun feeding them. They're always so...enthusiastic about being fed."

"That," Mac observed darkly, "is putting it mildly."

He opened the door with obvious reluctance, latched it carefully behind him and trudged across the yard in the direction of the calf pen, now converted to a pig feeder.

Jo stood at the window and watched him, her face quiet and thoughtful.

PUSHING OPEN THE DOOR of the feeder, Mac stepped gingerly inside, dragging a bulging burlap sack behind him. The smell assailed him at once, a sharp, earthy acrid tang that was, surprisingly, not nearly as terrible now as it had seemed when the pigs first arrived. He stood in silence, looking around. The calf feeder was a roomy building, roofed and enclosed on three sides and opening into a huge corral pen.

Under the roof was a long gravity feeder that was filled from the top, allowing the feed to run down into divided outlet at the bottom where the pigs could get at it. A galvanized metal water trough stood nearby, filled by a pump connected to the windmill outside.

There were pigs everywhere, snorting, tumbling in the straw, rooting in the dirt outside in the corral and sniffing wistfully at the empty water trough. Mac started to drag the sack across the enclosure, and the pigs suddenly became aware of his presence. About twenty of them galloped over to greet him, jostling around him, nibbling at his high rubber boots and cavorting about his legs.

"Git!" he shouted. "Git away, you awful little varmints!"

He opened the sack of daily protein supplement, hoisted it to shoulder height and dumped it into the feeder on top of the chopped grain while the pigs crowded around, watching with lively interest. Then he turned on the pump, sending a clear stream of water splashing into the long metal trough. The pigs launched themselves at it, climbing over one another's backs in their haste to get at the fresh, sparkling water.

"Thirsty, were you?" Mac muttered aloud. "No wonder. Go through a hundred gallons of water a day. I never saw anything like it."

He watched them drink for a while and then looked around with a questioning expression. Finally he opened the door, glanced back out over his shoulder to make sure that neither Joanna nor Keith were nearby and began to call softly.

"Sooo-ee! Soo-eeee! Here, pig, pig, pig..."

A few of the pigs cast him bright, curious glances, then went on drinking. He called again, and there was a sudden little eruption from the other side of the pen. A mass of straw flew into the air, and a pig crawled out from underneath, shook himself and then trotted across the enclosure, still shaking wisps of straw from his head.

Mac watched the pig approach, trying to stifle a fond little grin that tugged at the corners of his mouth. The small, plump hog was a comical sight with one droopy ear and a number of big black blotches splashed on his body like spilled paint, including one situated directly over his left eye. He headed briskly in Mac's direction with a look of great intensity on his small, pointed face.

Mac watched him come and cast another cautious glance over his shoulder before he knelt to greet the little pig. "So there you are," he murmured, scratching behind the droopy ear. "I wondered where you'd gotten to, you little devil."

The blotchy pig arched his back in pleasure like a cat and rubbed against Mac's rubber boot. Mac petted him a moment longer and then moved out into the open pen, still talking to the pig, which trotted cheerfully at his heels.

"We have to check for holes again, I guess," Mac said, pausing by the fence and addressing the pig, which looked up at him with an alert and interested expression.

Mac knelt, running his hand along a hollowed-out portion where the pigs had been burrowing, trying to dig their way out of the corral to get into the rich, inviting field of alfalfa beyond.

"Damn pigs," Mac continued, still speaking to the little blotchy hog, which was rooting contentedly nearby and returning at intervals to have his ears scratched. "Strongest fence I ever built and you're going to have it wrecked in another week. What do I have to put here to keep you in—land mines? I swear—"

"Hey, Mac," Keith's voice called from beyond the fence. "Who's there? We heard you talking to someone."

Mac straightened guiltily and looked over the fence. Jo and Keith were both standing there in the morning sunlight. Jo had a dark blue cardigan draped over her shoulders, and Keith still carried the little spotted puppy, which was nestled drowsily in his arms.

"Huh?" Mac said.

"Who are you talking to?" Keith repeated.

"Oh...just talking to myself. Getting old, I guess. At least I haven't gotten to the stage where I start answering back. Not yet, anyhow. Look," he went on, "these awful animals have just about dug under the fence again. I'm going to have to put a layer of tin or something in all these holes or these damn pigs are going to wind up in the next township."

"I don't know why you hate the pigs so much," Keith said, leaning on the fence and peering in at the busy pink swarms of feeding, fighting, squealing bodies. "I think they're neat. They're so smart."

"Smart!" Mac snorted. "Horrible things," he added.

Jo gave him a shrewd little glance, and a smile hovered around the corners of her mouth, but she said nothing.

They were distracted by the roar of an approaching engine and a flash of yellow as a little Jeep came tearing down the approach road and into the yard, pulling up with a flourish near the three by the corral fence.

"It's Peggy and Libby!" Keith called out joyously, watching in delight as the two tall, slender, red-haired girls, wearing blue jeans and T-shirts, climbed out of the Jeep and strolled toward them.

Jo smiled as well, tugging the cardigan closer around her shoulders and waiting while they approached. They had all seen a lot of the Lyndon girls since their return from college, and the rapport between her and the twins had been instant and mutual. Jo liked their warm, natural manner and their girlish high spirits, while they were drawn to her maturity and understanding and were greatly in awe of her courage and enterprise in purchasing the pigs and using them to solve Mac's financial problems.

As usual, Peggy was in the lead, her vivid face glowing with joy at the beauty of the morning and the pleasure of seeing her friends all together in a group. Libby, quieter and more reserved, followed a few paces behind her more extroverted sister. Apart from the obvious personality differences, the girls were absolutely identical, with delicate oval faces, sparkling green eyes, lithe shapely bodies and masses of springy, curly red hair. But Peggy usually let her wild, bright hair hang loose, with a colorful, twisted headband holding it back from her face, while Libby's unruly mane was tamed and subdued into a long plait that hung sedately down her back.

"Hi, guys!" Peggy called out, beaming at all of them. "What's shakin'?"

She climbed onto the corral fence and leaned over the upper rail to snatch Mac's cap off and plant a loving kiss on the top of his bald head. Libby, meanwhile, moved quietly in between Jo and Keith, gave Jo a shy, affectionate smile and lifted the puppy carefully from Keith's arms, murmuring and burying her face against its fragrant, warm body.

Peggy replaced Mac's cap and lingered on the fence rail for a moment, gazing at the pigs in the corral. "I just adore those pigs," she announced. "I think they must be an upper level of incarnation. They seem to be such well-integrated personalities, you know?"

"You're crazy, Peggy," Keith observed, looking up at her with an admiring grin.

"Keefer, you little squirt!" she shouted, climbing down and punching him on the arm. "When am I going to train you to show some respect for your elders?" She paused and studied him narrowly. "How come you're here, anyhow? Why aren't you in school?"

"Because it's Saturday," Keith said patiently.

"It's just heaven to be on holidays," Libby said, smiling at Jo. "We keep forgetting what day it is. Imagine being eighteen and not even knowing that it's Saturday."

"Saturday," Peggy repeated with exaggerated thoughtfulness. "Then tomorrow has to be Sunday." She grinned wickedly at the boy. "So, Keefer, my lad, are you up for it? Not losing your nerve?"

A sudden, uneasy current ran through the group, and Keith, Mac and the girls exchanged rapid glances. Jo looked around at all of them. "Why? What's happening tomorrow?" she asked slowly.

They all exchanged another glance, and then Keith said nervously, "Well, see, I'm...I'm going over to Gray's, and...and Peggy's going to let me ride her barrel racing horse. Just so I can...start learning to...to ride a horse, you know?"

Jo looked thoughtfully at his tense young face, knowing that he was lying. Worse, everyone else knew it, as well, and they were all conspiring to deceive her. She wondered what Keith was doing tomorrow with Gray and his daughters and felt a sudden flare of anger against Gray.

Why, she thought for the hundredth time, can't he just leave Keith alone? I've tried everything....

The tension was broken by the sound of another vehicle approaching. Jo peered around the corner of the house, and her heart gave a great leap and began thudding painfully in her chest when she recognized Gray's dusty dark blue truck.

He parked beside the girls' Jeep and strolled across the yard toward them, big and handsome in his jeans and a soft, faded old denim shirt. Jo shifted uneasily on her feet, wondering if the hammering of her heart was audible to the others standing nearby.

More and more he was having this effect on her, making her feel as light-headed and breathless as a girl. Worst of all, there seemed to be no way of controlling this reaction, even when she was furious with him about something. She was no longer fuzzy about exactly what she was feeling, either. In the midst of an argument she would look up at him and find herself wondering how it would feel to have those muscular arms around her, what it would be like to feel those power-ful, finely molded lips pressing hungrily against hers. . . .

"Hi, everyone," he said casually, and then turned to Libby. "I thought I sent you girls out to count calves, and then I find you over here instead, bothering the neigh-bors."

Libby smiled fondly and patted his tanned cheek. "We finished, Dad. There's fifty-seven calves in the south pas-ture. And we were down at this end when we finished, and Peggy wanted to stop in and see the pigs."

"Oh, did she? Well, Peggy, there's somebody up at the house who wants to see *you*."

There was a sudden, hard edge to his voice that made everyone glance at him in surprise. Peggy turned pale un-der her tan, and her lovely animated face went suddenly bleak and tense. She looked defiantly at her father. "What did you tell him?"

"I told him I'd find you and send you home." Gray looked at his daughter, his eyes as cold as steel. "Get rid of him, Peggy. I don't want him on my ranch. He'd better be gone when I get home."

Peggy stared at her father for a moment longer, then turned angrily on her heel and strode toward the Jeep.

"Coming, Libby?" she called without turning around, her hand on the door handle.

"No. . ." Libby said, looking troubled and almost on the verge of tears. "That's okay, Peg. I'll just . . . just stay here awhile and come later with Dad."

Peggy slammed into the Jeep, gunned the engine and roared out of the yard. The others stood silently, watching the bright flare of yellow disappear up the road.

Gray still stared into the distance, his jaw firm and set, until long after the vehicle was gone from sight. Then he gathered himself together and turned to smile down at Jo. "Well, Joanna," he said softly. "How's my favorite financial wizard on this beautiful May morning?"

Jo met his gaze, still troubled by the painful little scene that had just occurred, and by the obvious discomfort of Keith and Libby.

"I'm fine," she told Gray. "Let's all go up to the house and have a coffee break, shall we? I just baked some gingersnaps, and Keith says they're really good. He should know," she added. "He's already eaten about twenty of them."

The tension snapped, and Mac climbed over the fence to join them, kicking gently at the little spotted pig as it attempted to follow.

"Stupid pig," he said to the others. "Thinks it's a dog or something. Doesn't even know it's just a pig."

Jo gave him another quick, thoughtful glance, and then they all trooped across the yard toward the house, laughing and chatting together in the beaming warmth of the late spring morning.

Gray walked close beside Jo, and she was painfully conscious of the proximity of his big body. Once, when his hand brushed casually against hers, her flesh burned and tingled at the brief contact. Another time, in the midst of a teasing exchange, he rested his hard, heavy arm briefly across her shoulders as he laughed down at her, and a deep sexual thrill shot to the core of her being, leaving her feeling damp, uneasy and full of restless longing.

Oh, God, she thought helplessly. How can this be happening to me? And with *him*? I'm not ready for this. I'm really not.

They entered the kitchen, and the older people seated themselves around the table with the ease and comfort of old, trusted friends. Libby immediately dropped to her knees on the floor and crawled around, totally without self-consciousness, playing with the lively brood of fat puppies.

Keith shed all of his edgy, adolescent dignity and joined her, holding his sides and rolling on the floor, howling with laughter as Libby imitated the puppies' antics.

The three adults watched them, smiling indulgently, and sipped their coffee in companionable silence. Jo longed to ask about Peggy and her mysterious visitor, but remembering Gray's tense and angry face as he confronted his daughter, she restrained herself and decided instead to question Mac or Libby about it later in private.

I guess, she thought, everybody has trouble with their kids sometimes, even Gray.

She looked up at him with a teasing sparkle in her eyes. "So, Gray, I hear you're having a party that I'm not invited to. Now is that a neighborly thing to do?"

He looked at her, startled.

"Tomorrow," Jo said. "I understand from Peggy that something's going on at your place tomorrow, and Keith seems to be invited, but not me."

Gray smiled back at her. "Of course you're invited, Jo," he said. "I'd love to have you come to my house anytime you wanted to—any time at all."

Keith stiffened in terror, and Mac shot his neighbor a sudden glance of alarm, intervening hastily. "You can't go over to Gray's tomorrow, Jo. Those pigs are going to market on Monday morning, and we have to spend tomorrow afternoon getting them ready and washing them and everything.

Jo turned away from Gray's compelling gaze and looked at her uncle. "Don't worry, Mac. I'm not going over there. I just wanted to make sure I was invited, that's all."

She saw the tension in Keith's shoulders as he sat staring at the floor, all his laughter stilled, and felt a quick pang of regret, both for her teasing words and for the times in the past when she knew she had been too strict with him because of her own fears.

"Anyhow," she said briskly, "it's none of my business. I guess Keith is old enough to look after himself without his mother hovering around all the time watching him. Right?"

Keith glanced up at her in amazement, and Gray gave her a warm, delighted smile as she got up to refill their coffee mugs.

"Libby and I are taking the puppies outside," Keith announced. "She wants to see the big doghouse I'm building for Mrs. Brown and Alfred and Clarence."

The two of them went out, laughing and talking together, each carrying a puppy, and the three in the kitchen relaxed in the sudden peace and stillness.

"Gray," Mac began, his gentle, craggy face twisted with concern, "is Peggy—?"

"Please, Mac," Gray interrupted him. "I don't want to talk about it. I don't even want to think about it."

Jo looked at his square, rugged face, usually so full of cheerful teasing and good humor. But now his features were tense and brooding, his gray eyes darkened with worry.

"Gray," she said gently, "what's wrong?"

"Nothing I can't handle. I guess," he added, pushing his chair back and getting to his feet, "I'd better be getting home. We're branding tomorrow, and I need to start gathering cattle."

"I'll show you where the kids are," Jo said, pulling her cardigan on again. "Keith's building this huge doghouse over behind the Quonset...."

They left the kitchen together, talking quietly, and stepped out into the sunny farmyard, filled with a warm, springtime fragrance.

"Libby!" Gray called. "I'm leaving if you want a ride. Right now."

"In a minute, Dad," she called back, her voice muffled and far away. "Keith and I just have to catch—" Her words broke off in a shout of laughter, and Gray and Jo paused beside his truck and turned to smile at each other.

Jo looked up at him, and her smile faded. "Gray, I meant what I said. I know it's wrong for me to interfere too much in Keith's life, and I'm going to try not to."

"Good. You're doing the right thing."

"But," Jo continued doggedly, "I still haven't changed my mind about . . . about the kind of thing I suspect you might be getting him into. I hate the thought of danger for its own sake, and training a boy to think that he can't be having fun or acting like a man unless he's doing something dangerous. I know what it's like to lose a child, and I just can't stand . . . I just—"

Her voice broke suddenly, and Gray reached out and gripped her arm gently. "Steady, Jo," he murmured. "Steady. It's all right."

Jo stood quietly, trembling a little at the rich, tingling sensation of his warm, calloused hand against her skin, a warmth she could feel distinctly even through the heavy fabric of her sweater.

She met his eyes again, her face passionate with the depth of her conviction. "I mean it, Gray. If you're getting my boy involved in something, well, I know I can't be hanging around all the time to supervise. I just have to trust that you know what you're doing, and why. But if he gets hurt because of you, I want you to know that I'll never, ever be able to forgive you. Never."

He looked steadily into her eyes, his face quiet and intent. "Never is a long, long time, Jo."

"I know it is."

"Joanna McLean," he murmured, his voice suddenly husky, "if you were to get mad at me and never forgive me, I don't know if I could stand it."

She gazed up at him, stunned and almost frightened by the look of hunger that suddenly flared in his handsome face, and the depths of longing in his darkly lashed gray eyes.

Wide-eyed, she stared at him and then tried to pull away as he tugged her gently toward him, still gripping her arm, and drew her into the shadow cast by the open door of his truck.

"Gray," she murmured in protest. "Gray, please don't."

Then suddenly his lips were on hers, and her words were stilled, drowned in a wave of yearning that swept over her and left her numb and weak. She gave herself up to his kiss, loving it, loving the feel of his lips against her face and his hands on her body, and the sense that she was falling...falling into some place so deep and private and secluded that nobody had ever been there before....

"Joanna," he murmured, drawing away gently and brushing her hair aside to whisper into her ear. "Joanna, there are just so many things I want to—"

Shouts and laughter invaded the warm, secret place that had enclosed them for a moment. They heard Keith and Libby approaching across the yard, obviously followed by a whole troop of dogs, and sprang apart quickly.

By the time the young people reached the truck, Gray was leaning casually against the closed door, his hands in his pockets and his booted feet extended, whistling soundlessly between his teeth, while Jo stood rigidly beside the truck box, gazing at the horizon with an intent frown.

Keith cast a quick glance at his mother's flushed cheeks and her rapid, shallow breathing and then looked over at Gray. "Have you two been fighting again?" he asked suspiciously.

Gray turned to the boy with an injured look of innocence. "*I* don't fight," he protested. "Is it my fault if your mother just doesn't seem to like me?'' He grinned and tried to catch Jo's eye, but she refused to look at him.

"Well," Keith said firmly, while Libby stood nearby in troubled silence, "I think it's just stupid. I wish you'd both start acting like grown-ups and try to get along. After all, we're neighbors!"

"How about it, Jo?" Gray asked cheerfully, still grinning at her. "Want to try being a little more neighborly from now on?"

She met his glance almost involuntarily and bit her lip as she saw his dancing eyes and his warm, meaningful smile. "I think," she said firmly, "that I'd actually much rather just keep on fighting, thanks all the same." She bent, scooped the nearest puppy into her arms and cradled it defiantly as she marched off toward the house, refusing to look back.

Keith watched her go and then turned to Gray, his face full of apology. "She'll come around," he said. "She's really nice, honest she is. She just gets…sometimes she's…"

"It's okay, Keith. Don't worry about it." Gray dropped a fatherly arm around the boy's shoulders and gave him a brief hug, watching Jo's slender form as she opened the kitchen door and disappeared inside the house.

"I think you're right, you know," Gray added with a thoughtful, faraway smile as he turned to open the door of his truck and climbed inside.

"About what?" Keith asked, leaning against the truck and looking in at the big man.

Gray turned the key in the ignition, watched as Libby fastened her seat belt and then turned to smile at Keith. "I think she's going to come around," Gray said softly. "I really think she is."

CHAPTER SIX

"OKAY," MAC SHOUTED. "I've got the hose ready. You herd them down there into the corner and try to hold them there!"

"Easy for *you* to say," Jo muttered, stumbling along in her high rubber boots, panting with the effort of rounding up the squealing, excited mass of pigs.

The herd raced along the corral fence and pounded into the corner, packed along the fence, squirming and milling around, while Mac directed the stream of water over their backs and heads.

Suddenly, to Jo's amazement, the pigs began to calm, lifting their pink snouts, closing their eyes and standing quietly under the streams of water.

"Mac," she shouted, "Look at them! They like it!"

"It's about time they had a bath," he said grimly, aiming the hose with deadly accuracy at every patch of dried mud that was visible. "Filthy things," he added.

"They are not," Jo said. "Pigs are very clean animals, Mac, and you know it. If they're properly cared for and have enough room, they never foul their own sleeping area, and they keep their living space really clean."

"I have to admit," he agreed grudgingly, "that they've surprised me a little. Not," he added hastily, "that I'm saying I *like* them or anything. They're just . . . not quite as horrible as I thought they'd be, that's all."

The pigs were rapidly becoming pink and clean as they turned and preened under the arching sprays of warm water. Rainbows sparkled in the afternoon sunlight, and the mass of animals crowding in the corner grunted and squealed in pleasure.

Jo watched the process with satisfaction. "The book says that it's worth as much as five dollars a head at sale time just to have them clean," she told Mac. "I can see why, can't you? They look so much better."

"Yeah, sure," he muttered in disgust. "And now there's a big mud wallow underneath them, and in about two minutes those awful things are all going to be rolling in it and looking like little licorice pigs!"

"Oh, my goodness, you're right!" She began to run again, shouting and waving her arms. "Mac, you keep hosing them off while I move them up into the other pen!"

She panted with effort, her boots sticking and sucking deep into the mud with every step, but finally managed to herd the pigs into the next pen, which Keith and Mac had prepared earlier, lining it liberally with clean, dry straw. Still puffing, Jo closed the gate, latched it and leaned against the fence, looking through the rails with pleasure and relief at the corral full of shining, fat pigs, sunning themselves and rooting contentedly in the masses of fresh straw.

Mac joined her and surveyed the herd gloomily.

"Don't they look good?" Jo asked when she had her breath back. "We're lucky it was such a nice sunny day to give them their bath. The book says that if they take a chill, they can catch cold, just like people, and you can lose half your herd almost overnight. Pigs are very fragile."

"Fragile!" Mac snorted, still gazing over the fence at the squirming, squealing mass. "You and that damn book of yours," he added.

Jo heard the gruff affection in his voice and smiled privately, but said nothing.

"Say, Jo," he began, his tone elaborately casual, "that ugly little spotted pig, the one with the droopy ear...you know?"

"This one here? Trying to eat your boot through the fence?"

"Oh, is that where he is?" Mac asked, trying to sound surprised. "I didn't see him."

"That's where he is," Jo said dryly. "Right here underfoot, just like always."

"Yeah, I see him now." Mac nudged the pig gently with his boot through the fence, trying to get it to go away and join the others, but it looked up at him with bright, adoring eyes and rubbed eagerly against the board rail near his leg.

"Mac?" Jo prompted.

"Hmm?"

"Were you saying something about this pig here?"

"Oh, yeah." Mac gathered himself together with an effort and went on. "I don't think...I don't think we should send him to market along with the others."

Jo looked up at her uncle in surprise. "Really, Mac? Why not?"

"Well..." Mac hesitated again, then said, "He looks... kind of thin and sick, don't you think? I figured if we kept him for a while, he might fatten up a little. He's not going to make us any money if we sell him now. None at all."

Jo looked down at the plump, busy little hog in thoughtful silence and said nothing.

"Besides," Mac went on with a note of desperation creeping into his voice, "I was...I was reading that book of yours the other night after you went to bed, and it says..." He paused in obvious discomfort, then plunged ahead. "It says that when you...when you sell a bunch of hogs and buy a new bunch, you should always keep one back, kind of, to teach the new little ones where to eat and where the water is and all that. It helps them to...to settle down better and make the adjustment.''

Jo nodded, still thoughtful.

''It really says that,'' Mac argued, as if she had voiced disagreement.

''Okay, I believe you. It does sound like a good idea. But why this particular pig? I thought you disliked him even more than all the rest. You're always complaining about what a nuisance he is, getting in your way all the time and all that.''

''Oh, he is,'' Mac said fervently. ''He's the worst of the bunch. I hate him. I really do. But I just thought, since he's looking so thin and there's no profit in selling him, anyhow, that we should try to stand him for a while longer, just because...you know...''

His voice trailed off lamely, and he and Jo stood side by side, watching as the fat little pig stood on his hind legs, resting his tiny, sharp front hooves on the bottom fence rail and tried to squirm between the boards to get closer to Mac. He squealed happily, and his little curled tail frisked from side to side with great energy as he struggled.

''Git!'' Mac muttered down at him. ''Git away, you fool pig!''

Jo choked and turned aside to hide the laughter that she could no longer control. Finally she looked back at her uncle, her face carefully composed. ''Mac, you know, I think you're right,'' she said solemnly. ''He *does* look thin, doesn't he? And I think it's a really good idea, to have an older pig here when the new ones arrive.''

Mac relaxed visibly and plucked a straw from his hat-band, chewing on it in thoughtful silence.

''It's just a shame,'' Jo went on innocently, unable to resist, ''that it has to be *this* particular pig that we have to keep. I mean, knowing how much you hate him and all.''

"Yeah," Mac agreed, scowling fiercely down at the little hog who had given up the attempt to climb through the fence and was rolling happily in the straw, his small legs waving, his ears flapping, grunting in pure bliss. "I'll just have to try and stand the little nuisance for a while longer, I guess."

"Well," Jo said, gazing in satisfaction at the noisy pen full of pigs, "there they are. We haven't lost a single one, and they've all done well—doubled their weight in six weeks. Now they have the rest of the afternoon to dry off, and we'll give them an extra good feeding tonight, and tomorrow the truck comes to take them to the sale. And *then*—" she punched Mac's arm lightly and gave him a fond grin "—we should double our money. Almost three thousand dollars to go toward that bank loan. What do you think of *that*, Malcolm Burman, you old grouch?"

"I think you're a wonder, Jo," he said with sudden, quiet sincerity. "I really do. I'm starting to believe that maybe you really *can* save my scrawny old neck for me."

"Oh, pooh," Jo said cheerfully. "It's not just me. We're doing this together. We're a family, Mac."

Mac choked suddenly and turned away to brush furtively at his eyes, while Jo started tactfully toward the house, calling back to him over her shoulder. "Come on, Mac. That's enough work for a while. Let's go up and have a cup of coffee, and then we'll fill out the shipping form for the trucker."

"Okay." He fell into step beside her, and they strolled companionably toward the little house. "Jo...?"

"Hmm?"

"Didn't I hear Gray offering to haul the pigs to the sale for you?"

Jo went inside, washed her hands at the sink in the porch and moved into the kitchen to fill the kettle with water. "Yes," she said. "He offered. But I don't want... I don't like the idea of getting too dependent on him. We can look after ourselves, Mac. We don't need Gray Lyndon doing favors for us all the time."

Mac watched her slim, quick-moving form in troubled silence. "You still don't like him much, do you, Jo?"

"Well, I—" She avoided his eyes, struggling to control her voice. In spite of herself, she remembered the wild, sweet pleasure of Gray's kiss the day before and shivered in the warmth of the sunny kitchen. "I don't know, Mac. I guess he's all right. It's just that—" She hesitated, then changed the subject abruptly. "Mac, what was all that yesterday about Peggy? I wanted to ask you earlier, but I didn't like to bring it up while Keith was around."

Mac's face clouded. "That's a real shame," he said. "I know Libby feels just awful about it, and it's causing so many problems over there."

"I could see that." Jo set coffee mugs on the table and lifted down a tinful of cake to place it in front of her uncle. "But what is it? Who came to see her yesterday?"

"I guess you'd call him a boyfriend," Mac said, taking a piece of cake and munching on it gloomily. "But Gray sure wouldn't like to hear you call him that. Peggy met him last fall, just after the girls went to Calgary to university. He came down to visit her at the ranch over the Christmas holidays, and Gray just about threw him out of the house."

"Why?" Jo asked, seating herself opposite the older man and staring at him, wide-eyed.

"Well, see he's not...not the type Gray wants for his daughter. He's quite a bit older, for one thing—mid or late twenties, I guess—and he's a biker type. He has long hair and a big scar on his face and tattoos on his arms, and he wears a black leather jacket all the time."

"My goodness," Jo said. "No wonder Gray's upset. I think I would be, too."

"Well, maybe not," Mac said, his face still troubled. "The girls brought him down to meet me when he was here at Christmas time, and I really liked him. You can't always judge by appearances, Jo. I've got no doubt that this fellow has sowed some wild oats in his time. But when he was here he seemed like a real nice, intelligent young fellow, and he really loves that girl. You can see it all over him. He just worships the ground she walks on. And I think she feels the same way."

Jo considered this thoughtfully, sipping her coffee. "What does he do?" she asked. "Is he just a biker full-time or unemployed or what?"

"Neither. He's got a good job. He sells and services computers at a big store in Calgary and makes real good money."

Jo stared. "You're kidding."

"Everybody has to settle down eventually, Joey. And I guess this man's decided his wild days are over. He was telling me that he's saving his money, hoping eventually to buy his own shop. He just loves computers. He really gets into it when he's talking to you about them. I couldn't understand a word he was saying," Mac added with a grin.

"What's his name?"

"Rob Simmons."

Jo nodded, still thoughtful. "I wonder if he talks to Gray at all about computers and his plans for the future and how he feels about Peggy."

"Not likely. Gray hates him. I don't think he'd have the chance to talk to Gray about anything. Gray wouldn't even listen to *me* when I tried to tell him what I thought about the boy."

"Gray Lyndon," Jo observed grimly, "could be making a bad mistake, I'm afraid."

"That's what I'm afraid of, too." Mac met her eyes, his face troubled. "Peggy's always been a girl who knows her own mind and does what she wants. Has ever since she was born. If Gray pushes Peggy hard enough, God knows what's going to happen.''

"Isn't it strange?" Jo said absently, getting up to refill their coffee mugs.

"What's strange?"

"I don't know...life, I guess." She hesitated, trying to make up her mind whether she wanted a piece of cake and decided against it. "I mean, Gray's just full of advice on how I should be raising Keith. He can tell me everything I'm doing wrong, and he's ready to leap right in there and correct all my mistakes. And yet he doesn't seem to have the foggiest notion how to handle his own daughter!"

Mac was silent, chewing reflectively on a second piece of cake.

"What are you thinking?" Jo asked suspiciously.

"I'm thinking," Mac said, "that just because Gray's wrong about Peggy, that doesn't mean he couldn't still be right about Keith."

Jo refused to answer. She cleared the table, ran water over their coffee mugs and plates and stared out the window with a worried, brooding expression, gazing up the road in the direction of Gray's ranch.

I wonder, she thought. I wonder what Keith's doing, right this minute.

"Wow!" KEITH BREATHED, and turned to Gray, his eyes shining. "You built it! You really did! I thought you were just kidding me!"

"Well, sure I built it." Gray shifted awkwardly on his feet, delighted at the boy's obvious enthusiasm and touched by the look of hero worship in his eyes. "Didn't have much choice, did I?" he asked gruffly to hide the fondness in his voice. "Not with you bugging me about it every chance you've had these past weeks."

"Wow," Keith murmured again. He walked across the corral to inspect the new bucking chute at the end of the Lyndon girls' barrel racing arena. Gray had just finished it that morning, and the wood was still fresh-smelling and unpainted, but the chute was firm and sturdy, with the posts firmly planted and the gate hanging straight and true.

"See how it works?" Gray said, coming up beside the boy. "This little gate on the end opens into the holding pen back there, and there's a wing outside it. So we run your steer up the fence and into the chute, and then you get your bull rope on him and get set and everything, and when you're down and ready, we open the big front gate here—" Gray swung it open to demonstrate "—and there you are out in the arena, bucking and spinning while the crowd roars."

Keith laughed in delight and moved around to test the latch on the big gate.

Gray watched him, grinning privately. Already the boy walked with a look of manly confidence, even a little swagger obviously taking pleasure in picturing himself on the bucking, whirling, massive animal in the middle of the rodeo arena.

Slowly Gray's grin faded, and his face clouded with concern. "Keith..." he began.

"Yeah, Gray?" the boy asked, kneeling by the gate, too absorbed to turn around.

"Keith, your mother isn't going to be happy about this."

"So?" Keith looked over his shoulder. "We just won't tell her, that's all. What she doesn't know won't hurt her."

Gray came up beside the boy, his face still troubled. "I don't like to hear you talk about your mother that way, Keith."

"I know," Keith said, instantly contrite. "I'm sorry. I really love my mom. She's a great person, and she's always good to me, and life's been awful hard for her, too, looking after Mandy and me all by herself all those years, and then when Mandy died..." He paused and Gray waited. "But I get so *sick* of her fussing over me all the time and worrying about every single thing I do!" He looked rebelliously at Gray. "I should be able to do some things, too, like other guys, and not just be tied to her apron strings all the time because *she's* scared."

"Well, I don't know, Keith. I mean, of course I think you should be able to do some things that other boys do. But I hate the thought of going behind her back like this."

"Well," Keith said stubbornly, "there's just no other choice."

"Sure there is. We could at least tell her what we're doing, and if she forbids it, I could respect her wishes. That's what I *should* be doing, Keith."

"Well, go ahead. Tell her if you want to," Keith said quietly. "And I can guarantee she'll forbid it. And when she does, then I'll just go over to Jerry Walter's place and learn to ride bucking stock over there, and I won't tell you or mom or anybody about it."

Gray looked down at the grim young face and knew absolutely that the boy meant what he said. He hesitated, picturing the lively, rollicking Walter ranch with its brood of reckless boys and the wicked black Angus stock that they practiced rodeo events on.

Every time he saw the Walter boys at least one of them was sporting a plaster cast or a new set of stitches on some portion of his body. They just looked on injury as a way of life.

Gray pondered, still gazing absently down at the passionate young face in front of him, so much like Jo's, thinking of how this boy should be trained, carefully and properly, so he could enjoy the sport while also learning to avoid injury. And then he thought of Jo's own vivid, earnest face... her sweet, curving lips and blue-green eyes and

the golden dusting of freckles over her delicate cheekbones. He remembered with restless, urgent longing the way
he'd felt yesterday, kissing her, and he heard her voice, telling him that if this boy was hurt because of him, she'd
never, ever forgive him....

"Oh, hell!" he muttered aloud, shaking his head wearily. "I guess if you're going to do it, you might as well learn
to do it right. But, Keith, I want to tell your mother about
this just as soon as we can. I hate deceiving her like this.
She's a classy lady, your mom is, and she deserves to be
treated fairly."

"Okay, okay," Keith agreed hastily. "You said you'd
teach me, and then I'd enter a rodeo next month. We'll tell
her then. After the very first rodeo, we'll tell her what I'm
doing, and when she sees that I'm not hurt or anything, then
maybe she'll..."

His voice trailed off and his eyes lighted with excitement
as he looked off across the field, where a cloud of dust was
rising against the pure blue arch of prairie sky.

"Here they come!" he shouted.

He ran across to open the gate into the holding pen, and
Gray watched him, smiling. The cloud of dust swept nearer
and materialized into a small, tightly packed herd of young
steers, pounding along the fence line, followed by Peggy and
Libby, both mounted on tall sorrel geldings. The girls rode
with the effortless grace of a lifetime in the saddle, and they
worked together easily, one taking the point to hold the animals bunched along the fence line, the other bringing up the
rear to keep them moving briskly.

The lively Hereford steers raced into the pen and began to
mill and bellow, while Keith, wild with anticipation, pulled
the outside gate shut behind them and latched it securely.
Libby reined in beside him, sitting her horse easily as it
danced from side to side, its sides heaving and dark with
sweat.

She smiled down at the boy. "You *sure* you want to do this, Keith? These steers look awful feisty."

"I'm sure," the boy said. "Hi, Peggy," he called as the other twin approached slowly on her big horse.

"Hi, Keefer," she said. "Ready to get killed?"

He grinned up at her, and she smiled back, but her face wasn't as animated as usual, and there was a bleak stillness about her eyes that wasn't at all like Peggy. As Gray approached them, carrying a wide, flat-braided rope, her face tightened and she wheeled her horse and rode off toward the barn without a word. Gray watched her go with a tense, troubled expression and then turned back to find Libby's eyes resting quietly on him.

"Well, what are we waiting for?" he asked brusquely. "If this kid's so anxious to get himself wiped in the dirt, we might as well get a steer in the chute and let him go at it."

Keith trembled, his face pale beneath its tan and blazing with excitement.

Libby slipped from the saddle and loosened the cinches, then turned to her father. "I'll just go and give him a quick rubdown, okay, Dad? Then I'll be right back to help."

"Sure, Lib. We're not going to start right away, anyhow. I'm not putting this boy up on a steer until I've told him a little bit about it."

Libby led her horse away, and Gray called after her, "Don't water him for a while, Libby. He's still too sweated up, and it's not safe for him to drink."

She looked back over her shoulder, rolling her eyes and giving Keith an eloquent "aren't parents stupid" glance that made Gray burst into hearty laughter before he turned back to the boy.

"Okay, Keith. Now this is your bull rope, and it goes around the animal's belly like this. And this divided part here, that's your handhold...."

A few minutes later, when the girls returned, walking close together and talking quietly, Gray and Keith were squatting side by side on the dusty ground of the home-made arena, deep in a conversation accompanied by lively demonstrations on Gray's part and bright, eager questions from Keith.

"No, no," Gray was saying. He stretched the rope over his leg, handhold uppermost. "It goes like this, see? And then you fit your hand in like this." He demonstrated, sliding his hand into the divided portion of the rope, palm uppermost, and gripping it tightly. "And wrap the loose end of the rope around it a couple of times."

"How many times?" Keith asked, watching with intense concentration.

Gray grinned down at the boy. "Not too many, or you'll get hung up and have one arm two feet longer than the other."

Keith's eyes flickered, and he glanced up with a frightened look. "What do you mean, 'hung up'?"

"That's what every rodeo cowboy is most afraid of. That's when you get bucked off, but you can't get your hand free of your rigging, and you get dragged alongside the animal while he kicks at you. Men have been killed that way."

Keith nodded, shivering a little, and Gray looked down at him with concern. "Keith...are you sure you want to do this? There's no law saying you have to, you know. If you'd rather wait, it might be best to—"

"No! I've waited long enough. I want to do it today!" The boy stared back, his eyes blazing. "You promised! And if you don't—"

"Okay, okay," Gray said mildly. "No need to get all upset. I guess we'll give it a try, then," he added, glancing up at the girls, who stood quietly side by side, watching Keith. "See if you girls can find a quiet little one to run in for the first time, okay? Nothing too frisky."

Libby grinned. "They're *all* frisky, Dad," she said cheerfully. "They've been out on green grass for a couple of months, and they're rarin' to go."

Peggy caught the flicker of fear that appeared again in Keith's eyes and leaned toward him. "Don't be scared, Keefer," she whispered. "I've ridden lots of them. It's fun."

"Okay," he said, squaring his shoulders and taking a deep breath. "If a dumb *girl* can do it, I guess I can."

Peggy laughed and then ran off to help her sister. Keith watched as Gray and his daughters selected a small Hereford steer from the group in the pen and ran it down the fence and into the bucking chute, latching the gate quickly behind it. The glossy animal bellowed and rolled its eyes, straining furiously at the rails that enclosed its body.

Keith looked nervously through the bars at the steer, while Gray straddled its body, one foot on a rail on each side and bent to fit the rope into place.

"He looks...so much bigger now that he's in the chute," the boy commented.

Gray grinned down at him. "They always do."

Libby dropped another rope over the animal's hindquarters and pulled it gently up the other side, but didn't tighten it. "This is called the flank strap," she told Keith. "It's pulled up and tightened just as the gate opens, and it tickles him and makes him buck harder."

Keith swallowed and licked his lips apprehensively. "Do we want him to buck harder?"

"Relax, Keefer. This little guy can't hurt you. He's just a baby."

"I *am* relaxed," Keith said with dignity, pulling a leather glove onto his hand. "It's just that this is my very first time, okay?"

"Sure, Keith," Libby said soothingly. "It's always hard the first time. But you'll be great."

"Okay, Keith," Gray told him, stepping out of the center of the chute and climbing down onto the rails at the back. "You come up here and straddle the rails above his back, like I was doing."

Keith obeyed and found himself balanced above the little steer, which was still heaving and snorting in the narrow confines of the chute.

"Here," Gray said, handing him a dusty little white sack. "This is rosin, makes your hand stick to the rope. Slap a little of it on your riding glove."

Keith slapped the bag mechanically against his palm, and small pungent clouds of rosin dust rose above his glove. Then he bent to fit his hand carefully into the braided handhold, just as Gray had shown him, and looked down between his knees at the curly red-brown hide rippling with muscles and quivering in outrage. He could smell the warm, dusty scent of the animal and the rich, mingled scents of leather and manure, of dust and rosin and sunshine.

He felt a strange mixture of emotions as he balanced there with the sun beating warmly on his back and the other steers bellowing in the pen behind him. He felt terror and an urgent desire to escape, accompanied by wild, almost unbearable excitement. Above all he had a feeling that, after this day, nothing in his life would ever be quite the same again.

Gray watched him, his eyes concerned, his rugged face quiet. "Well, what do you think, son?" he asked. "You really want to do this?"

"You bet I do," Keith said, squaring his jaw and trying to smile, although it was a shaky effort.

"Okay, then. Just set yourself down on his back. Easy, don't get him scared...easy now..."

Holding his breath, Keith eased himself down onto the animal's back as Gray held him and supported his shoulders.

"Nod when you're ready," Gray said tensely, "and remember everything I told you about keeping your balance and not leaning down into the spin when he starts whipping his body around!"

Keith looked at the older man, his eyes blazing with excitement, his face so pale that the freckles stood out distinctly across his taut young cheekbones.

Gray returned his gaze in sudden dismay. Keith looked so much like Joanna just then, and his boyish shoulders felt so thin and fragile under Gray's big, callused hands. He caught an echo of her voice, like a whisper on the wind, saying, "Never, ever forgive you..."

Oh, my God, Jo, he thought. I'm sorry, sweetheart, but I have to do this. I wish I could make you understand.

But he had no more time for second thoughts. Keith stared straight ahead and nodded tightly, Peggy jerked the latch on the flank strap, and Libby, out in front, flung the big gate open.

The steer hesitated and then, seeing the gate open to freedom, the animal flung itself out into the arena, intent on ridding itself of the burden on its back. It jumped and kicked a couple of times, arching its wiry little body and flinging its head from side to side while Keith hung on grimly, his body jerking around as if he were a marionette.

The three by the fence shouted encouragement as dust billowed from the animal's flashing hooves and the cowbell attached to Peggy's flank strap clanged loudly. After a few seconds, the steer dropped its head and flung itself into a tight, vicious spin, whirling rapidly clockwise, pulling Keith's thin body farther and farther down into the swift rotation.

"Straighten up!" Gray shouted. "Lean away from the spin!"

Keith apparently heard him through the dust and confusion. They could see him make an effort to pull himself up and lean away to his left. But, as he did so, his hand loosened its grip on the braided handhold of his rope, and he was flung into the air, sailing a few feet and landing flat on his face in the dusty arena.

The flank strap loosened, then trailed off, and the little steer, relieved of both irritants, trotted to the end of the arena near the holding pen and stood quietly, its sides heaving.

Gray and his daughters ran toward Keith's prone body, which lay still and inert on the ground. Gray got to him first and knelt beside him, running expert hands over the boy, leaning forward to call to him. "Keith! Can you hear me? Keith, are you okay?"

There was a terrible moment of silence, and then the boy nodded his face in the dirt, moaned and dragged himself up onto his elbows, gasping for breath.

Gray turned to his daughters, who were both kneeling beside him, their faces pale with alarm. "He's okay. Just had the wind knocked out of him. Give him a couple of minutes to get his breath back."

Keith moaned again and pulled himself up onto all fours, his head hanging, still gasping and panting. After a few moments, he shook his head awkwardly from side to side and struggled to get to his feet. Gray slipped an arm around the boy's thin shoulders and helped him, steadying him on his feet and walking him slowly around in a circle.

Soon Keith was recovering his breath and moving easily on his own. He shook off Gray's arm, walking experimentally back and forth, testing his body for injury. Finally he turned to the others who still watched him anxiously. A slow grin spread over his face, and his teeth flashed white against the dirt that coated his cheeks. "What happened?" he asked.

"You were falling down into the spin," Gray said. "And when you tried to get out of it, you overcorrected and flew out the side door."

Keith nodded, considering. "But I stayed on quite a while, didn't I?"

"Keith, you did great. Best I've ever seen for a first ride. I think you've got a real, natural talent there. Right, girls?"

Peggy and Libby pressed closer, hugging the boy with sisterly warmth and heaping praise on him, echoing their father's words.

Keith listened, still grinning, and tugged at his riding glove. "Well," he said finally, "what are we waiting for? Let's get him in again, okay? *This* time, he's not going to beat me!"

Libby smiled at him and gripped his elbow, and Peggy pounded him warmly on the back as he strolled back to the bucking chute between the two girls. Gray watched the new ease and confidence of the boy's stride and the jaunty, masculine set of his shoulders, and smiled.

Jo's face flashed into his mind again, as it did a hundred times a day, haunting his dreams and his waking hours. I'm doing the right thing, Jo, he told her silently. I know for certain this is the right thing for this boy and, dear God, I hope that someday I can convince you of it, too.

He knew it was a dangerous thing he was doing. Not for Keith, who was young and resilient, but for himself. Because he was beginning to realize more and more that this woman was coming to mean a very great deal to him. And if he ruined his chances with her over this, he knew with desolate certainty that he would regret it for a long, long time.

He hesitated for a moment, lost in thought, his face taut and troubled, brooding about how Jo would have reacted if she had been here just now and seen her boy flung onto the ground, his slender body lying so still in the dust of the arena.

His face clouded with pain, and he shivered at the thought of her seeing that. But when the young people called to him, he shook his head, gathered himself together and moved over to the pen to help them load the little red steer back into the bucking chute.

CHAPTER SEVEN

JO STOOD IN THE SHADE of the roofed enclosure behind the
auction market, breathing in the pungent aroma of straw,
manure, dust and tightly packed animals. She walked down
the central aisle, which was bordered on both sides by pens
full of squealing, excited pigs, bleating sheep and calves
bawling plaintively for their mothers.

Finally she reached her own set of pens, paused to con-
sult her buyer's card and frowned critically through the rails
at her new acquisitions.

They looked, she decided, even better here in the pen than
they had in the sales ring, and she was pleased with her day's
work. The price had been so good.

Her thoughts were interrupted by the sound of a brisk,
strong tread in the aisle behind her, and an arm dropping
around her shoulder. Even without turning around she knew
exactly who that arm belonged to. She could tell by the
pounding of her heart and the sudden quickening of her
breathing. But she kept her face carefully noncommittal,
grateful for the dusky seclusion of the big barn. "Hi, Gray,"
she said dryly, still examining the pigs. "How are you today?"

He chuckled, standing close beside her. "What a
woman," he marveled. "Cool as a cucumber. Watching you
today, anybody would think you'd been to two hundred
livestock sales instead of just two."

Jo laughed with him and tried to keep her voice under
control, despite the unsettling effect that his nearness al-

ways had on her. "I make it a policy," she said cheerfully, "to try never to make a complete idiot of myself twice in the same way." She hesitated and then smiled up at him. "After all," she added, "there's always all kinds of *new* ways to make a complete idiot of myself. Why repeat the old ones?"

He returned her smile, looking down into her eyes. "Joanna, my girl," he murmured softly, "it's awfully hard to picture you making a fool of yourself. No matter what you do you always look twice as capable as anybody else I know."

"Oh, come on, Gray. Quit teasing me. You're always doing that."

"I'm not teasing," he protested indignantly. "I mean every word. Look at what you accomplished today, for instance. I happen to remember what you paid for those pigs you sold today, Mrs. McLean. I was there when you bought them, remember?"

Jo nodded. "I remember."

"And I know that you more than doubled your money in six weeks, and you bought another hundred, bidding like an old pro, by the way, and you bought them *under* market value." His arm was still resting across her shoulders, and he gave it a little warm squeeze, drawing her close to him. "Now don't try to tell me you're not one smart lady."

"I was lucky today," Jo told him, thrilling at the feel of his big, hard-muscled body against hers and struggling not to let her reaction show. "It was just the market trends, that's all. It's like the stock market. These pigs here—" she indicated her new, tiny pigs, snorting and shuffling and playing in the musky depths of the pen "—are called weaners. And the weaner market was flat today. But the ones I sold are classified as porkers, and two of those buyers had strong orders for them, so they bid each other up..."

Her earnest voice trailed off, and she looked up at Gray, who was still holding her, and laughing so hard that there were tears in his eyes.

"*Weaners* and *porkers*!" he said, choking with laughter. "Jo, Jo . . . you're a treasure. You're more fun than anybody I've ever met."

"I don't see," Jo began a little stiffly, "what's so hilarious about—"

"Come on," he interrupted, taking her elbow and guiding her out into the sunlight. "Let's get out of here and get some fresh air."

They strolled side by side across the sales yard, which was crowded with people and activity. Groups of men were standing around exchanging jokes and conversation in the warm afternoon sunlight. Deals were being concluded and money was changing hands while trucks and stock trailers of all sizes were backing up to the loading chutes to collect livestock, and the whole scene was underscored by a steady chorus of animal noises and dusty clouds from the pens nearby.

Men passed them, greeting Gray with boisterous friendliness and looking at Joanna with sidelong, cautious glances that reflected a new and growing respect.

"How," Gray asked, leaning against the side of the office building and continuing their conversation, "did you ever get to know so much about livestock and markets and . . . and weaners and porkers?"

Jo looked up at him suspiciously. His voice was calm and interested, but his eyes still danced with lively amusement.

"I bought books," she said with dignity. "And studied the markets and talked to some other accountants and market analysts, and I decided that this was something Mac could go into with a minimal outlay, since he already had an adequate feeding and sleeping facility. And I was interested in the rapid turnover and short-term profit projection. I knew that was what he needed. And so far," she concluded, dropping her eyes under his direct, admiring gaze, "things are working out just as I'd planned."

"All I can say is, you're a terrific woman for a man to have on his side," Gray told her, his voice quiet and sincere for once, all the teasing gone. "Mac's lucky that you came along when you did. Real lucky."

They were silent for a moment, watching the colorful whirl of activity all around them.

"Have you had any lunch?" Gray asked abruptly.

Jo shook her head. "I was going to go out for a hamburger, but the weaner price was so good and I didn't want to miss any, so I just . . . let it go."

He nodded. "Me, too. Want to run downtown for a bite to eat? We can have lunch, and I'll drop you back here at your car later, and you can still be home well before supper time."

She hesitated. "Gray, I really shouldn't stay. Keith will be home soon, and Mac's going to be wondering—"

"Come on, Jo. It's only two o'clock. How much difference will an hour make? Come have some lunch with me and celebrate your successful sale."

"Well . . . all right."

He looked down at her in mock surprise. "Just like that? You're sure mellowing, Joanna McLean. I was prepared to plead for fifteen minutes, and you just say, 'all right,' just like that?"

She grinned up at him, her eyes sparkling. "Well, if it's not enough of a challenge for you anymore, Gray, I could always . . ."

"That's fine," he assured her hastily. "I wasn't complaining. Believe me, I wasn't complaining."

Jo laughed, and the prairie sun on her face felt almost unbearably warm and sweet as Gray took her arm and guided her across the sales yard toward his truck.

THE RESTAURANT was cool and attractive, surprisingly elegant for a small prairie town. Jo commented on it and Gray shrugged.

"This is a rich area, Jo. It may look dry and barren, but this is some of the best farm and ranch land in the world. There's a lot of money around here. And it helps, too, with the sales yard—they get a steady traffic from the city, coming out to deal in livestock."

She nodded, still looking around with pleasure as they waited for their meal. Her face grew suddenly thoughtful, and Gray, always alert to her expression, caught it at once. "What are you thinking, Jo?"

She met his gaze, her eyes still wide and thoughtful. "I'm just trying to remember the last time I did this."

"Did what?"

"You know...had a meal in a restaurant with a...a man, just for pleasure, you know. Not a business lunch or anything, just a treat, like this."

He watched her intently. "And how long has it been?"

"You know, I honestly can't remember." She laughed awkwardly. "I guess I'm not much of a social butterfly, Gray. It's been so long that I feel like I'm fifteen again on my first date, and I'm afraid I'm going to do something wrong or act really dumb."

He smiled tenderly across the table at her, his eyes deep and gentle in the flickering light of the little candle lamp between them, and reached out to cover her hand with his own.

"You don't have to worry," he said, his voice a little husky. "Just be yourself. Everything you do is fine with me."

She gave him a little tremulous smile in return, and he set out to relax her by asking her about her first date and telling her about his. Before long they were exchanging hilarious reminiscences and laughing over their meal as if they had known each other all their lives, and Jo forgot all about her nervousness.

They were, in fact, having such a good time that she was reluctant to do what she had intended to do when she accepted his invitation. She had planned to use this opportunity to find out exactly what Gray was doing with her son and what he was planning for Keith.

She sipped her coffee and frowned briefly, remembering. Keith had come home the day before with his clothes torn and filthy, and he'd told some ridiculous story about slipping and falling when he was trying to saddle Peggy's horse. And this morning he had been limping and holding one arm a little gingerly, obviously trying to hide his pain from her.

"...all of a sudden?" Gray was saying.

"Pardon?" Jo asked, collecting her thoughts hastily and looking over at him.

"I said, you were a million miles away there. Where did your thoughts wander?"

"I was just wondering." She hesitated, studying the candle flame intently, and then looked up, meeting his eyes. "I was wondering what Keith was doing yesterday over at your place. That's all."

"Why?"

"Well, because he came home in such a mess, and I could tell that he was sore, and I just wondered..." Her voice trailed off, and she paused, looking at the candle again.

"Jo, if you really want to know," he said quietly, "I'll tell you all about it. And if you want to come and watch, you're welcome. I don't want to do anything behind your back. You know that. I respect you too much for that."

Jo nodded, still not looking at him. "But..." she began.

"But we have a real big difference of opinion here," Gray finished the statement for her. "You know that I have a different view of what's right for Keith than you do. And I don't know if we're ever going to agree. I think it's best if we just leave it alone."

"It would be best," Jo said stubbornly, "if you'd just leave *him* alone."

"Jo, if it isn't me," Gray told her gently, "it'll be someone else. He'll go wherever he has to, to learn what he wants to learn. I happen to think it's best for him to learn from me."

"If you'd leave him alone," Jo argued, "he wouldn't have any need to get involved in all this in the first place. He never had the slightest interest in horses or rodeo or anything like that before he met you."

"But then," Gray said reasonably, "he might have decided to get involved in something else, something even *more* upsetting to you. Can't you just let go a little, Jo? Just have some faith and let him live his life."

"Not if he's going to get hurt," she whispered, staring across the table at the big man opposite, her eyes dark with fear and pain. "I'm not a terrible, possessive mother, Gray. I have no problem with allowing him his privacy, and I don't interfere with his choice of friends or anything like that. But I can't *bear* the thought of him doing reckless, dangerous things and being hurt or . . . or . . ."

Her voice broke, and Gray took her hand again, looking at her thoughtfully across their scattered, empty plates. "Jo, let's just let it go, okay? Let's talk about something else."

"All right," she said, drawing her hand back and meeting his eyes with a level gaze. "Shall we talk about Peggy instead?"

His face clouded, and he made an abrupt gesture with his hand. "Now that," he said, "is the *last* thing I want to talk about."

"Why, Gray?"

He looked down into his coffee cup with a dark, brooding expression and didn't answer.

"Why?" Jo persisted. "Are you afraid I'll say something you don't want to hear? Do you really think it's fair, Gray," she continued gently, "that you have so much advice to give me about Keith, but you won't let me say anything at all about Peggy?"

He looked up, meeting her eyes with an unhappy expression. "What could you say about it? All you know is what you've heard from other people . . . from Mac, and Libby, I suppose. You've never actually met this . . . this creep who's hanging around her."

Jo ached for him, hearing the pain and despair in his voice, but fairness and a concern for Peggy forced her to go on. "How can you be so sure about him, Gray? I mean, have you ever taken the time to talk to him, to get to know him, to try to understand what Peggy sees in him."

"I know what she sees in him." He toyed with one of the bread sticks from a basket on the table, turning it end to end, finally breaking it savagely between his strong brown fingers and tossing the pieces back into the basket. "This guy is just her way of rebelling and showing me that she can do as she damn well pleases. She's been that way ever since she was born. Libby's always been quiet and shy and anxious to please, but Peggy was a little hell-raiser before she could even walk."

"But how can you say that? How can you be so absolutely certain their relationship is just . . . some kind of rebellion on Peggy's part when you don't even know this man?"

"I don't have to know him. A man just has to look at a guy like that to know what he is and what he wants from a girl. Why can't he stick with his own kind? Why chase after someone like my daughter?"

"Gray . . . Mac met this fellow, and he liked him. He said he thought . . . Rob was a nice person and very sincere about his feelings for Peggy."

Gray stared at her in silence, and Jo began to feel uncomfortable under his piercing, angry gaze.

Her cheeks flushed, and she waited, ready to make a sharp reply if he challenged her. But he pushed his chair back wearily, got to his feet and reached for the bill. "Let's go, shall we?" he said. "I think our hour is up."

Jo stood up, shrugged into her jacket and walked beside him out of the restaurant, glancing in troubled silence at his taut, erect figure and his clean-cut, remote profile.

"WELL, THEY SURE LOOK GOOD," Mac said, leaning on the fence rail and looking in satisfaction at the pen full of busy, happy little pigs. "Funny," he added, "how small they look. Makes you realize how fast the other ones grew. They were this size just a couple of months ago. Now look how much bigger than these little guys that ugly spotted one is."

As if aware that he was the subject of their conversation, the larger pig with the droopy ear tossed them a busy, distracted glance and returned to his task. He was patiently herding the smaller pigs toward the straw-lined sleeping area, clearly making an attempt to show them the difference between the eating place, the sleeping place, the play area and the place to deposit wastes.

Despite his best efforts, little pigs kept escaping his surveillance, darting away from the group with happy squeals and diving headlong into feed and water troughs, or wallowing gaily in the mud around the water outlet.

Jo giggled. "Poor thing. He looks like a kindergarten teacher all alone with a hundred pupils to look after."

"Serves him right," Mac said gruffly. "About time he had some responsibility besides sleeping in the sun and making a nuisance of himself. Ugly thing," he added as an afterthought.

They both watched in silence as the spotted pig cast them another distraught glance and then rushed across the pen to interrupt a sudden noisy battle that had just erupted amid a group of little pigs. Small pink bodies whirled and lunged everywhere as the combatants made earnest efforts to bite one another's tails.

"Vicious little monsters," Mac muttered. "That's the way," he urged on the bigger hog, who was nipping firmly at the little pigs and herding them away toward the other side of the pen. "Give it to 'em!"

"We'll have to hang up some tires for them," Jo said, frowning as she watched the lively scuffle. "The book says that if they have some hanging tires to play with, it discourages tail biting."

Mac choked on his reply, struggled to keep his face straight and nodded. "I imagine it would," he agreed solemnly.

Jo cast him a sideways glance. "Go ahead, laugh. But the book worked with the first batch, Mac. They really did well, that first bunch," she added cheerfully. "They sold better than I expected."

"I have to admit," Mac said, "that this is beginning to look like not too bad an idea. With a calf crop you have to wait till fall before you get any cash flow at all. But these horrible things, they start to put money in your pocket in no time."

"Well, Malcolm Burman!" Jo said, turning to him in mock amazement. "I believe that's the first hopeful thing I've heard you say in the two months I've been here!"

He shifted awkwardly on his feet and avoided her eyes, a little smile tugging at the corners of his mouth. "I'm not *optimistic*, mind you," he warned her. "I still figure the bank's going to get my ranch before the snow flies. But at least it feels good to be putting up a bit of a fight. I hated just rolling over and dying without trying to hang on somehow."

"Mac," Jo said, smiling up at him and linking her arm through his, "we've barely begun to fight."

They exchanged a glance of rare love and gentleness and then turned aside in mutual embarrassment and started off toward the house.

"Who's that?" Mac asked, peering down the road.

"Where?" Jo said, squinting and staring in the direction he indicated.

"On the approach road. Somebody coming on horseback. Must be one of the twins."

Jo shaded her eyes and stared into the distance. "I don't see a thing," she complained. "You have eyes like an eagle, Mac."

But by the time she reached the house, checked the plump chicken roasting in the oven and started peeling potatoes for their supper, a tall sorrel gelding trotted into the yard, and Jo recognized the bright, flaming mane of hair on the slender girl riding the horse, although she still couldn't tell which twin it was.

The girl rode over to the corral and dismounted with lithe, effortless grace. She said a few words to Mac, who was hauling sacks of protein supplement into the chop house, and went with him to inspect the new group of little pigs, leading her horse. Then she looped her reins over a corral post and started in the direction of the house.

Jo peeped out behind the curtain, watching the girl approach, and decided that her visitor was Peggy. The twins were so identical that it was difficult to tell them apart and would be almost impossible if they dressed exactly alike. But Libby usually wore quieter colors, and she kept her hair braided or tied back in a ponytail, while Peggy's hung loose in a wild, springing mass, as electric and full of energy as the girl herself.

Today Peggy had a colorful calico bandanna tied around her forehead, and she wore a vivid tie-dyed shirt of brilliant orange with her jeans. She looked exotic, and extraordinarily beautiful. Jo let the curtain drop and returned to peeling her potatoes, thinking about the twins as she waited for Peggy's knock at the door.

The girls had returned home for the summer shortly after Jo and Keith arrived, and Jo had seen a lot of them since. For some reason that wasn't entirely clear to her, the girls had formed a strong attachment to Jo, and they liked to come, singly or together, and visit, content just to sit in the kitchen, sipping coffee and chatting with her while she worked.

Jo was fairly confident that she could tell them apart by now, even without the telltale clues of dress and hairstyle. There was a difference in the essential attitude with which they approached life, and as she got to know them better, it grew easier and easier to recognize.

Libby was quiet and serene, her eyes calm, thinking more than she said. Peggy, on the other hand, was vibrant and defiant and tended to plunge into situations with more energy than forethought. Jo was beginning, she realized, to love both of them far more than she liked to admit. They felt almost like daughters ... and just a few years older than the daughter she had lost....

Her thoughts were interrupted by a brisk knock at the door, and the girl popped her head inside.

"Anybody home?" she called cheerfully. "Yummy! Something smells wonderful."

"Just a roasting chicken," Jo said with a smile. "Come in, Peggy." She hesitated. "It *is* Peggy, isn't it?"

"Yes, it's Peggy. I just wanted to—"

She was interrupted by the arrival of Keith, who came up from the basement carrying a cardboard box and looking gloomy.

"Hi, Keefer," Peggy said, sitting at the table and accepting a cup of coffee from Jo with a warm smile before she turned back to the boy. "Why the long face?"

"Well, it's just time to...Mac and I are going over to the Campbells before supper to take them their puppy."

As he spoke, a furry head popped over the edge of the box, and the puppy surveyed them suspiciously, his blunt little nose quivering.

"Poor Keith," Peggy said sympathetically. "I know you hate to part with them, but you can't keep *all* of them, you know."

"I know," Keith said morosely, cradling the box close to his chest with one hand and caressing the puppy's small silken ears.

"Besides," Peggy went on, "think of the terrific home he's going to have. Those little Campbell kids are just going to love him."

Keith brightened a little. "Do you think so, Peg?"

She nodded solemnly, sipping her coffee. "I saw Mrs. Campbell in town the other day, and she said the kids are so excited that they can't even sleep, and they're getting books from the library about how to look after puppies, and they've made a special bed for him and bought a bunch of puppy toys, and they're fighting over what to name him."

Keith looked down at the soft, warm little body in the box. "You hear that?" he murmured. "You're going to have a great life, little guy. You're going to have all kinds of fun."

Jo gave Peggy a quick, grateful glance, and they all looked up as Mac came into the porch, brushing dust from his jeans. "What time's supper, Jo?" he called into the kitchen.

"Oh, let's see," Jo paused, and checked her wristwatch. "About an hour, I guess. Maybe a little more."

"Good. Ready to go, Keith? I've got the truck right outside."

Keith nodded and left with his uncle, still carrying the puppy in its cardboard box. The two women in the kitchen could hear his eager, boyish voice fading into the distance, telling Mac what Peggy had said about the Campbell children and their plans for the puppy.

Soon they heard the departing roar of the truck engine, and then they were alone in the silent, sunny kitchen.

"Thanks, Peggy," Jo said softly. "I'm sure that's going to make this easier for him."

"He's such a great kid," Peggy said absently, stirring sugar into her coffee. "We really love him. He feels just like a little brother." She was silent a moment, gazing at the blue square of window above the sink, and Jo knew she wasn't thinking about Keith.

"Peggy," she said.

"Yes?" The girl turned, and looked directly at Jo with her brilliant green eyes.

"Peggy, did you want to…talk about something with me? Something specific?"

"Well, yes. I guess I did." Peggy hesitated, frowning at the calendar on the opposite wall, her face troubled. Finally she turned back to the other woman. "Jo, I'm not sure how much you know about…about Rob."

"Well," Jo began carefully, "I know a little. I know that Mac's met him and likes him and that your father doesn't approve of him at all."

"That," Peggy said bitterly, "is putting it mildly."

Jo was silent, rinsing the potatoes under the tap and chopping them into a saucepan as she waited for Peggy to continue.

"It's just rotten prejudice on his part, you know," Peggy said. "Because Rob looks like a biker, not a cowboy, and his hair's a little long, and he wears a leather jacket, Dad's sure he does drugs and belongs to the Hell's Angels and God knows what else. It's so *stupid*!''

''Peggy,'' Jo said gently, ''you have to try to be fair. That's not your father's only objection, and you know it. This man is a lot older than you—''

''Eight years,'' Peggy interrupted. ''Big deal.''

''It's a big deal,'' Jo said firmly, ''when it's your daughter and she's just eighteen.''

''Nineteen,'' Peggy said. ''Our birthday is next week.''

''Okay, nineteen. That's still awfully young to be making this kind of decision.''

''Jo, lots of my friends are nineteen, and they're already raising kids!''

''And do you envy them?''

Peggy met her gaze thoughtfully. ''Not much,'' she admitted. ''I don't think motherhood at eighteen is all that terrific actually.''

''Well, maybe that's what Gray is concerned about for you, Peg. Maybe he wants to make sure you have a chance to enjoy your youth, get an education, have some fun and independence before you get tied down.''

''Yes, sure,'' Peggy argued. ''I can validate all that. But if I had a nice twenty-year-old boyfriend from the next ranch, he wouldn't object at all. It's just Rob that he's so upset about.''

She hesitated and looked pleadingly at the older woman. Jo set the saucepan on the stove, turned the heat on under it and poured herself a cup of coffee, sitting down opposite Peggy and looking at her with thoughtful sympathy.

''Jo, you'd like him, too, if you met him,'' the girl said earnestly. ''He's just the sweetest guy, and he's kind and funny and good to me, and he makes me feel...'' Peggy hesitated and then blushed, a rare occurrence for her. ''He makes me feel like a princess,'' she said softly.

Jo smiled at her, moved by the tender expression on the girl's lovely face. "Well, that's the most important thing of all, I think," she said gently.

Peggy looked up at her gratefully and went on, encouraged by her reaction.

"Jo, it's okay in the winter while we're in school and living in the city, because then I can see him whenever I want. But it's still *three months* till school starts again," Peggy said tragically, "and I've only seen him once since April. I can't stand it. I just can't."

"You mean your father won't even allow you to see him? Not at all?"

Peggy shook her head bitterly, and her glorious mane of hair tumbled around her flushed face. "You know he came to see me last weekend when Libby and I were down here looking at the pigs, and Dad came down and told me I had to send him away?"

Jo nodded.

"Well, we had a big fight after that, and Dad was so mad...he said he never wants Rob near the ranch again and that if he catches me with him in the city, he'll stop paying for my education. It was awful."

"Oh, Peggy...I wish there was some way I could help."

"Well," Peggy began slowly, "there is, actually. That's why I came to talk to you."

Jo tensed, certain of what was coming, and dreading to hear it.

"You could help," Peggy said, "by letting me see Rob sometimes. I mean, letting me call him from here or meet him here once in a while and not telling Dad about it."

Jo was silent, and the girl gazed across the table at her with naked pleading.

"We could tell Dad you're...teaching me to sew or something," Peggy went on, her words tumbling over one another in her eagerness to say what she wanted. "It wouldn't matter what we said as long as it involves *you*. Dad's so crazy about you that he'd believe anything you said."

Jo glanced up at the girl, startled by her words, and then let it pass. Instead, she shook her head slowly. "No, Peggy," she said. "I'm sorry, but I can't do that. I'm willing to help you any way I can—by talking to your father on your behalf or meeting your boyfriend or whatever I can do. But I won't lie to Gray."

"I don't see why not," Peggy said bitterly. "I don't see why *you* should have all these scruples while he—" She hesitated and put her hand to her mouth, obviously regretting her hasty words.

"While he's disobeying my wishes regarding Keith?" Jo asked quietly. "Is that what you were going to say, Peggy?"

The girl nodded, with her head lowered. "I'm sorry," she murmured, still not looking up. "I don't want to get Keith in trouble or anything. It just seems to me that Dad is perfectly willing to do things behind *your* back, with Keith, so I don't see why you should be so—"

"There's a difference," Jo said. "I agree that I hate what he's doing with Keith, and I wish he'd stop, and I've told him so. But he's not lying to me, Peggy. He'd be quite willing to involve me if I wanted to go and—" Jo shuddered and paused briefly, then collected herself "—if I wanted to watch," she concluded, trying to keep her voice steady. "And I feel I owe him the same courtesy. I have no objection to having you meet your boyfriend here. But if Gray asks me about it, I won't lie to him on your behalf."

"All right," Peggy said, her voice bleak. She pushed the coffee mug aside and got slowly to her feet. "It was worth a try, anyhow. I'd better be getting home," she added tonelessly.

"Peggy," Jo began, aching at the misery in the girl's voice. "Would you like me to...to talk with your father? Maybe I can..."

Peggy laughed mirthlessly. "Forget it, Jo. He's the stubbornest person in the world. Once his mind's made up, you can't change it. Nobody can."

"I'm afraid for you," Jo told her simply. "I'm afraid you'll do something foolish, Peg. And I'd hate to see you get—"

"Don't worry about me," the girl interrupted, her face pale and composed. "I'll be fine, Jo. Just fine."

She walked swiftly out of the little house and across the yard, mounted her horse with lithe, easy grace and cantered away down the approach road, her hair flaming in the slanting rays of afternoon sunlight.

CHAPTER EIGHT

ONE MORNING IN EARLY JUNE rain began to fall on the prairie, surprising and delighting Jo. Somehow, she had pictured this adopted home of hers as an eternal desert, buffeted by brutal winters and hot, searing summers. She hadn't expected the balmy springtime breezes, the mild days beneath skies of endless blue and the green bloom of fields, starred with wildflowers, that rolled to faraway, misty horizons. And she hadn't expected that there would be rain.

The rains were welcome because the prairie was growing dry by late spring, and on some days the wind whipped huge clouds of dust that rolled along the skyline like dark thunderstorms. They had planted a little garden behind the house, and the tender green plants, growing in their tidy rows, needed moisture to take root and grow, and so this gentle early-morning rain was a special delight.

Jo went to the kitchen door and stood hugging her arms, looking out with pleasure as the first drops fell, hitting earth so dry that they bounced up into the air again in big, dusty bubbles. She breathed deep of the fragrance, an indescribably beautiful scent of freshness, of flowers and damp earth and sage. Finally, regretfully, she turned back into the kitchen to prepare their breakfast.

Keith sprinted for the school bus with his gym bag over his head, and Jo watched for a moment as the bus backed around and started down the road, sending sheets of water spraying past its heavy tires. She smiled, feeling happy and contented for no particular reason and went back to mixing and kneading dough for the whole wheat buns she was baking. Keith had reached the age when he was hungry all the time, and Jo baked buns twice a week, just to have something on hand for him to eat that wasn't what she considered "junk food."

She pounded and shaped the solid, elastic mass of dough, feeling a deep, warm kinship with the millions of women, through countless generations before her, who had done exactly the same thing. She began to sing softly to herself and looked up with a smile as her uncle appeared in the doorway, holding a large, flat cardboard carton.

"Mac, you look so nice! What a handsome guy."

Mac grinned at her, his seamed, weathered face creasing in a wry smile. "Nice of you to say so, Joey. But I'm pretty realistic about this broken-down old cowboy."

"Don't say that," Jo protested loyally. "I mean it, Mac. You really look terrific. I can't remember seeing you dressed up like this except when you came to see me in Vancouver last winter, and I was too upset then to be able to..."

Her voice trailed off, and she returned to her energetic kneading of the bread dough. Mac set the carton down on the table and crossed the kitchen to take his truck keys from a rack near the window. He wore a fine gray wool suit in a western cut, polished gray riding boots and his old-fashioned gabardine topcoat, and he did, in fact, look handsome and distinguished.

"Sure you won't change your mind and come with me?" he asked. "You've been stuck pretty close to home for a long time. Wouldn't you enjoy a day in the big city?"

Jo shook her head. "Thanks, Mac, but I'd really rather stay home. I have all kinds of things planned for today, and I'm just setting this bread dough to rise, and somebody has to water the pigs before noon."

"Little nuisances," Mac muttered darkly. "Cattle, now, they look after themselves. Those pigs have to be waited on hand and foot."

Jo chuckled. "Hand and hoof, you mean." She waved at the big, flat carton. "Did you finally decide?"

He nodded. "I'm taking all five of them. I might as well. Why hang on to them?"

"Oh, Mac . . ." Jo tipped the ball of dough into a bowl, buttered the top of it and looked up at her uncle in concern. "Even the one of the old homestead? I thought you didn't want to part with that one."

He shrugged. "The dealer said he could sell it for five hundred, and God knows, we need the cash. I could always do another one."

He looked over at his niece, trying to smile.

"Stupid thing, anyhow, for a grown man to be doing, painting watercolors. I can't believe that people are willing to pay hundreds of dollars for the silly things."

"They're not silly. They're good, Mac. Really good. You're a talented man."

"Sure. A talented man on the verge of bankruptcy." As if regretting the sudden, bitter edge to his voice, he drew himself together, reached for his package of paintings and turned to Jo. "This rain is really settling in and turning cold," he told her. "I'll toss a few bales of straw into the pen for the little pigs before I go, so they can burrow into it if they need to."

"Oh, Mac . . . I can do that. You're all dressed up."

He waved a hand at her. "Don't be silly. Why go out in the rain when you don't need to? Besides, it's clean straw, and it'll only take a minute."

"Well, okay. If you insist. Drive carefully, and good luck with your paintings," Jo called after him.

She covered the bowl of dough with a clean cloth, set it to rise on a chair near the radiator and checked her watch.

Then she went to the window and looked down at Mac's tall, spare body, moving carefully in his dress clothes as he tossed a couple of bales of straw into the calf shelter that housed the new batch of little pigs.

Finally he brushed off his pants, hurried into his truck and drove carefully out of the yard, splashing through a small lake of water that had accumulated near the gate. Jo leaned out to gaze down the road as his truck was swallowed up in the wind-driven gusts of heavy rain. Even after he disappeared completely she continued to stare out into the rain at a world so uniformly gray and wet that there was nothing to distinguish land from sky.

It was, she supposed, a depressing sight—the bleak prairie and the deserted ranch buildings, sodden and silent under the steady downpour. But Jo didn't feel at all depressed. She felt cozy and comfortable, full of energy and delighted at the rare prospect of a day all to herself to use exactly as she pleased.

And, as she had told Mac, she had all kinds of plans. She hurried to tidy the kitchen and took a pack of meat out to thaw for supper. Then she switched on her computer, which had long since been set up in a corner of Mac's living room and sat down at it with a smile of anticipation.

For weeks she had been toying mentally with a new chess strategy, but she had been so busy with farm accounts and housekeeping chores that she hadn't had time to test it. Now she switched on the monitor and loaded the chess program, which allowed her to challenge the computer. Her new game plan was daring and innovative, involving a solid frontal advance of all the pawns as a unit rather than leaving them behind to protect the king, and she was certain that with some refinements it would prove difficult to overcome.

At the back of her mind, as she concentrated on her game, was a memory of Gray Lyndon, telling her that he was looking forward to their chess match. She knew that sooner or later she was going to find herself in a position where she would have no choice but to respond to his challenge, and for some reason it was terribly, desperately important to win that challenge.

The screen swam in front of her eyes briefly as she remembered their kiss the other day in the sunshine...the feel of his lips and his body and the strange, aching hunger that had haunted her ever since. Jo was frightened by her deep, restless longings, and she had been determined, after that kiss, to be firm in resisting any further advances. But she hadn't needed to resist. When they had gone to dinner after the sale, he'd made no move to renew the contact and had been cold and distant when they parted—still angry, Jo supposed, over her comments about Peggy.

She shook her head and returned her attention to the game, noting in dismay that the computer had just captured her knight.

Okay, she told herself. This can work, I think, but the backup pieces have to be carefully watched and protected *all* the time. No lapses of attention allowed here...*and no more thinking about that man....*

She forced all her concentration onto the game and watched in delight as her little army of foot soldiers swept forward, side by side, boldly challenging the opposition. The strategy was risky, even foolish-looking, and it left a lot of weak, unprotected areas behind the lines that would have to be shored up by special moves. The computer won the first two games, but Jo was still pleased with the way the attack worked. She jotted notes in a scribbler, suggesting alternate moves, and set the program to begin again.

She was so absorbed that she lost track of time, and her dough was almost spilling over the sides of the bowl when she remembered to punch it down, shape the buns and set them to rise again. In the kitchen she looked out at the cold gray rain, checked her watch and frowned thoughtfully.

If the pigs were huddled inside, unable to play and root in the sun, they might well be filling in their time by eating more. And when they ate, because of the rich protein supplement mixed with their chopped grain, they got thirsty. And when they were thirsty, Jo recalled, they were quite capable of emptying their big water trough in just a few hours.

I'd better go out now, she decided reluctantly, and see if they need water. Poor little things, they have to depend on us for everything.

She tugged on a light nylon windbreaker over her sweater and jeans, stepped into her high rubber boots and let herself carefully out of the house. Then she sprinted across the yard, splashing in the puddles, exhilarated by the gusts of cold rain beating against her face.

She reached the calf shelter, unlatched the door and stepped inside, blinking in the sudden silence and the dim mustiness of the enclosed space. She looked around, puzzled.

There were no pigs in the building. It was silent, deserted, empty of life.

This is ridiculous, she thought. Maybe they've all burrowed into the straw to keep warm.

She looked at the fresh drifts of straw that Mac had tossed into the pen. There was no way, she realized in confusion, that those piles of straw could completely conceal the bodies of a hundred active pigs.

Hesitantly she walked over to the open side of the building and peered out into the rain. The corral beyond was empty, as well, except for a dim shape on the other side, which Jo recognized as Mac's spotted, droopy-eared pig, huddled forlornly beside the fence. Jo tugged the hood of her windbreaker over her head and crossed the pen to stand beside him.

"What is it, Droopy?" she asked aloud. "What's happened? Where are they?"

The pig gazed up at her, his intelligent little eyes filled with an expression of anguish that was almost human. Then he looked down at the fence again, and Jo saw instantly what had happened.

Near his sharp pointed hooves was a hole dug under the bottom rail in a corner that Mac had obviously missed when he was reinforcing the corral fence to contain the pigs. The hole was too small for Droopy's bulky body to fit through, but it had allowed all of the new little pigs to escape into the freedom of the alfalfa field beyond the corral.

Shivering with cold and with a sudden terror that gripped her stomach and made her feel sick, Jo climbed onto the fence and peered out into the field. There were little pigs everywhere, wandering about aimlessly or huddling together for warmth in the big, exposed area of rain-washed land. They were clearly not enjoying their new freedom. Many were shivering uncontrollably, and they looked lost and forlorn as they milled and trotted around in the sodden alfalfa crop.

It had been easy enough, Jo realized, for them to get out. They had just followed one another as they had burrowed under the fence. But, although by now they probably regretted their escape and longed for the cozy dry straw and the warm food and water in their pen, it wasn't nearly as easy to find their way back.

Paragraphs from her book on *The Care and Feeding of Market Hogs* began to nag painfully at her mind, and she tried to ignore them. But it was hard to forget all the dire warnings about the delicacy of pigs and the danger, especially when they were small, of getting them wet or chilled.

Frantically she climbed off the fence and ran to open the wide gate that opened into the field. The wind caught it from her hands and blew it shut again, and she hurried, muttering under her breath, to find a board to prop it open with. Then, slipping and stumbling in her haste, she hurried out into the field and tried to round up the pigs and herd them back through the gate and into the safety of their enclosure.

The little pigs, chilled and terrified, resisted her attempts, scurrying away from her and running into one another, milling about in the big field and refusing to group or to move in any specific direction. Jo ran and panted, almost sobbing with frustration as the pigs eluded her again and again.

Her hood slipped back, and the driving rain soaked her hair, matting her curls flat against her head, dripping down inside her collar in icy trickles. She summoned all her patience and tried once more, moving the mass of squealing, frightened little pigs carefully against the fence, and then trying to ease them down toward the gate. But they panicked and spurted out past her legs in a sudden rush. She whirled in an attempt to stop them, lost her balance and fell headlong.

By now she knew she was crying, because the tears on her cheeks were warmer than the icy rain that pelted her face and body. She pulled herself awkwardly up on all fours and knelt, gasping, dripping mud and water, soaked to the skin. Then, slowly and wearily, she dragged herself to her feet, gathered her last reserves of strength and ran clumsily off across the field after the terrified herd of pigs.

GRAY DROVE along the road to his ranch, peering out beyond the sheets of water that washed over the windshield of his truck, his face quiet and thoughtful.

He felt a little lonely, he realized, even somewhat depressed, maybe because of the rain. Not that it wasn't welcome, of course. Prairie ranchers never complained about rain, no matter how poorly timed or inconvenient it might be. But the day was so gray and bleak, so damp and cold, and he longed for a little warmth and lightness in his life.

His face tightened, and he gripped the steering wheel harder, thinking about Peggy and how unpleasant the atmosphere was around his house these days. Peggy was avoiding him, barely speaking to him, and Libby looked at him all the time with those sad, disappointed eyes. . . .

He neared the turnoff to Mac's ranch and gazed wistfully at the buildings huddled silently in the rain. He knew Joanna was home alone today, because he had spoken with Mac briefly in the hardware store and learned that his neighbor was on the way to Calgary, planning to spend the day in the city. Gray felt a yearning, almost overwhelming in its urgency, to stop in and visit her. He wanted to see her sweet, laughing face with its delicate dusting of freckles, hear her voice and look into those blue-green eyes. He wanted, more than anything, to hold her in his arms again and kiss her lips and be allowed to discover the hidden pleasures of her slender, shapely body. . . .

He shook his head wearily, resisting the temptation to turn the steering wheel.

He knew he was on dangerous ground here. He had been attracted to women all his life, but never like this. No other woman had ever been so able to haunt his dreams and waking hours and make him weak with longing, and he feared the depth of his feeling for this particular woman—because he knew the feeling wasn't returned.

Jo disapproved of so many things about him: his views on raising children, his whole attitude toward life. She'd endured his kiss the other day—maybe even responded to it a little—but as soon as she'd had the chance she pulled away from him again, just as she always did . . . withdrew herself to a safe distance and then looked at him with those cool, thoughtful eyes. It hurt him, that coolness, and the growing certainty that he would never be able to get close to her. . . .

His gloomy thoughts were interrupted by a sudden flicker of movement just behind Mac's corrals. He slowed the truck and strained to make out what it was that he'd seen.

There it was again—a flash of motion, dimly seen through the pounding sheets of rain, like a person, running. But who would be running around behind Mac's corrals in a downpour like this?

He thought of Joanna, all alone in the house, and felt a flicker of uneasiness. Still tense, he backed his truck around in a spray of water and headed up the road again, pulling into Mac's yard and driving down to the corrals. Gray parked the truck and pulled on his yellow riding slicker, stored behind the seat, which covered his body from his head to the tops of his rubber boots. Then he unlatched the door and stepped into the calf shelter.

As soon as he saw the emptiness of the building and registered the absence of the pigs, his uneasiness hardened into real concern. He ran out through the corral, seeing the open gate and the field beyond, and the soaked, muddy figure stumbling through the alfalfa.

"Jo!" he shouted through the driving gusts of rain. "Jo, are you all right?"

She heard him and turned, then came struggling wearily toward him across the field.

At any other time, Gray thought, this would, possibly, have been really funny. She was coated in mud from head to foot, black with it, only her eyes glinting in her darkened face. Her rubber boots had come off, probably stuck deep in a puddle somewhere, and her stockinged feet were smeared with clumps of dripping soil. But Gray saw the shivering of her slender body and the exhausted droop of her shoulders, and didn't feel at all like laughing.

"Poor girl," he murmured, drawing her soaked, shaking form into his arms and holding her against him like a child.

"Poor girl," he whispered again, his lips close to her muddy cheek. "How long have you been out here?"

She rolled her head against his chest and choked, trying to answer. "I don't . . . I don't know. A long time."

She pulled back a little and looked up at him, her beautiful eyes in that mud-streaked face tragic and imploring. "Gray . . . they're going to catch cold. They won't go back in, and they'll get sick, and Mac will lose—"

"Hush now," he said. "None of that talk. We'll get them back in."

"But I can't . . . they won't . . . they keep on . . ."

Gray looked at her with aching tenderness. She was almost incoherent with exhaustion and trembling violently, and he wanted nothing more than to take her into the house, look after her, see that she was warm and dry again. But he knew her well enough by now to know that she would never allow herself to be cared for until the pigs were safely inside the shelter.

Gray stared with narrowed eyes at the field full of huddled, shivering pigs, assessing the situation. Then he turned back to Jo.

"It'll be easier with two of us," he told her. "We'll move them just like cattle, with one of us at the rear and one at the point. They're too cold and tired to put up much of a fight, I think. Wait a minute," he added. "I'll be right back."

He ran inside the calf shelter and reappeared almost at once, carrying a four-by-eight-sheet of plywood easily in his big arms. Then he came back to Jo and looked down at her in concern. "Are you sure you're up to this?" he asked. "I'm really worried about you, Jo."

She shivered and coughed and then tried to smile, although it was a bleak effort. "I'll be fine," she said. "Just tell me what to do."

"Okay. You just move over here a little and keep them against the fence. I'll go up and herd them into a bunch and then stay behind them and bring them down along the fence and through the gate. Just don't let the front ones veer away and get back out into the field.''

She nodded and watched as he moved across the field, his slicker flapping around his boot tops, carrying the big board in front of him like a shield and using it to scoop the little pigs up into a group along the fence line.

"Here they come!" he shouted. "Hold them along the fence, Jo!"

She moved over and waved her arms feebly, keeping the little pigs bunched along the fence line as they trotted wearily through the puddles toward the gate.

The bobbing mass of muddy pink backs flowed through the gate and into the corral pen, and Jo watched, almost faint with relief, as they rushed gratefully toward the warmth and protection of their roofed enclosure.

She showed Gray the hole where they had escaped, and he wedged his big piece of plywood down against the lower rails to block the opening.

"I'll come out later and repair it properly," he told her. "But that should hold them for now, not that I think they'll be too anxious to get out again today."

She nodded and trudged slowly beside him into the enclosure to look at the shivering masses of little pigs who huddled together in corners or burrowed frantically into the straw. Her mud-smeared face twisted in concern.

"Gray look at them. Some of them are coughing already, and their tails are all hanging straight down, not curled at all. They're sick, Gray."

"They'll be all right," he told her soothingly. "It's warm and dry here and they've got all kinds of feed and water. They'll be okay, Jo. Anyhow," he added, "there's nothing more that we can do for them now. Let's worry about you, shall we?"

He unlatched the door, put an arm around her and stepped outside. Suddenly she sagged against him and would have fallen if his arm hadn't been supporting her.

"Jo!" he said in alarm. "What's the matter?"

She looked up at him, and even under the layers of mud he could see the paleness of her face. "I'm sorry," she whispered. "I'll be all right in a minute. I just . . . need a little rest. . . ."

He picked her up in his arms and carried her as easily as if she were a child, marveling at the lightness of her body.

Especially, he thought with a small grim smile, considering that she was weighted down, right then, with at least ten pounds of mud and water.

He reached the house, held her awkwardly against him while he turned the knob and kicked the door open, carrying her inside and closing the door behind him with his foot. Then he eased her gently into a sitting position on the bench near the washstand and looked down in concern at her muddy, matted head. She was hunched forward on the bench, too weak to move, her hands dropping listlessly between her knees, her body racked by occasional violent shudders.

"Oh, Jo. . . you poor thing. What am I going to do with you?" he murmured.

Rapidly he stepped out of his boots and stripped off his raincoat, hanging it on a hook by the bench. He took a towel from the sink and rubbed it briskly over his face and his dripping, dark hair and then turned his attention back to Joanna.

With reluctance he realized she was too weak and chilled to do anything for herself and that he was going to have to look after her, even if she hated him for it later.

"Wait right here," he told her urgently, grabbing the nearest heavy coat and wrapping it around her shivering body. "Don't move," he added, realizing as he said it how stupid it sounded.

How could she move? She was too weak to stand up, for God's sake.

He ran into the bathroom, moving swiftly in his stockinged feet, and started the hot water running into the tub. As an afterthought, he grabbed the bottle of bubble bath on the ledge and dumped a liberal amount into the running water. A steamy cloud, pleasantly scented with violets, grew and filled the little room, and Gray ran back out into the porch. She was sitting exactly as he had left her, slumped on the bench, huddled inside the heavy coat.

"Jo..." he began hesitantly.

She looked up at him, her eyes dull and uncomprehending, miserable with cold and exhaustion.

"Jo, we've got to get those wet clothes off you and get you clean and dry, or you're going to get really sick. Now, do you think you can undress yourself?"

She made a feeble movement, lifting her trembling hands to the zipper on her windbreaker, and then let them drop again.

"Okay," Gray said, taking a deep breath and drawing her gently to her feet. "Forgive me, sweetheart. It looks like I'm going to have to do it."

She was so limp and chilled that she was hardly aware of his actions, Gray realized. Working quickly, trying to be detached and professional about it, he took off her jacket, tugged her sodden, dripping sweater over her head and unbuttoned her shirt.

When he reached for the zipper of her jeans, she whimpered and pulled away, striking out feebly at his hands, trying to work the zipper herself. But her hands were too cold and stiff to function properly, and she gave up, standing silently with her face averted as he unzipped her soaked, muddy jeans and eased them down over her hips.

Gray kept talking, murmuring to her soothingly, hardly aware of what he was saying, just trying to make comforting sounds to relieve the dreadful awkwardness of the moment.

He realized, to his shame, that in spite of his best efforts he wasn't able to ignore the beauty of her body. Because she was so slender and quick-moving, and she tended to wear loose, casual clothes, he had always had an impression, somehow, that her figure was spare and boyish. He was surprised by the delicacy and lushness of her body as he clumsily unhooked her bra, and she stood naked except for her wet, mud-stained panties.

Hastily Gray wrapped the coat around her again. But that one brief glimpse had been enough to show him the unexpected fullness of her breasts, still firm and youthful even though she had borne two children, and her trim, narrow waist above the soft swell of her hips.

His mouth went suddenly dry, and he lifted her into his arms, wrapped cocoonlike in the big coat, and carried her into the bathroom. The water was rising high in the tub, with a sea of bubbles billowing and washing over the sides, and the room was so warm that the tiles and mirrors were beaded and running with steam.

Gray propped Joanna up on the big hamper, switched the taps off, tested the water and then turned back to her. "Well," he said with forced heartiness, rolling his sleeves up over brown, heavily muscled arms, "*this* is sure going to feel good. Right?"

She looked up at him in silence, her blue eyes desolate in her dirty face. Gray lifted her to her feet, pushed the coat back from her shoulders and let it fall to the floor. He gripped the elastic of her panties and pulled them cautiously down over her hips while she bit her lip and kept her face turned away from him. Gently Gray lifted her and eased her down into the hot soapy water, and she immediately sank up to her chin, closing her eyes and sighing.

"Oh, God..." she whispered, so low that he could barely hear her.

He took the washcloth and used it to soap her body, trying to pretend that this was fifteen years ago and she was one of his little twins, having her nightly bath. He cleaned the mud out of her ears, scrubbed her fingers and her feet, washed her back. Then he took the container of shampoo and lathered her muddy hair, rinsing it with the shower head until it was squeaky clean, and toweling it vigorously until it stood up around her head in little damp, springing tendrils.

All the time, she kept her face turned away from him, enduring his touch in silence, letting him do the things she was unable to do for herself. Gray was touched by the trusting, childlike way she yielded to him, obediently offering herself up to be cared for. He had always thought of her as such a brisk, no-nonsense kind of woman, sometimes even intimidating in her competence. This new vulnerability was almost unbearably moving and filled him with a swelling tenderness that he could scarcely contain.

"Joanna," he whispered, hardly aware of what he was saying. "Oh, Joanna, you're so beautiful, such a beautiful woman."

He lifted her carefully from the water, stood her on the bath mat and began to dry her hastily with a huge bath sheet. But she was a little recovered by now and pushed him away, clutching at the towel and pulling it tightly around her body.

"I can...do this. I'm better now," she murmured huskily.

He hesitated, unsure of what to do. He didn't want to leave her alone in the bathroom, for fear she might still collapse or pass out or something. And yet, now that she was feeling stronger, it all seemed intensely intimate—their proximity in the hot, scented little room, and the nakedness of her warm pink body.

"Really," she said, her voice a little firmer. "Please, Gray, leave me alone for a few minutes, okay? If I need anything," she added, seeing that he was still hesitant, "I'll call you right away."

"Promise?"

"Promise," she assured him dryly.

"Can I get you anything?"

"Just my terry cloth robe, please. It's hanging on the back of my bedroom door. And my slippers are there, too."

Gray hurried to fetch her long, heavy robe of pale blue terry cloth and cast a quick, guilty glance around her neat, attractive bedroom. This room fascinated him, as did everything about Joanna. A few times in recent months, when he was visiting Mac and she was away, he had even tried to think of ways to get inside it for a minute. He would have loved to spend time looking at her books and pictures, absorbing the atmosphere she had created for herself, trying to understand her better.

But knowing that she was waiting, he was forced to content himself with that one rapid, curious glance at all the things she used and treasured, and then he hurried back down the hall to the bathroom.

"Here's the robe," he said, placing it carefully across the hamper. "Anything else?"

"I...I don't think so," she said awkwardly. "Thanks, Gray."

He looked down at her in silence. She still clutched the big towel firmly around her shapely body, and in the steamy warmth that surrounded her, the color was returning to her cheeks and lips. Her damp hair stood up around her head, already drying in a halo of curls touched with gold by the light overhead.

He smiled. "That's just the way my kids' hair used to look after a bath," he told her. "A mop of little curls, like that, except that theirs was always carrot-red, not dark like yours."

She shifted nervously on her feet and continued to look up at him, her blue eyes pleading. "Gray," she began, flushing with embarrassment, "I'd like to ask you—"

He reached out gently and put his fingers over her lips. "Don't say it, Jo. You don't have to say anything. I've already forgotten the whole thing. Everything."

She met his quiet, sincere gaze with gratitude, and then dropped her eyes, still gripping the towel with trembling fingers.

"After all," he went on, with the old teasing note creeping back into his voice, "I think this evens the score, don't you?"

Her cheeks flushed a rich pink, like summer roses. "Okay," she murmured, "that sounds good to me. We've both...and now we'll just forget it. *All* of it," she added firmly, looking up at him with an urgent appeal.

"Sure we will," he said soothingly. "All of it."

But as he closed the bathroom door gently and went out to the porch to clean up her muddy clothes, he realized he had lied to her.

Never, as long as he lived, was he going to be able to forget the sweet, trusting way she had given herself into his hands and let him care for her, or the look and the feel of her lovely, slender nakedness.

CHAPTER NINE

JO STOOD BY THE SINK, gripping the edge of the counter and staring into the mirror. She still felt weak and a little sick, and she was frightened by the heaviness of her limbs and by the oppressive, awkward difficulty of moving, which contrasted sharply with her dizzy light-headedness. Her head felt like one of those helium-filled balloons, clutched by children in amusement parks, and if she wasn't careful, her head might just come loose and drift up somewhere around the ceiling. Then Gray would have to come in and get it down for her....

She choked on a hysterical little giggle, coughed and went on staring at herself, her eyes bleak.

Oh, God, she thought, remembering. He *undressed* me...right to the skin and put me into the tub and scrubbed me like a little kid. How could I possibly have allowed it? But I had no choice. I couldn't even move. It was as if I were frozen inside a block of ice and I had to let him chip it away so that I could breathe....

Her cheeks burned with shame, and she wondered how she would ever be able to face him again with this knowledge hanging in the air between them. He'd promised he would forget about it, but Jo knew it would be on her mind forever, haunting her every time she saw him, reducing her to a paralysis of embarrassment.

The easiest thing, she decided, would be simply never to see him again. She could certainly organize her life so that she wouldn't have to encounter Gray Lyndon.

But right now he was outside the bathroom door, and she had to go out there.

Gloomily she considered her options. She could call to him through the door, tell him she was fine now and could he please go away because she wanted to rest. But that wouldn't work. He wasn't going to leave until he'd satisfied himself that she was fully recovered and able to function properly.

She could run into her bedroom, draw the shades, turn the light out and climb into bed, telling him that she was going to have a nap and would be fine when she woke up.

Still gazing unhappily at herself in the mirror, she considered this idea. It was certainly attractive. She wouldn't have to see him again, and she *was* tempted by the thought of sinking into a warm nest of blankets and pillows, resting her poor, pounding head, and drifting off into a deep, healing sleep.

But, she thought miserably, chances were he'd hang around waiting until she woke up, and then Mac or Keith might come home and hear the whole story from him, instead of her.

At any rate, she decided, whatever she did, she was going to have to do it soon. The scented, humid warmth in the little enclosed room was becoming oppressive, and she was really starting to feel dizzy and faint. She gave one last unhappy glance in the mirror and turned away to run water from the shower head into the tub, amazed by the swirls and gobs of wet dirt that still coated the bottom.

I guess I must have been a real mess, she thought with a shudder.

She finished tidying the bathroom, took her robe from the hamper and belted it around her waist. Then she put on the slippers he had brought her and pulled the door open a few inches, peering cautiously out into the hallway.

There was no sound or sign of activity in the rest of the house, and she had a sudden, wild hope that he might have gone home after all and left her alone. But when she crept down the hallway and out into the living room, she saw with a sinking heart that Gray was kneeling beside the fireplace, feeding kindling into a pile of logs and encouraging the fire with little twists of newspaper.

Jo watched as the flames caught and flared high, and he got to his feet and began to gather an armful of pillows and sofa cushions, arranging them carefully on the braided rug in front of the hearth.

As he turned, he caught sight of her, sagging in the doorway, with one hand clutching the doorframe. He tossed the last of the pillows down and came rapidly across the room toward her, his face taut with concern.

"Jo! You look awfully pale. How do you feel?"

"I . . . I'm not sure. I felt fine for a little while, after . . ." She hesitated, wretched with embarrassment, and then struggled on. "After my bath I felt all right, but now I'm . . . a little dizzy."

"It's just your body, trying to adjust to all the sudden temperature changes. The important thing is to keep warm and rest. Come on," he said briskly. "I've built a fire and put these pillows down here. You can lean back against the sofa, and I'll bring you a drink to steady you."

Helpless in the face of all this strength and capable fussing, she let him lead her over and settle her in a soft nest of cushions, cozily covered to her chin with a big knitted afghan, reclining comfortably against the front of Mac's soft old couch. Then she watched as he went out into the kitchen, took a bottle of Mac's good sherry from the cupboard, poured her a generous drink and strolled back into the living room to hand it to her.

"Thanks," she said, accepting the glass and watching as he settled himself in a low chair opposite her, stretching his long legs in relaxation, resting his stockinged feet on the hearth. "Aren't you having a drink?"

He shook his head. "I don't need one. I haven't been through what you have this morning. Besides," he added with a grin, "I have to keep all my wits about me today."

"Why?" she asked, sipping the drink and sighing in bliss as the fiery sweetness of the rich liquid exploded through her, warming her body and chasing away the shaky cobwebs in her head.

"Because," he said with a grin, "I thought, once you were feeling better, you might consider a little chess match. What better way to pass a rainy afternoon?"

Jo looked over at him sharply.

Gray had always possessed this amazing ability to behave as if whatever had happened between them most recently had never occurred at all. Whether their last encounter had ended with a bitter, angry fight or with a kiss, the next time she saw him he seemed able, somehow, to be nothing more than calm and friendly and casual.

But this, she thought, was the absolute limit—Gray Lyndon sitting across the hearth from her like an old, trusted friend or a brother chatting easily about a chess match after the experience that they had just shared!

"Gray..." she began, biting her lip and looking down at her hands.

"What, Jo?" He looked over at her, studying her bent head. "You weren't by any chance going to talk to me about something I've already forgotten, were you?" he asked gently. "Because if you were, there's no point. If I've already forgotten it, then it's gone? Right?" She sipped her drink and didn't answer. "Right?" he persisted.

"Right," she said, her voice almost inaudible.

"Good." He turned away again, gazing in pleasure at the leaping flames, glowing green and blue and scarlet in the dusky midday light. "I love looking at a fire," he commented dreamily. "You know, I could just sit here for hours, relaxing like this, with you over there, and do nothing but watch the fire."

Jo stole another glance at him, peeping over the rim of her glass at his face as he gazed into the hearth. His square, sculpted features were lit by the bronze glow from the fire, softening their firm planes, and his big, strong body was relaxed and easy in the old armchair. Golden light flared in his curly dark hair and flickered across his lips and cheekbones.

To her utter amazement, Jo was assailed suddenly by an urgent rush of sexual desire so intense that she almost gasped aloud.

She made a small, awkward movement, setting her glass down so hastily that it nearly spilled. Gray glanced over at her in quick concern. "Something wrong, Jo?"

"No, I'm all right. I'm fine. I just . . ." Her voice trailed off, and she stared down at the pattern in the rug near her hand, bewildered by the pounding strength of her passion, trying desperately to control herself. A swarm of images battered against her mind, pressing unbidden into her consciousness: memories of how his hands had felt, big and hard against her naked skin and the tender way he had cared for her, the unbearable sweetness of their kiss that day in the sunshine. . . .

Somehow Jo felt as if every sight and emotion was magnified and intensified by the darkened seclusion of the room, by their warm, intense privacy in this swimming world of rain and mud, by the richness of the liquor coursing through her veins. She was sharply aware of the graying curls peeping out from his shirt collar, of his tanned hands lying casually on the chair arm, of her own nakedness, burning beneath the soft, caressing fabric of her robe. . . .

She made a quick, frantic little movement, trying to dispel the tumult of emotions and regain some control over herself.

"Jo?" he asked again with a note of anxiety in his voice. "Are you sure you're all right?"

"Yes, I'm fine. I'm just worried about—" She paused, searching desperately for a way to finish the sentence.

He was looking at her so intently. What if he could tell what she was thinking?

"I was . . . I just remembered those filthy clothes of mine out in the porch. I should do something about . . ."

As she spoke, she began to struggle to her feet, and he reached over to put a hand on her arm. "Relax," he told her. "I already did that."

"You did?" Jo looked up at him, trembling at his touch, feeling her body melting into a sweet, delicious weakness. Finally she pulled her arm away and tried once again to gather her thoughts. "What did you do with them? They were so dirty."

"While you were finishing your bath and drying your hair, I soaked them in the sink out in the porch and then tossed them into the washer with about a gallon of detergent." He looked at his watch. "They should be ready to go in the dryer by now."

"Oh." She hesitated and then stared at him again, her eyes wide. "My buns! I forgot all about them! I had—"

Once again she struggled to get up, and he restrained her. "You'll have to forget those buns, I'm afraid, Jo. They were running over the sides of the pan and down onto the floor when I found them, and I just had to scrape the whole mess into the garbage."

Jo picked her drink up again and took a nervous little sip, avoiding his eyes. "It sounds," she said, trying to keep her voice light, "as if you've taken care of everything."

"Well, I tried. And it sounds as if *you*—" Gray smiled at her and got to his feet "—are feeling a whole lot better all of a sudden."

"What do you mean?" Jo asked in alarm, watching as he strolled across to a cabinet built into the wall by the fireplace.

"I mean," Gray called back over his shoulder, rummaging busily in the cabinet, "if you've got the energy to be brooding and fretting about housekeeping, I figure you're just about totally recovered. So *now*—" he came back across the room, carrying a chessboard and a little wooden box containing the playing pieces "—we'll see who's the better man, Joanna McLean!"

Jo watched in silence as he folded himself down on the floor opposite her, set the chessboard on the rug between them and began to arrange the chessmen. His head was bent, and she could see his dark, springing curls, dusted with gray, close enough to touch, and his strong brown fingers as he set the little pieces into position.

"Okay," he said finally. "Who goes first?" He looked up at her with a cheerful, teasing grin, but as he caught the expression on her face, his smile faded and his eyes became suddenly intent. "Jo?" he whispered.

She stared at him, wide-eyed and helpless, with everything that she was feeling there in her face for him to see.

Gray gazed back at her for a moment, speechless with wonder. Finally he lifted the chessboard and set it carefully aside. "I think," he murmured huskily, "that this game can wait for a while. Don't you?" Then he reached out and gathered her gently into his arms.

She shivered in fear and excitement as she felt his strong arms close around her and allowed herself to be drawn in and crushed against his body. She was still experiencing that same strange sensation, a kind of heightened awareness in which every touch, every scent and sound was intensely powerful. The feel of his strong fingers, cupping her head and caressing her cheeks, the rippling bulge of muscles in his big arms, the clean, outdoor scents of rain and sun that mingled in his soft flannel shirt and his curly hair against her cheek, the husky murmur of his voice in her ear—all of these were almost unbearably vivid and poignant.

And beyond these immediate sensations there was another, more distant feeling, created by the pounding sea of rain beyond the windows and the crackling warmth of the fire in the hearth. Jo felt that they were the only two people left on the planet, marooned on this tiny oasis of light and warmth in a wide, terrifying sea of harsh, gray cold.

She clung to him, straining her body against his, holding him closer and closer to her. His lips found hers and he kissed her, gently at first and then with rising passion. She felt her head begin to swim, and her spirit seemed to rise of its own accord beyond her control and float toward him, yearning for him....

His hands began to move over her body, pushing the robe aside and stroking the naked skin beneath, running along the length of her slender back, moving slowly around to cup her breasts gently, slipping down along her thighs.

"Gray," she whispered. "Gray...!"

But she had no idea whether she was trying to protest or was urging him to hurry. She was lost, drowning in sensation, drifting on a warm, rich tide of desire and urgency.

"It's all right," he whispered back, his lips pressing close to her ear so that she felt his warm breath on her cheek. "It's all right, sweetheart, it's all right."

Suddenly she felt herself being lifted, held against his body, carried away. She had a sensation of helplessness, of total yielding to whatever was going to happen next, as if no other world had ever existed and her whole life was contained inside this little house on this rain-washed, dusky afternoon.

He carried her down the hallway and into her bedroom, placed her gently on the bed and turned to lock the door. Then he drew the covers back, peeled her robe from her body and tucked her in between the bedclothes. In her state of heightened awareness, the cool sheets burned and tingled against her body, and a shudder ran through her.

She turned on her side, curled up and lay watching him, wide-eyed and silent, as he stripped off his clothes. There it was—the beautiful, virile male body that she had seen so long ago, it seemed, on the night she had first come here. But then she had been terrified, and now all she felt was an overwhelming, hungry desire.

His movements were deliberate and calm, without haste, but as he peeled down his undershorts and stepped out of them, it was obvious that he was feeling some urgency. Jo looked up at him as he stood by the bed, his big, hard body taut with desire, and she smiled.

He smiled back and pulled the covers aside, climbing in beside her. "Are you laughing at me, Joanna?" he murmured, taking her into his arms.

She giggled against his chest. "I was just thinking what it must be like for men. I mean, it's pretty hard for you to conceal how you're feeling, isn't it?"

He chuckled. "It is when there's a woman like *you* around, that's for damn sure." He held her close to him, running his hand luxuriously down her back and over the curve of her hips. "I've had this problem," he confessed, "ever since I met you."

"What problem?" she asked, burrowing against his curly mat of springing, frosted chest hair.

"The problem of my body reacting to your presence, like it's doing right now, and threatening to embarrass me in front of other people."

She pulled away a little and looked up at him in surprise. "You're kidding. Even during all that fighting?"

"Oh, Jo," he groaned, drawing her close to him again and continuing his long, slow caresses. "Even during all that fighting. No woman has ever affected me the way you do. I can't ever remember wanting anybody so much. I've been almost crazy sometimes with wanting you...."

His voice trailed off, and his movements grew more deliberate, more insistent. Jo had always suspected that he was a passionate man, and he seemed now to yield totally to his passion. He gave himself over to enjoyment of her body, letting his hands and his mouth explore the textures and surfaces of her skin, drawing the covers back to look at her and delight in her.

Jo was astounded by the surging intensity of her response. She had never felt so lifted out of herself, so completely given over to sensual pleasure. She turned to him, running her fingertips over his broad, muscular chest and his steel-hard thighs, fondling and caressing him until he was huge and erect with desire.

He gasped with delight at her touch and increased the tempo of his own movements, responding to the pounding inner rhythms that drove them both. Finally, when neither of them could endure it any longer, he rolled over and lifted his big body above hers, lowering himself gently inside her.

Jo felt him enter and moaned in pleasure. Nothing she could remember in her entire life had ever been quite this satisfying, she thought. But soon all thought was gone, swallowed up in pounding waves of joy that swelled and mounted and became her whole world. She rode on a rising tide of exultation to a point where the wave crested at an unbearable, dizzying height, sparkling in sunlight—and broke, then ebbed in a long, slow, throbbing rhythm that left her spent and gasping.

When she was able to breathe again and remember her own name and think with some degree of clarity once more, she rolled her head on the pillow to look at Gray. He lay on his back with his eyes closed, still breathing heavily, and Jo watched him, enjoying his clean-cut profile, the crisp silvery hair at his temples and the firm, sculpted shape of his lips.

She reached out gently to place a fingertip against his mouth, and he opened his eyes and smiled at her, his darkly lashed eyes crinkling at the corners.

"Well, well," he murmured. "Who's this in my bed?"

"It's *my* bed," Jo pointed out, smiling back and continuing, idly, to trace the outlines of his face with her fingers. "And, you know, I don't remember inviting *you* into it."

A teasing sparkle appeared in his eyes. "Is that so? Well, I don't recall you fighting all that hard to keep me out."

She sighed and assumed an injured tone. "I know. I just decided that it was inevitable. You're so much stronger than me—obviously it was futile to put up any resistance. I just had to grit my teeth and go along with it."

Gray chuckled. "Beyond a certain point that's probably true, you know. There was definitely a point of no return for me back there, I'll admit. What a woman," he added, addressing the ceiling in hushed tones of awe. "My God, what an incredible woman."

"Oh, stop it," Jo said cheerfully, and pushed at his big body with her hands. "Come on. Get up."

"What?" he asked, his voice injured. "Just like that? No encores?"

"Certainly not," she said, pretending to be shocked.

"Well, then," he murmured drowsily, drawing her close to him and rolling onto his side, "let's just have a little nap, okay? C'mon, snuggle up and sleep for a while."

"Gray, we can't! What if we fall asleep and Keith comes home and finds us here? Gray, we've got to—"

"What time does the bus get here?" he asked.

"Usually just after four."

"Okay. It's not quite two o'clock now. I'll set your alarm for three, and we can nap for an hour, and that still gives us an hour to get up and get decent before he comes home. How's that?"

Jo hesitated, still feeling a twinge of panic, but reluctant to leave the coziness of the bed. Her body felt warm and heavy, sweetly drowsy, and the idea of a nap, nestled in Gray's strong gentle arms, was almost irresistible.

"All right," she said finally. "Just for an hour. And make sure you set that alarm properly."

"This is amazing. Absolutely amazing," he commented to nobody in particular as he propped himself on one elbow to adjust the clock radio. "This woman is actually becoming a reasonable person. If you keep this up," he added, speaking to her over his shoulder, "it's even possible I'm going to start liking you a little bit, you know."

"Not much danger of that," Jo murmured sleepily, cuddling close to him as he got back into the bed and closing her eyes. "We're too different, Gray. You might like me for ten minutes, and then we'd be fighting again."

"Why don't you try me, sweetheart?" he murmured. "Just try me, and see how long I can..."

But she was already asleep, her shapely breasts rising and falling softly as she breathed with a quiet, even rhythm. Gray leaned over her, tucking the blankets up around her shoulders and looking down at her as she slept, his face gentle and thoughtful.

"I love you, Joanna," he whispered to her as she slept. "But I wonder if you're ever going to let me tell you how I feel."

He was silent for a moment longer, studying her sleeping form with aching tenderness. Finally he wrapped a big arm around her, drew her close to him, moving carefully so as not to disturb her, and closed his eyes.

KEITH CAME NOISILY into the porch, stamping mud from his boots and opening the door to shake out his jacket.

"Mom?" he called into the kitchen. "Hey, mom? You in there?"

"In the living room," his mother's voice called.

Keith's two spotted puppies came hurtling noisily up the basement stairs to greet him, twisting their plump bodies in paroxysms of joy, as if he had been gone for years instead of just hours. Mrs. Brown followed more sedately, her tail wagging with quiet dignity, and licked his hand. Keith knelt to greet the puppies, took an apple and a glass of milk from the fridge and wandered into the living room.

"Wow," he said as he entered, "this rain is really awesome. You should see the school yard, mom. There's a big lake covering the whole football field, and—"

He stopped dead, the apple halfway to his lips, and stared.

There was a warm fire crackling in the fireplace, and his mother and Gray Lyndon sat opposite each other in high-backed wooden chairs at a little card table pulled up near the hearth, concentrating on a chess game.

They both glanced up, smiling, as he entered, and Keith looked at them, still surprised. There was something different about his mother—something hard to put his finger on. She was dressed in the same clothes she always wore around home, jeans and sneakers and a warm sweater, but her eyes seemed unusually bright, and her cheeks were flushed.

"Gray stopped by for a visit," she was saying, "and since it was such a cold, rainy afternoon, we decided to have this famous chess match he's been talking about for so long."

"Yeah? Who's winning?" Keith asked, dropping onto the couch and looking at the chessboard with interest.

"I am," Gray said placidly.

"He is *not*!" Jo said. "He's cheating!" Keith understood, now, the pinkness of her cheeks. She always looked like this when she was angry with Gray.

"C'mon, mom," Keith said reasonably, getting up to poke a log farther into the heart of the fire. "How can anybody cheat at chess?"

"It's not easy," she said, "but this man can do it. He's trying to castle his king after he's already moved it once."

"I *didn't* move it," Gray protested hotly. "I was going to move it, and then I changed my mind and put it back. And you know it."

They glared at each other across the table, and Keith lounged on the couch, shaking his head. "You two are incredible," he said. "I never saw two people fight so much and over such stupid little things. I'll bet you guys couldn't do anything together without fighting about it."

Gray grinned lazily at Jo and then turned toward the boy, leaning comfortably back in his chair. "That's not entirely true, Keith," he said. "There are some things your mother and I do really well together."

Keith saw his mother's body tense, and her cheeks flared pink again as she cast Gray a sharp, warning glance.

"Like what?" the boy asked curiously.

Gray paused for effect while Jo continued to stare at him tensely. "Well, like moving pigs, for instance," he said finally with another teasing glance at her. "When it comes to chasing pigs around, we're just a hell of a team, your mother and I."

Keith laughed. "When do you two ever chase pigs around?"

"Today," Jo said promptly, clearly relieved. "I went out just before lunch, and all the new little pigs had crawled out under the corral fence and gotten into the alfalfa field. And I couldn't get them back in until Gray came along and helped me."

"Lucky for you," Keith said absently. "I thought Mac fixed all those holes," he added.

"He did, but they made a new one," Jo said, her voice gloomy.

Keith looked at her in concern. "Will they be all right, mom? I mean, will they catch colds or anything?"

"I hope not," Jo said softly. "I truly hope not, Keith." She hesitated. "We went out to check on them just after—" Inexplicably she blushed again and stumbled over her words. "Just after we...we..."

"Finished our lunch," Gray supplied helpfully.

"Right," Jo said with relief. "Just after lunch, and they were all burrowed into the straw and didn't look so cold anymore, but a few of them were still shivering, and some were coughing, too. We just have to wait and see, I guess."

Gray, meanwhile, was studying the chessboard, pondering his move. "Aha!" he shouted so suddenly that the other two in the room jumped a little and looked at him in alarm. He leaned expansively in his chair, beaming at Jo. "Check," he announced, moving his rook into position. "Let's see you wriggle out of *that* one, Ms. McLean."

Jo frowned, studying the playing pieces with intense concentration. She bit her lip, poised her hand slowly over the board and lifted her queen, moving it a few squares to the left. Then she glanced across the table, stifling a chuckle at the look of sudden consternation that appeared on Gray's face.

"All right," he said finally in disgust. "It's going to take me an hour to figure out how to counter that one, and I've got to get home now and do my chores. We'll have to finish this later."

"How?" Keith asked. "Are you just leaving the whole game set up over there till the next time you come or what?"

"The wonders of modern technology," his mother said. "We've been entering all the moves on the computer as we went along, and now we'll just store the unfinished game and recall it when we have a chance to play the rest of it.''

''Wow,'' Keith said, impressed. ''Neat.''

Gray got up and went into the kitchen, returning immediately with his long raincoat, which he pulled on as he smiled at Joanna. ''Thanks for the game and the nice visit, Jo,'' he said softly.

''That's fine,'' she murmured, turning her face aside and busying herself tidying the chess pieces away into their box. ''Thank you for helping me with the pigs.''

''Well, I'd better be going,'' Gray said, but he still lingered in the doorway, clearly reluctant to leave this comfortable place with its bright, crackling fire, its cheerful occupants and the pleasantly challenging chess game. ''Bye, Jo. Bye, Keith.''

''So long, Gray,'' Keith said casually, bending to lift one of the puppies into his lap. ''See you Saturday.''

''Why?'' Jo asked, pausing on her way into the kitchen. ''What's happening on Saturday?''

Suddenly the cozy little room was electric with tension. Keith flushed and shifted uneasily on the couch, and Gray looked at him with a calm, steady gaze. ''I thought we had a deal, Keith,'' he said quietly. ''I thought you promised me you'd tell your mother.''

''I was going to tell her,'' Keith said, his face pale beneath the tan. ''Honest, I was. I just…didn't get around to it yet, that's all.''

''Tell me what?'' Jo asked, looking from one to the other.

''Keith?'' Gray prompted him gently.

''It's just…'' Keith hesitated, and cast his mother a glance that was half pleading, half defiant. ''It's nothing to make a big deal about. I'm just going to a rodeo with Gray on Saturday, that's all. Over at High River. No big deal.''

''Why are you going?'' Jo asked.

''Well, just for the fun of it. Just to see what it's like.''

"Keith..." Gray began, but the boy cast him a glance of such naked, impassioned pleading that he subsided, his face troubled, and said no more.

There was something in the atmosphere of the room, something hanging unsaid in the air between them, that troubled and frightened Jo. She looked from the man's grave, quiet face to the boy's tense expression.

"There's something else," she said quietly. "Something you're not telling me." Again she looked from Gray to Keith. Neither of them spoke. Her face tightened with fear. "I don't want him to go," she said to Gray.

"Mom!" Keith shouted. "*Why* do you always have to be so *damn*—!"

"Keith!" Gray said sharply. "Don't talk to your mother like that!"

Keith subsided, his face twisted with misery, and looked down bleakly at the puppy, which was standing in his lap and trying to lick his face.

Gray stood, big and quiet in the doorway, and looked directly into Jo's eyes. "I'm taking him with me, Jo," he told her gently.

Her fear throbbed urgently through her and hardened slowly into anger. "Even after I've told you I don't want you to?"

"I'm afraid so. I promised him I'd take him and I'm going to."

She stared at him, and their eyes met and held in a silent, bitter challenge. Finally Jo turned away, her shoulders slumped helplessly.

"All right," she said in a toneless voice. "If that's what you're planning to do, what else can I say?"

"Jo..." Gray reached out and held her arm, pressing it urgently. "Jo, why are you so opposed to this? What's wrong with letting the boy go to a little small-town rodeo on a nice summer afternoon? What could be more wholesome than that? What could possibly be your objection?''

''You don't understand,'' she said in that same flat, defeated voice. ''I could never make you understand.''

Gray glanced over at the silent, miserable boy on the couch and then back to her. ''Try me,'' he said gently.

''Gray, ever since Keith started getting interested in this... this 'sport,' as you call it, I've taken the trouble to learn something about it by reading everything I could find.'' She gazed up at him, her eyes earnest and pleading. ''And I know that it's dangerous and addictive. I also know, even though I don't want to hear any details, that Keith's tried a little of it over at your place, and if you start taking him to actual rodeos, the next thing we know he's going to be wanting to *enter* them, or whatever you call it, and ride in the rodeos!''

She paused, breathless with emotion, and stared down at the floor, trying to control her trembling. Over the top of her head Gray and Keith exchanged a quick, significant glance, and then Gray turned back to her, putting an arm gently around her shoulders.

''And would that be the worst thing in the world, Jo? If he were to enter a rodeo? In, say, the boys' steer riding, for instance?''

She stiffened, shrugged his arm away and then looked up at him, her eyes blazing. ''Those kids get *killed*, Gray! They get trampled and rammed into fences and have whiplash in their necks from being tossed around on those awful animals.''

''Jo that only happens to one in ten thousand. It's far more dangerous to drive a tractor, for instance, or ride in a plane, than to ride in a rodeo. In fact,'' he added, ''that's how most rodeo cowboys get hurt. Not riding bulls or bucking horses, but being hurt while they're traveling from one rodeo to the next.''

"That's a stupid argument," Jo said stubbornly. "Saying that it's all right to do something dangerous just because it's not quite as dangerous as something else you might be doing. There's no logic to that kind of thinking."

"Well, I think," Gray told her steadily, "that there's not a whole lot of logic to *your* kind of reasoning, Jo."

"What do you mean?"

"I mean, the idea that we can keep somebody safe by never, ever letting them do anything dangerous. Jo, people fall on their own stairs and drown in their own bathtubs and get crippled by their own lawn mowers. Nothing is safe. I think," he went on with passionate sincerity, "that beyond a reasonable caution, we just have to live our lives with some faith that bad things aren't likely going to happen and stop all this worrying all the time."

"Great," Jo said bitterly. "That's a lovely philosophy, Gray. So why don't you let Peggy be with the man she wants to be with and stop interfering in her life and making her miserable?"

His face tightened. "That's entirely different. That's something that could affect her whole future."

"Oh, I see. And you're saying, then, that a broken back or multiple paralysis isn't going to have any real effect on Keith's future?"

They stared at each other, breathing hard, locked in combat.

"Look," Keith said wearily, getting up from the couch and cuddling the puppy close to his chest as if for comfort. "Just *stop* it, okay? I won't go, mom. I'll stay home and be safe if that'll make you happy."

"No, Keith," Gray said quietly. "You'll go so your mother can learn there's nothing to be afraid of." He looked at Jo. "Why don't you come with us, Jo? You might even surprise yourself and wind up enjoying the day."

"Thanks for the invitation," Jo said, pushing past him into the kitchen and beginning to rummage busily in the cupboards and refrigerator. "But I have better things to do with my day."

Keith hesitated at the top of the basement stairs, his face lighting suddenly. "Does that mean I can go?"

"Yes," Jo said wearily. "You can go."

Keith gave a shout of joy and clattered noisily down the steps, singing a scrap of rock music at the top of his lungs. Alone in the kitchen Gray and Jo stood quietly, looking at each other.

"Jo..." he began.

"Don't say it, Gray. Please don't say it. Just go, okay? Maybe we'll talk later after I've had time to adjust to this."

"Jo, I just want you to know that I—"

"Please," she interrupted him. "I'm not up to a discussion about it just now. I think this is one of those situations where we're both partly right, but neither of us wants to admit it, and it's best just to leave it alone for a while."

"And what about this afternoon?" he asked.

"That has nothing to do with *this*! Nothing at all!"

"But it has something to with us, Jo. Is it going to happen again?"

She met his eyes with quiet challenge, and he waited for her answer.

"Not if I can help it," she said finally, turning toward the counter to begin chopping celery. "Goodbye, Gray."

He hesitated in the doorway, obviously wanting to say something further and then apparently thought better of it, letting himself out into the rain and closing the door softly behind him.

CHAPTER TEN

THE RAIN ENDED the next afternoon and was followed by days so rich and mellow and lovely that Jo wondered why anybody would ever choose to live anywhere but on the prairies. Every morning the sun rose early and beamed slanting rainbow colors across the misted grass, waking the songbirds nesting in tiny hollows on the surface of the prairie and the cattle, who stirred and circled and began to graze, placid humped shapes in the gentle light of dawn.

As the sun climbed higher in the sky, it turned bright copper and blazed forth a heat that coaxed out the tufted summer grasses and the lovely pastel wildflowers. By midday, when the sun was directly overhead in a vast cloudless sky, the cattle and horses stood sleepily, basking in the warmth, switching their tails lazily at flies and drowsing in peaceful silence.

Jo went for long walks on the prairie, lifting her face to the sun and letting her spirit rise and expand in the huge silence, the warmth and peace and solitude. But when she told Mac how she loved it and how she wondered why everybody in the world didn't want to come and live here, he merely snorted. "Sure, sure, it's nice in June. Wait till August when it's as dry as powder and the wind howls every day."

Jo stood at the sink, washing the breakfast dishes and staring absently out the window, her face bleak. Mac was growing more cynical and discouraged all the time, it seemed. And Jo suspected that the sickness among the little pigs had been especially hard on him. He had never admitted that this experiment might work or that he was counting on the pigs to help him ease his dangerous burden of debt. But he must have been, Jo thought miserably, drying the last of the plates and stacking them neatly in the cupboard. He must have been, or this wouldn't have hit him so hard. Poor Mac.

It was difficult for her not to feel guilty about this new disaster. She knew, rationally, that it was nobody's fault, and yet it had been her idea to try the pigs in the first place, and she was the one who had pushed the project and talked Mac into going reluctantly along with it. And the pigs had been in her care when they escaped from the corral and got chilled.

She put away the dish towel and the drying rack, wondering what Keith was doing. Usually, by this time on a Saturday morning, he was already lounging in the living room, his two puppies playing in his lap as he ate cereal and chuckled at cartoons. But this morning there was no sign of him, although Jo could hear him moving about, busy with some project of his own down in his basement room.

Probably, Jo thought, he's afraid to show his face for fear I'll change my mind and tell him he can't go to the silly rodeo with Gray today....

Gloomy thoughts seemed to be assailing her from all sides this morning. She felt a longing to escape, and giving one last quick look at the kitchen, she took her sweater from the hook by the door, tossed it over her shoulders and stepped out into the yard.

As always, the incredible warm stillness and beauty of the prairie morning almost overwhelmed her. She stood for a moment on the front walk, delighting in the misty sweep of land rolling off on all sides to a vanishing horizon, the drowsy, sun-drenched hum of insects underlying a warbling chorus of bird calls and the sweet scent of grasses and sage freshly washed by rain.

She took a deep breath and smiled, feeling her spirits lift in sudden happiness. Then she looked down toward the pig shelter, and her smile immediately faded. Mac appeared from inside the building, carrying a heavy burlap sack, which he tossed into the back of his truck. As Jo watched, he rested for a moment against the box of the truck and then, thinking himself unobserved, lifted his cap and scrubbed his hand wearily across the top of his bald head.

When he turned to trudge back inside the building, his movements were slow and labored, and Jo noticed, with a painful jolt that almost brought tears to her eyes, that for the first time she could ever remember, Mac was looking really old.

She paused, composed her features carefully and then walked down to the shelter, stepping into the murky, pungent depths of the big, open building and looking for her uncle. He was leaning against the self-feeder, staring gloomily at the masses of small, listless hogs.

"How many?" she asked.

He hesitated, looking at her miserably.

"Come on, Mac," Jo said. "I saw you putting them in the back of the truck. How many were there?"

"Three," he said.

Jo felt a sharp stab of panic, and controlled it instantly. "Okay," she said calmly. "That's seven that have died so far, but according to what the vet says, we're not likely to lose any more. This kind of flu usually runs its course rapidly. He said that all of them that were going to die would likely be dead by now."

"Sure, Jo. But you're forgetting what else he said."

She stood silently, staring at the pigs, not wanting to hear what her uncle was going to tell her.

"He said," Mac continued relentlessly, "that the real danger isn't in how many die. It's the fact that the ones that survive are going to take such a setback that they won't gain much at all, and we're going to lose most of our investment. Right?"

"I guess that's what he wanted to warn us about," Jo agreed reluctantly. "But I haven't given up hope, Mac. We still have two or three batches to go, and if we do really well on those, we could make up for—"

"Joey, Joey," he said sadly, shaking his head, "you're such a stubborn little optimist. You probably wouldn't give up with disaster staring you right in the face. But there comes a time when even *you* have to face reality."

"Well," she said firmly, "call me stubborn if you like, but I just happen to believe that we haven't reached that point yet. We'll do what the vet said to do with these pigs—give them lots of water and plenty of feed and extra vitamins and finish them out as well as we can, and then make enough on the new ones that we can meet most of that outstanding note, even after we pay all the expenses. Wait and see, Mac. You just wait and see."

But she knew that her brave words had little impact on him any longer. He listened, nodded and then turned away, wandering over to unlatch the door and step out into the sunlight.

Jo watched him go, feeling a great, aching sadness that threatened to engulf her. Mac looked so lost and filled with sorrow these days. And as he moved around the land and the buildings that he had loved all his life, he was like a man saying goodbye to what he treasured most in the world.

Helpless misery washed through her, leaving her empty and desolate, and a sob caught in her throat. She felt a sudden, urgent longing for Gray, for his strong arms around her, his teasing eyes laughing into hers and his cheery, capable way of comforting and helping and making things better. But then she remembered that she was angry with Gray, too, and that there was nothing in her world anymore, it seemed, for her to cling to or draw comfort from.

She turned, hearing the door open again, and saw Mac coming back in with a sack of the rich, ruinously expensive vitamin supplement that the vet had recommended for their pen full of sick and shivering little pigs.

Jo watched as he tore off the string tab on the top of the sack, hoisted it and upended it into the feeder. She saw him looking at something across the pen with a bleak, unhappy expression, followed his gaze and stiffened with fear.

"Oh, no," she whispered, wide-eyed, putting her hand over her mouth in alarm.

Their big spotted hog, already twice as large as the little pigs that milled about and pressed against his flanks, was standing listlessly in a corner with his head lowered. There was none of the vibrant energy and good cheer that usually marked his presence. His eyes were dull, his ears drooped even more than usual and his big body looked rough and thin. As Jo watched, he was gripped by a sudden spasm of coughs that left him heaving and gasping, his mouth open.

"Mac, I didn't know he was sick, too. When did he—?"

"Last night," Mac said briefly, "when I checked them before bedtime, was the first time I noticed him coughing."

"Mac..." Jo fought back tears as she gazed at the spotted hide, normally so sleek and fat. "He'll be all right, Mac. He's bigger and stronger than the others. He'll get better."

"Who cares?" Mac said with a shrug, feigning indifference. But his eyes, as they rested on the weary, pain-racked body of the spotted hog, were dark with worry. "Stupid thing, anyway," Mac muttered. "He was supposed to be looking after the others. If he'd been doing his job properly, none of this would have happened."

Jo heard the pained concern in her uncle's voice and remembered the big hog standing miserably in the rain by the hole in the fence, looking up at her with such guilt and anguish in his small, bright eyes.

She felt like crying, and knew that by now it wouldn't take much at all to get her started. She blinked her eyes rapidly and turned to leave, stumbling toward the door in her haste to get out of this building, away from all this misery.

"Gray's outside," Mac warned her. "Just got here. I guess he's come to pick up Keith."

Jo nodded, took a deep breath and stepped out into the sun-splashed farmyard. Gray was leaning against the front fender of his truck, chewing thoughtfully on a straw and singing to himself as he waited for Keith. As soon as he saw Jo emerge from the pig shelter, he straightened and strolled toward her.

Jo watched him approach, moved in spite of herself by the way that the mere sight of him seemed able to affect her so profoundly. He wore clean, faded jeans, a dark blue plaid shirt and a wide, tooled-leather belt with a big shining trophy buckle of some kind, and he looked extraordinarily handsome and virile. As usual he was bareheaded, with the sun glinting in his crisp dark curls and highlighting his tanned cheeks. Jo was assailed by a sudden, helpless yearning to throw herself into his arms, pour out all her troubles and draw comfort from the warmth and strength of his big body.

He saw the unhappy look on her face and paused, his eyes dark with sympathy. "How many altogether?" he asked.

"Seven," she said, her voice breaking a little. "Three more died this morning."

"Oh, Jo, I'm so sorry. Is there anything I can do?"

He reached out to put an arm around her shoulder, and she shivered and drew away. If she ever allowed herself to yield to his touch again, knowing how much she longed for it all the time, she was afraid she would never be able to resist him.

"There's nothing that anyone can do," she said. "We just have to let it run its course and then assess the damage at market time, I guess."

"Jo..." he began, his face still troubled and concerned as he looked down at her.

But they were interrupted by the arrival of Keith, who came running out of the house, his face blazing with excitement, carrying a jacket and his school gym bag.

Jo examined her son critically. He looked like a miniature replica of Gray, with the same lean-fitting jeans, a bright plaid shirt and a leather belt and buckle. Jo wondered where he'd gotten the buckle. Probably Gray had given the boy one of his. There seemed to be a whole complex relationship between this man and her son that she knew little about.

And Keith seemed different somehow on this warm summer morning—taller, and rangier, with a new shadow of a mustache on his upper lip and a strangely mature, husky timbre to his voice. Jo felt a sense almost of panic, as if she were helplessly watching her son slip beyond her into a frightening, masculine world where she could no longer protect him from all the terrible dangers of life.

She stood for a moment in the sunlight, thinking about Keith when he was small. He had been such a sweet baby, chubby and dimpled and happy, gripping his spoon in his fat hand and banging it on the tray of his high chair and clutching his little yellow fabric duck that he dragged around everywhere, tugging at its beak and its feet until they were nothing but orange shreds....

"Mom?" Keith was asking her in concern. "Earth calling mom?" He waved a hand in front of her eyes. "Hey, is there anybody in there?"

Jo blinked, gathered herself together with a little start and smiled at him mistily. "I was just thinking about when you were a baby. Remember your little yellow duck that you loved so much?''

''Oh, *no*,'' he moaned, shifting his feet in embarrassment and staring down at the ground, his cheeks flushed. ''Don't start with the *duck*, okay, Mom? *Please!*''

Jo reached out to ruffle his hair, but he dodged away from her hand. ''All right,'' she said in resignation. ''Go ahead, have a nice day.''

She watched as he hurried around and tossed his gym bag into the back of the truck.

''What's in there?'' she asked.

''Oh,'' he said vaguely, ''just...stuff. Bye, Mom,'' he added, climbing hastily into the passenger side of the truck.

Gray hesitated, giving Jo a searching look, and she met his eyes steadily. ''I'm allowing him to go with you, Gray, but I'm warning you. I don't want him anywhere near those animals. I don't want you getting him involved in anything foolish.''

Gray continued to look at her silently. Finally he reached out a gentle hand, cupped her cheek and gave her a tender, private smile. Jo shivered at the quick flare of passion in his eyes and felt her knees weaken suddenly. She was relieved when he opened the door and stepped into the truck, starting it up and wheeling around in the dusty yard.

They both waved, and Jo waved back, then stood staring down the road long after the truck diminished in the distance, grew as tiny as an insect and finally toppled over the edge of the far horizon and out of sight.

THE SUMMER EVENING was mellow and dusky, perfumed with the rich, spicy nighttime scents of lilacs and petunias that drifted in through the open kitchen windows. A curved scrap of moon hung in the sky, as delicate and transparent as a baby's fingernail, and the only sound was a steady, sweet chorus from the crickets, accompanied distantly by the booming of bullfrogs in the slough down beyond the alfalfa field.

Jo and Mac sat peacefully together in the small living room, busy with their own pursuits. Jo was seated at her computer, working on her new chess program, frowning in concentration as she entered moves and assessed their results. Across the room Mac had his easel set up beside the card table, and all his painting equipment scattered across the surface of the table. With sure, delicate strokes he was reproducing a pair of pronghorn antelope standing with their heads up, silhouetted against a prairie sunrise.

Jo stared at the screen, biting the end of her pen and thinking deeply, charting moves and consequences. Finally she entered a choice on the computer keys and smiled as the computer beeped, whirred briefly and then settled in to plot its response. She was challenging her computer at the upper level of the chess program, where on occasion it had taken as long as twenty minutes to decide on its next move.

Jo sometimes tried to imagine how many moves and combinations of moves the tiny microchips could analyze in twenty minutes, but it was impossible for her mind to encompass. Still, she frequently beat the computer at the lower levels of play and, on a couple of memorable occasions, had actually come close to winning at this upper program setting. She loved the challenge of it, and the sheer fun of pitting her mind against the machine.

She remembered her unfinished game with Gray, which had, she recalled, been a lot of fun, too. He was a formidable opponent, a keen and skillful player, with a daring, unconventional style that sometimes took her breath away and sometimes made her giggle in delighted astonishment. And he responded with such vibrant energy, shouting and gloating when he took one of her key pieces, clapping his hand to his forehead and loudly bemoaning his gullibility when she trapped him into making a bad move.

Jo smiled to herself. Actually Gray was a lot more fun than the machine and not nearly so predictable....

While the computer was thinking, she got up and wandered across the room to lean against Mac's chair and watch his deft, sure hand as he stroked in the texture of the antelope hide.

He dipped his brush into a jar of water cleaned it and turned to smile up at her. "Well, Jo, what do you think?"

"It's lovely, Mac. If I had enough money, I'd buy it myself, but your prices are far too high for me."

He chuckled. "Go on. You're just humoring the old man." He searched among his blocks of compressed colors for the shade of brown that he wanted and then went on without looking up, his voice deliberately casual.

"You know," he said, "I remember reading a while ago that pigs are more like people than any other animal. I mean," he added hastily, "their constitution and all. This article said they even use pigs to test drugs and medicines because they're likely to react to them just about the same as human beings do."

"I think I remember reading the same thing," Jo said absently. "I'd forgotten until you mentioned it." Her computer beeped, and she hurried back to see what move it had chosen. "Look at that! Why would it move the queen up there? That's just suicide, unless it's planning to...oh, *I* see..."

She frowned, thinking deeply, and was hardly aware that Mac was speaking to her until he called her name a second time. "Pardon, Mac?" she asked, looking around at him. "Sorry, I wasn't listening. I'm trying to figure out—"

"I was just asking," he said idly, frowning at a band of cloud along the horizon in his painting, "what you'd do for Keith, say, when he was little if he had flu or a bad cold."

"Oh, I don't know," she said vaguely. "There's not much you *can* do really except keep them warm and bundled up and give them aspirin and sponge them off with rubbing alcohol if they get feverish . . . lots of liquids and vitamin C—that sort of thing."

Across the room Mac nodded thoughtfully and returned to his painting. Then, just as the last twilight glow faded and summer darkness rolled across the prairie, they heard a vehicle drive into the yard.

Jo tensed, wondering if Gray would be coming into the house. Her heart pounded, and her mouth went suddenly dry. She forgot all about her chess game, which had been so absorbing until now, and about the harsh words they had recently exchanged, about her concern over his relationship with Keith—about everything but the thrilling, heart-stopping knowledge that he was nearby, and that, in just seconds, he might walk into the room.

But, with a mixture of relief and disappointment, she heard the truck door slam and the engine start up again as the big vehicle pulled out of the yard and off down the road. Immediately Keith's steps sounded on the walk outside, and the kitchen door slammed.

"Keith?" Jo called.

"Hi, Mom. Hi, Mac." As always when Keith entered the kitchen, the fridge door opened instantly, and they heard him rummaging for something to eat.

"Did you have a good day?" Jo asked, her voice carefully casual.

"Great!" he said from the kitchen, his voice muffled by whatever he was chewing on.

After a few seconds, he appeared in the entry to the living room, and the two adults stared at him, speechless. His clothes were dusty and smeared with dirt, and one shirt-sleeve hung open from shoulder to elbow in a long, ragged rip. But his eyes were bright with suppressed excitement, and his young, thin body was taut with emotion.

Mac looked quietly over at Jo, who finally gathered herself together and found her voice.

"Keith! What on earth happened to you! Are you all right?"

The boy hesitated, clearly torn by conflicting emotions. Then, with an expression half fearful and half exultant, he brought his hand out from behind his back, holding up a small trophy.

Jo stared at the trophy, wide-eyed and stunned. It had a marble base, and a small wooden column topped by a tiny gilt figure of a man riding a bucking bull.

"Keith, that's great!" Mac said warmly. "Where'd you place?"

"Third," the boy said proudly, barely able to contain himself. "But only four guys made it," he added, compelled by honesty.

"You mean," his uncle asked, "only four kids were entered? That's hard to believe."

"No, there were lots entered. Almost thirty. But it was real rough stock and only four guys made it to the whistle. You see," he went on earnestly, turning to his mother, "you have to ride for eight seconds, Mom, and then they blow a whistle to let you know you've made it. If you buck off before eight seconds, you don't get any points. And only four guys stayed on long enough, and I got more points than one of them, so I won this trophy, and—" he paused for effect "—*ninety dollars* prize money!"

Mac exclaimed in pleased surprise, and the boy flushed with delight.

"I can't believe this," Jo said finally, her voice cold. "I just can't believe you've done this."

The boy stared at her, deflated, and tensed himself for an argument. "Mom, you knew I was going to the rodeo. I didn't sneak behind your back or anything."

"You certainly did. Both of you did, you and Gray. I knew you were going to the rodeo, but I had no idea you were going to... to *ride* something. In fact, I expressly told Gray that I didn't want—"

"Mom, it's fine! There's nothing wrong with it! It's the most fun I've ever had, and there's nothing for you to be so scared about. Guys don't get hurt, Mom. They really don't. I wish you'd come and watch sometime and see for yourself."

"You're saying this isn't dangerous? No risk of getting hurt?"

The boy nodded eagerly, still clutching the trophy in his hands.

"Then," Jo said quietly, "tell me what happened to your clothes."

"Well..." he shifted awkwardly on his feet. "Well, the steer bounced around a little in the chute, you know...." He looked over at Mac, who nodded in understanding. "But Gray pulled me up before I could get banged up at all. Only my shirt caught on a nail inside the chute, and then, after my eight seconds were up, my rope loosened and he threw me off in the dirt, but I didn't get hurt, Mom. Not a bit."

She looked intently at his vivid, animated face. "And what's next, Keith? Are you and Gray going to just keep doing this in spite of the way I feel about it?"

He met her eyes with strangely mature composure and a quiet, even look of challenge that was new and deeply disturbing to her. "Next," he said, "are two more rodeos, the next two weekends, at Nanton and Okotoks, and I'm entering both of them. And after that—" he drew a deep breath and plunged on "—is the Calgary Stampede."

Jo stared at him. *"The Calgary Stampede!"*

"Yeah." Keith grinned in spite of himself, his eyes sparkling with excitement. "Gray already has me entered, and you should see the money and the prizes you can win. It's just incredible.''

"Over my dead body," Jo said grimly.

"Mom, please, don't be like this. Mom, if you only knew what it means to me—"

"Keith, I've watched the Calgary Stampede on television. I've even seen it in person a couple of times, years ago. And the boys' steer riding there is a terrifying thing. They put those young boys on animals that buck as hard as . . . as Brahma bulls almost.''

"Gray says I can do it," the boy said stubbornly. "He says I have a lot of natural ability, and if I keep practicing and get a couple more rodeos under my belt, I could even win something at Calgary.''

Jo switched off the computer abruptly and got to her feet, her face closed and silent.

"Mom?" Keith asked hesitantly.

"You're not going, Keith. I absolutely forbid it, and I don't want to discuss it anymore.''

"Yes, I am," he said, his cheeks flushed, his breath coming hard. "I'm going, Mom. I'm sorry, and I really hate to hurt you, but I'm going to live my own life like other guys do, whether you like it or not. You just say the word, and I'll leave tonight. Right now.''

"Leave!" she exclaimed, tense with fear. "Where on earth would you go?''

"To Gray's. I could go and stay there, ride to school on the bus and everything. Gray really cares about me," Keith said calmly.

"Cares about you!" Jo echoed bitterly. "He's got a strange way of showing his concern, doesn't he? Trying to get you killed?''

"I'm *not* going to get killed, Mom. I just wish you wouldn't be so scared all the time. Gray says—"

"I don't want to hear *another word* about that man," Jo said, struggling to keep her voice level. "Or any of this nonsense about you leaving or anything. We won't talk about it any more tonight, Keith. Have a bath and go to bed. We'll talk in the morning when we can both be a little calmer and kinder to each other."

"Mom, if you'd just—"

"No more, Keith. I mean it."

There was no mistaking that tone in his mother's voice. He turned with his trophy dangling listlessly from his hand and trudged through the kitchen toward the basement stairs.

Jo watched him go, overwhelmed with sudden, sickening terror at the sight of his ragged, torn shirt and the dirt ground into his jeans. She thought of the danger he had risked, how close he might have come to being maimed or crippled, and her breath caught in her throat.

Mac watched her with concern. "Jo..." he began hesitantly.

"It's all his fault, Mac," she said. "Gray's, I mean. How can a boy that age be expected to resist when a man that he hero-worships is filling his head full of such big ideas and telling him it's the right thing? I don't blame Keith. I blame Gray."

"Jo, you're on pretty dangerous ground here, you know. You could drive the boy away."

"No, I won't," she answered calmly. "I know how I intend to deal with this situation, Mac."

"What are you going to do?"

"I'm going to go over in the morning and have a little talk with Gray Lyndon. I'm going to tell him how I feel about what he's doing to my son. And then I'm going to—"

She choked suddenly, stopped speaking and hurried along the hall toward her room, while Mac watched her slender, departing form in troubled silence.

THE NIGHT WAS STILL and silent and utterly dark. A wisp of cloud crossed the tiny crescent moon like tattered lace, and even the crickets and bullfrogs seemed to have gone to sleep.

Mac tiptoed cautiously around the darkened kitchen, afraid to put a light on for fear of waking Jo. He took the big flashlight that always sat on a shelf in the porch and sheltered the beam with his hand, gathering the things he needed. With his arms loaded he paused in the doorway, frowning in concentration.

Aspirin, rubbing alcohol, chocolates, and there's lots of sacks in the chop house, and a book to read...lamp and extension cord...maybe a hot water bottle would be a good idea....

He tiptoed back into the kitchen, folding his long body awkwardly down onto the floor to rummage under the lowest pantry shelf and dragged out a big blue rubber sack with a stopper attached. He paused, resting on his bony knees and thinking, and then took the water bottle over to the sink, letting the water run in a tiny trickle so that it wouldn't make any noise. Patiently he waited for it to get hot and then filled the bottle.

Finally he set all his supplies carefully on the floor in the porch, took his old work jacket from the hook and shrugged into it. Then, still moving with infinite caution, he gathered his things again, let himself stealthily out the door and latched it soundlessly behind him.

He moved across his farmyard in the deep velvety blackness with a sureness born of a lifetime of familiarity. He knew every mound and tussock, every irregularity on this piece of earth. He had walked it in storm and shower, in baking heat and bitter cold, in every hour of every season since the days before his memory began.

Mac went into the chop house, gathered a pile of clean burlap sacks and added them to his burden. Then he approached the old calf shelter where the pigs were now housed and let himself quietly inside, working the latch awkwardly with his arms full of equipment.

He stood for a moment, blinking in the inky, warm depths of the building, listening to the soft, rustling sounds in the straw as pigs moved and shuffled restlessly, and the occasional coughs and wheezes of the ones that were still sick.

He plugged his extension cord into the outlet by the door and played it out over his arm, threading it through the low rafters above him as he picked his way across the massed, huddled forms of sleeping hogs. He stepped carefully among them, trying not to disturb them. When he reached the far side of the pen, using his flashlight at its lowest setting to guide him, he looked around and then moved along the wall and knelt down.

The big spotted hog lay there on his side, gasping and shivering helplessly. Mac flashed the light over the animal, whose little black eyes, bright and feverish, rolled back and looked up with an imploring expression. But, sick as he was, when the hog recognized Mac he gave a hoarse little grunt of adoration and struggled to rise, churning his legs uselessly under him.

"Stop that, you fool thing," Mac muttered huskily, and gave the pig a gentle push with his hand. "Don't you even know enough to lie still when you're sick?"

He plugged the lamp into the extension cord, casting a warm little pool of light that bathed his stooping, kneeling figure and the suffering animal on its bed of straw. Then he began to work, moving awkwardly in the constricted space, shaking out blankets and covering the pig's shuddering body, fitting the hot water bottle carefully against its thin flank, rubbing the droopy ears tenderly. As he worked, he talked constantly in a rough, affectionate monotone.

"Stupid pig. Going and getting sick. Just what I'd have expected of you. Don't even have the sense of a flea. Now have to go and lose sleep over you, sitting up all night trying to keep you alive.''

He dampened a cloth with rubbing alcohol and wiped it gently over the thin skin by the pig's ears and on his belly. As the liquid cooled and soothed his pain-racked body, the pig closed his eyes in relief and sighed, a sound that was almost human. But then, almost at once, he grew chilled and began to shiver again, and Mac had to move quickly to get the hot water bottle back into position.

"Not that *I* care," Mac went on hastily, as if someone had voiced an opinion and he was defending himself. "What does it matter to me if one more stupid pig happens to live or die? It's Joey I'm thinking about. That poor girl is just about at the end of her rope. She's seen enough of death and loss, and she can't stand much more."

The pig rolled his head to one side and seemed to be listening. He cocked his drooping ears and followed Mac's face with his intelligent little eyes, trying hard, through his mist of pain and fever, to pay close attention to this beloved face and voice.

"That's why she's treating the boy the way she is, you know," Mac went on, still murmuring to the pig as he bundled the sacks into place. "She knows it's wrong, and under any other circumstances she'd keep her fears under control. She's a terrific woman, Joanna is. It's just that she's lost so much, and she can't live with the idea of that boy being hurt. She just can't bear it. So now, if *you* go and die," he added severely, "how do you think she's going to feel? Answer me that. Huh?"

He went on patiently, murmuring in a soothing, monotonous voice as he worked over the prone body of the sick animal, trying vainly to stabilize its body temperature.

"Listen," he muttered finally. "This isn't working. Now I'm going to give you a whole bunch of aspirin, and you're going to take it, you hear? What I'm going to do, you see,

I'm going to grind it up into a powder and mix it with a couple of chocolates. You *know* how much you love chocolates, and then you're going to eat it. You hear me?''

Suiting action to words, he crushed several aspirin in a dish he'd brought with him and mashed two big chocolates in with the white powder. They were maraschino cherry chocolates, a flavor that Mac had long ago determined was the spotted pig's special favorite, though he seemed to like almost every kind of candy except nougat and licorice.

The hog's ears perked a little as he smelled the tantalizing aroma of chocolate and cherry liqueur, and he lifted his head to sniff feebly at the dish Mac offered him.

"*Eat*, damn you!" Mac urged, his face tight with the intensity of his concern.

Obediently the spotted pig licked up most of the sweetish, dark mixture, and Mac hurried to fetch a dish of water for him to drink.

Then he resumed his position, kneeling and looking down at the animal's twitching, shuddering form. The pig's eyes closed, and he drifted into an uneasy sleep. Mac settled in the straw, took his book and held it close to the lamp, trying to read.

Finally he gave it up and shifted in the straw, making a little mound of sacks to rest on and pulling up a couple of others to cover him against the evening chill. He rested in the pool of light cast by the tiny lamp and put one hand on the restless, suffering body of the pig.

Then he lay back with his other hand beside his head, gazing up at the dim, cobwebbed rafters. His face was drawn and tense with misery, and his eyes, in this private, unguarded moment, reflected his agony at the multitude of losses that he faced—losses, he sometimes thought, that were almost too much for one man to bear.

CHAPTER ELEVEN

JO SAT LISTLESSLY over her third cup of coffee, gazing out the window.

Strange, she thought, how Sunday morning always has a special feeling about it somehow, even if you spend it exactly the same way you do every other day.

The morning was warm and glorious, a symphony of blue and gold, so rich and lovely that it seemed almost to mock her in her depression and anxiety. It was a morning to be happy and carefree in, to lift your face to the sunshine, and sing and dance, and feel young and wonderful.

But life isn't like that once you're grown up, Jo thought gloomily. Life is just one problem after another it seems. Get one thing worked out and something else goes wrong.

Suddenly appalled by this uncharacteristic pessimism, she forced herself to get out of her chair and hurry across the kitchen to dump the sour dregs of her coffee mug into the sink. Then she went outside to feel the warmth of the early sun. She stood on the front walk, absorbing the peace and stillness of the prairie morning, firmly resolved not to give way to the old, black unhappiness that had dogged her footsteps so much of the time since her daughter's death.

Mac approached from across the yard, and Jo looked up with a smile. "Hi, Mac," she called. "You were up early this morning."

"I was?" he asked, pausing to unlatch the gate.

"You certainly were. I heard you moving around in the kitchen just when it started getting light outside. It must have been right around four o'clock or so."

"Yeah, well..." He hesitated, standing by the gate. "I couldn't sleep. I was hungry, I guess. Got up looking for something to eat."

Jo shaded her eyes against the slanting, early-morning rays of the sun to look at him and exclaimed aloud in concern. "My goodness, you *must* have slept badly, Mac. You look so tired."

He smiled wearily, his eyes darkened smudges in his craggy face. "That awful, eh?"

Jo was still watching him in concern. "You'd better have a nap this afternoon."

"A *nap*!" he snorted scornfully. "Just like an old lady. Fat chance."

Jo smiled at him affectionately. "Well, at least come inside and have a cup of coffee. I'm just making a fresh pot."

"Now *that*," he said fervently, "is something I could definitely be enthused about."

Inside the kitchen Jo looked thoughtfully across the table at her uncle. Though his seamed, weathered face was sagging with exhaustion, he seemed strangely at peace, almost happy.

"How are the pigs this morning?" she asked.

"Oh...getting better. I think you're right. There aren't any more of them going to die, I don't think."

"Oh, good," Jo said. She hesitated, afraid to ask about the big spotted hog.

Almost as if he had read her mind, Mac reached for a slice of toast and said casually, "You know that big ugly pig, the one with the spots and the droopy ears?"

"Of course," Jo said. "I was just wondering how he was."

"Well, he seems a little better. His fever must have broken in the night sometime. Just now, when I went out there, he was up on his feet and eating."

Jo looked at her uncle, her eyes shining. "Oh, Mac, I'm so glad!"

"Why?" he asked gruffly. "Who could possibly care about that big old nuisance, anyhow? Now that he's eating again," Mac added, spreading strawberry jam on his toast, "our feed bills are probably going to double. He's such a glutton."

Jo let this pass and got up to refill their coffee cups. "What do you think about the rest of them?" she asked over her shoulder.

"It's too early to tell, Jo. Almost all of them have been sick, and even though they're getting better, they've taken a bad setback. We'll just have to wait and see how it turns out."

She nodded thoughtfully.

Mac hesitated and gave her a cautious glance. "Are you still planning to go to Gray's this morning?"

Her face clouded and she bit her lip. "Yes, Mac, I am."

He sipped his coffee and said nothing.

"Why?" Jo asked, gazing over at his gleaming bald head as he bent above his plate. "Look at me, Mac."

He looked up and met her eyes, his face tired and quiet.

"You think I should just leave it alone, don't you, Mac?"

"Joey, Joey..." He shook his head wearily. "I don't know what to think. I know that life is just too complicated to figure out, and it's hard enough to decide what's right for our own lives, let alone everyone else's. I just want you to be happy, sweetheart. Whatever you decide you need to do, I'm with you all the way."

She flushed, surprised and moved by the loving tenderness in his voice.

"I just wish..." he began moodily, and paused.

"What, Mac?" she urged. "What do you wish?"

"I wish someone could do something to help Peggy," he said. "Sometimes I think that poor kid is suffering more than any of us, and there's nobody to help her."

Jo glanced at him in surprise. "What makes you think that? Has she said something to you?"

"Not in so many words. But I've known those two ever since they were babies, Jo. And Peggy's always been the lively one, full of life and fire, you know? And lately she's just...like a dead person. There's no life to her at all. I worry about her."

Jo frowned in concern. "I didn't realize it was that serious. I thought it was just...you know...one of these adolescent love affairs and that she'd get over it before too long."

Mac shook his head. "I'm afraid it's far more than that. Peggy isn't a girl to do things halfway. Never has been."

"I've tried to talk to Gray about it," Jo said. "He just won't listen. He feels so absolutely certain that he's doing the right thing for her by cutting this relationship off, and there's just no way to convince him otherwise."

"Strange, isn't it," Mac commented casually, "how clearly we can see the error when it's somebody else's kid involved?" He reached hastily for another slice of toast and refused to meet her eyes.

"Mac," Jo began stiffly, "I really don't think there's any parallel in these two situations. None at all."

"I don't know," he said. "I honestly don't know. I've never had children, and I always regretted it...." Mac paused, and Jo glanced up at him in surprise. "But," he continued, "as I get older, I can see, more and more, that raising them must be just about the hardest thing anyone ever has to do. You want so badly to do the right thing, and yet sometimes it seems that no matter what you do it's wrong. I can't judge anybody's decisions. I just wish," he added plaintively, "that everybody could be happy. That's all."

"Well, that would certainly be nice," Jo agreed with a wistful little smile.

They were interrupted by a sudden uproar on the basement stairs, and they both looked up in alarm as Alfred and Clarence, Keith's pair of fat spotted puppies, erupted from the stairwell and into the kitchen. The two puppies were fighting over a battered old carpet slipper of Mac's, with each one gripping part of it firmly between sharp, tiny teeth. They circled nosily in the kitchen, growling fiercely, both puppies digging back on their haunches with ears laid back and eyes bulging while the old slipper stretched between them, huge and floppy, threatening at any moment to pull apart at the seams.

The unhappy tension in the kitchen broke and drifted away on a tide of merriment, as Mac and Jo leaned back in their chairs and howled with laughter.

"No wonder they made so much noise on the stairs," Jo said, choking and wiping her eyes. "It can't have been easy coming upstairs in tandem like that."

Mac reached down gently, trying to detach the nearest puppy from the slipper, but was met with opposition so fierce that he gave up and left them to it. "I needed new slippers, anyhow," he told Jo.

"Coward," she said, smiling at him. Then she looked at her watch and began to hurry about the kitchen, clearing the table and stacking dishes in the sink. "If those two are upstairs," she said, "Keith won't be far behind, and I wanted to get away before he's up. I just don't feel like another argument this morning."

Mac nodded. "Take the truck," he said. "I don't need it this morning and that back road is dusty this time of year."

"Even after all that rain?"

Mac laughed. "This dry old prairie soaks up rain like a sponge. Two days after a rain, you can hardly tell it ever happened."

"Well, you can tell by looking at my garden, that's for sure. Everything out there is shooting up like Jack's beanstalk."

Hearing more sounds from the basement, and Keith's voice as he said something to Mrs. Brown, Jo hurried to get her sweater from the hook and toss it over her shoulders.

"I'll be back soon," she said, and then hesitated. "Tell Keith I love him," she added. "And tell him I think it's...I mean, I'm really proud that he won a trophy, even though I don't approve of how he did it. Tell him that, Mac, would you?"

The older man nodded, smiling gravely at her. "I'll tell him," he promised.

Jo drove Mac's truck along the prairie trail to the neighboring ranch, delighting in the warmth and freshness of the morning and refusing to allow herself to think about the purpose of her errand, or the possible outcome of this confrontation with Gray.

She rolled down the window and rested her arm on the sill, letting the gentle breeze waft over her, lifting and stirring her curly hair. A big jackrabbit sprang out of the brush beside the trail and bounded off across the prairie, disappearing in a patch of brush at the base of a coulee.

Overhead, a hawk circled and swooped closer, diving gracefully in soundless flight, clearly expressing an interest in getting a closer look at the rabbit. But soon it gave up and soared high again, drifting on the warm air currents, ceaselessly scanning the prairie below for any sign of movement.

There were masses of flowers on the rolling land in a bewildering variety of species and colors, and Jo thought again, as she often did these days, that she'd like to get a book and learn to identify all of them. She was, she knew, becoming dangerously attached to this wild, barren, lovely place, and she dreaded the thought that they might soon have to leave it. It was so hard to consider all the things that would have to be done—finding a place to live, enrolling Keith in a new school, making the rounds of all the accounting firms, looking for a job....

If it's this hard for me, she thought, after just a few months here, what must it be like for Mac? The poor old dear. I know it's on his mind all the time, but he never says a word about it anymore....

Still busy with her own thoughts, she drove into Gray's big, sprawling ranch yard, pulled up and parked by the house, getting out of the truck and looking around hesitantly. Gray's house was beautiful, a huge two-story fronted with fieldstone gathered from his own land and surrounded by a spacious fenced yard with wide lawns and flower beds that showed signs of neglect. The place was silent and deserted in the early-morning warmth, with no trace of life anywhere.

Maybe, Jo thought with relief, they've all gone away somewhere and I can just go home....

She stepped up onto the broad, shady veranda, walked around and paused by the kitchen door, her heart hammering loudly in her chest. Finally she knocked and waited tensely, but there was no answer. She knocked again and then peered inside. The inner door stood wide open, so Jo opened the screen door and stepped cautiously into the kitchen.

"Hello?" she called. "Anybody home?"

Her voice echoed in the silent house, and she crossed the kitchen to look into the big, cluttered living room. The twins, she knew, were a lot of help to Gray with the outside work and the business of the ranch, but they were both slapdash, indifferent housekeepers, and the rooms showed evidence of an extremely casual approach. The house was lovely and could be a showplace, with its huge rock fireplace, its graceful bay windows, sunken living room and huge country kitchen.

Jo had been in the house several times, once for Gray's branding, twice along with Mac for neighborly chats and coffee and once to collect Keith after one of his mysterious visits with Gray and the girls. Every time she saw the place she had to resist a strong urge to roll up her sleeves and start tidying, to scrub and straighten and go somewhere to browse through wallpaper samples....

It's none of my business, she told herself firmly, what Gray Lyndon's house looks like.

Obviously there was nobody home, and Jo fought down a ridiculous impulse to steal up the stairs and into Gray's room. She found that she was yearning, almost desperately, to look at the bed he slept in, open his closet and bury her face among his shirts, touch the things that he used every day.

Horrified at herself, she hurried out of the house, across the veranda and down the steps. Then she heard voices coming from the direction of the barns and saw the twins approaching across the ranch yard. They were walking close together, side by side, and arguing bitterly in low tones.

As the girls drew nearer, Jo could see, however, that Libby was doing most of the talking. She held her head close to her sister's and seemed to be arguing vehemently, pressing some strong case while Peggy listened with downcast eyes and shook her head from time to time. The tone of Libby's low, sweet voice carried clearly in the gentle morning air, but Jo was unable to make out her words.

As they approached the house, the twins suddenly became aware of Jo's presence and moved apart quickly, falling silent and looking up at her as she stood by the gate.

"Hello, girls," Jo said casually. "Isn't it a beautiful morning?"

They both smiled and murmured something in reply, but Jo didn't hear what they said. She stared into their beautiful, vivid faces, so strangely identical and yet so vastly different in expression. Libby's gentle face was pale and drawn with concern, and she gazed up at the older woman with an agonized, pleading expression that made Jo want to take the girl into her arms and soothe and comfort her.

Peggy, on the other hand, looked silent and withdrawn, with a cold, determined line to her generous mouth that spoke of a decision reached and a resolve that couldn't be weakened by anyone. Jo trembled a little, wondering what the girl was planning to do. She had a feeling, looking into their unhappy faces, that something terrible was about to happen—something that none of them could do anything about.

"Is everything all right with you two?" she asked, trying to keep her voice light. "Anything I can do to help with anything?"

Libby looked urgently at her sister as if willing her to speak, but Peggy just shrugged and smiled. "Everything's fine, Jo. Just fine," she said quickly. "Can we help you with something?" she added politely.

Jo hesitated, wondering if she should press the issue, and decided against it. Mac was probably right. There was no way anybody could change Peggy's mind once she'd decided on a course of action. Jo just wished she could shake this cold, frightening premonition of disaster.

"Well," she began hesitantly, "actually, I was just wanting to...to talk something over with your father, if he's around, and not too busy."

"Sure," Peggy said easily. "He's down in the arena, working his new rope horse. Just over there," she said, pointing to the edge of a large rail enclosure that was partly visible beyond the corrals.

"Do you want us to go with you, Jo?" Libby asked. "We can show you how to get there through the corrals."

"No thanks. That's fine, Libby. I'll just take the long way around. It's a nice morning for a walk, anyhow."

Libby nodded, and the twins moved through the gate and up the walk toward the house. Jo watched them for a moment and saw that, as soon as they were out of hearing up on the veranda, they resumed their furious, quiet argument, with Libby talking earnestly and Peggy listening, her shoulders stiff and stubborn.

Jo turned aside and walked slowly down through the sunshine toward the arena. She was glad of the distance she had to walk, because, for some reason, she could barely control the pounding of her heart. Her palms were damp, she was breathing rapidly, and she realized, too late, she really had no idea what she was going to say to Gray.

All she knew for certain was that she couldn't bear the dangerous activity that he was deliberately involving her son in and that she was prepared to do whatever was necessary—make threats, deliver an ultimatum, have a temper tantrum—anything that would finally make him understand how desperately this mattered to her so that he would leave Keith alone.

Still tense and agitated, she approached the fence of the big arena and peeped through, staying behind the holding pen at the end so that he couldn't see her. Just in front of her was a new structure built of fresh green wood, and after some study and pondering, she realized that it was an exact replica of the chutes used at rodeos to hold bucking animals in place while cowboys got set to ride them. Her anger flared again, hot and searing, almost blinding her with fury.

This is new! He just *built* this! He built this whole thing for *Keith* so that he could learn to ride those awful animals! God, the man has so much gall....

She drew a deep breath, crept closer and peered through the rails of the fence. Gray was in the arena, mounted on a rangy young bay gelding with a white star on its face and high white markings on its legs. Jo realized that this was the first time she had ever seen Gray on horseback and, despite her anger, she looked at him for a moment with curiosity and a warm surge of admiration.

The horse was obviously young and skittish, and Gray was riding it with a complicated hackamore of braided rope, handling the horse skillfully as it shied and danced from side to side. The man's body was so easy and comfortable that he seemed at one with the powerful animal, swaying and balancing with each movement of his mount. He wore his old, faded denim work clothes that, rough though they were, could never quite disguise the beautiful, powerful lines of his hard, muscular body.

A vision crept unbidden into her mind, a memory of that body, naked and rigid with desire, filling her little bedroom with fire and beauty while the rain pounded against the windows, and her own body yearned and surged with longing....

Jo's mouth went suddenly dry, and she took herself firmly in hand, drew a deep breath and climbed up onto the fence.

The horse saw her first, throwing its head up alertly and nickering as she appeared. Gray turned and looked at her, startled. Then he nudged the horse with his knees and reined it around gently, trotting across the arena to where she sat on the top fence rail. He reined in beside her and looked over into her face. As soon as she saw his square, rugged features beneath the brim of his straw hat, the sun glinting on his strong cheekbones and the steady warmth of his gray eyes, Jo felt the old weakness spreading through her, drowning her anger and her resolve in a warm flood of desire.

Oh, God, she thought wearily. It would be so much easier if he didn't have this effect on me all the time. Why am I so weak? Why can't I just get over it . . . ?

"Look, I want to talk to you," she said, more sharply than she had intended.

"Okay," he said calmly. He slid his leg over the saddle and stepped gracefully from the horse, looping the reins loosely over a fence rail and standing beneath Jo as she sat on the upper board. "Come down here," he said. "We might as well sit in the shade while we talk."

He led her over past the bucking chute to a rough bench that was built against the fence in the shade and gestured to it. Jo sat down, and he seated himself casually beside her, leaning back against the fence, putting his hands into the pockets of his jeans and extending his booted feet comfortably as he waited for her to speak.

She hesitated, wondering if she could trust her voice, uncertain of what tone to take and how to begin. She looked around helplessly and caught sight of the fresh green lumber in the bucking chute. Her anger flared again, quick and hot, washing through her and strengthening her to do what she knew was necessary.

"That thing is new," she said, gesturing toward the chute. "You just built it this spring."

"Yes," he said. "Just about a month ago."

"You built it for Keith," she went on, her voice low and tightly controlled, "so he could practice riding steers."

"That's right," he agreed quietly. "I did."

"And yesterday," she continued, her voice rising a little in spite of herself, "you took him to a rodeo and, against my *express wishes*, Gray, you entered him in the rodeo."

"Yes," he said again in that same quiet, steady tone, "I did."

She hesitated and, to her dismay, felt her anger threatening to evaporate again in a flood of miserable tears. She fought to keep herself under control and turned to look up at him, her beautiful eyes pleading. "I thought," she murmured, "that you...cared about me. I thought you had some respect for me at least."

He met her gaze steadily. "I think I've made that pretty obvious, haven't I, Joanna?"

"No!" she burst out. "You haven't! All you've done is mock me and make a fool of me by ignoring everything I say and undermining my authority as a parent and..." She paused, out of breath, her chest heaving, her cheeks flushed.

"Jo, please..." He put his hand on her shoulder, and she shrugged it off impatiently. "Jo," he began again, "the boy wasn't hurt. He was on top of the world when he went up to accept that trophy. I wish you'd been there to see it, Jo. The kid was about ten feet tall."

"Yes," she muttered bitterly, "and his shirt was torn where he got caught in the chute, and his clothes were filthy because he got mashed into the dirt, and now—" she looked up, her eyes blazing furiously, "he says you're taking him to other rodeos and entering him in the *Calgary Stampede*, of all things!"

"That's true," Gray said, meeting her angry gaze with unwavering calm. "I am."

"I forbid it," Jo said coldly. "I won't allow it, Gray. You have to tell him that the plans have been changed and that he won't be going."

"I'm sorry, Jo. I won't do that."

Unable to contain herself, she leaped to her feet and paced angrily in front of him, turning to confront him with her hands on her hips and her whole body electric with outrage. "How can you sit there and *say* that? This is *my* son we're talking about, Gray. And I hate what you're getting him involved in. I've told you before how much I despise this whole macho nonsense about real men having to go out and do foolhardy, dangerous things to prove their manhood. I just *hate* it. And I'm warning you again that if you insist on going ahead with this, then I'll...I'll have to..." She hesitated, searching for words, almost too angry to think.

He sat and watched her quietly, his eyes following her with a calm, steady gaze as she paced in front of him. "I love you, Jo," he said.

"I'll have to—" she continued, and then broke off and stared at him, startled and confused. "What...what did you say?"

"I said that I love you. I've never loved anyone the way I love you. You mean the whole world to me. Do you ever give any thought to that?"

She continued to stare at him in stunned silence, unable to believe her ears.

"Doesn't it mean anything at all to you, Jo? Have you just forgotten about it? We made love, remember? We went to bed together," he said, leaning forward, his eyes dark and intense with feeling. "Have you just forgotten about it, put it out of your mind somehow? Because," he added grimly, sinking back against the fence rail behind him, "I sure as hell can't. Not for a second."

She licked her lips and tried to answer. "Of course...of course I haven't forgotten," she whispered. "It meant something to me, too, Gray. I don't...I don't just do that sort of thing as a matter of course, you know. But," she added, her voice strengthening a little, "I don't believe that you love me. If you cared about me, you wouldn't cause me this kind of pain."

"Jo, it's *because* I love you that I have to do this," he told her gently. "I'm trying to help you. Can't you see that? What you're trying to do to that boy is wrong, Jo, and I think you know it yourself. But you've suffered a terrible loss, and it's made you afraid of life. I want to help you get over that fear, for your own sake as well as Keith's."

She stared at him silently, thinking about his words, while he returned her gaze with steady compassion.

"I know it's dangerous what I'm doing," he went on. "Not because of any harm that might come to Keith, because I honestly don't think he's ever going to be badly hurt. It's dangerous because I might lose you over it, and any chance I could have had, possibly, of winning your love. But I have to take that risk, Jo, because I believe I'm right, and a man isn't worth anything if he's afraid to do what he believes is right."

"Gray, what gives you this . . . this overwhelming confidence? How can you be so sure all the time that you're right and everyone else is wrong? With Keith, with Peggy—all the time, you're just absolutely certain that you know what's best for everybody."

"We all have to follow what we believe to be the right course of action," he said quietly, "if we're people of integrity, Jo. But if somebody can prove to me that my position is wrong, I'm willing to change in a minute."

"I don't believe that. I don't believe you'd change, ever, no matter what anybody told you. You're too arrogant and too stubborn."

Gray smiled at her as she stood in front of him, her blue eyes sparkling with anger, her dark, sunlit curls framing her flushed, passionate face.

"Well," he said slowly, "you're hardly one to talk, you know. I swear, you could give lessons in stubbornness to a mule, Joanna McLean. But," he added, his brief, teasing smile fading into seriousness again, "I mean it, Jo. Prove to me that I'm wrong and I'll be happy to do it your way."

"And how do I prove it? *After* Keith is crippled or . . . or . . ." She choked briefly and then went on, "After that happens, then do I get to have the hollow satisfaction of hearing you say that you were wrong? Is that how it works, Gray?''

"Nothing bad is going to happen to Keith," he told her firmly. "I'm going to take him to these rodeos and see that he's properly instructed and has the best possible equipment, and he's going to have a great time and feel good about himself and develop a sense of purpose and self-esteem to carry him through these tough adolescent years, and nothing is going to harm him. And someday you're going to tell me I was right."

Jo looked at him for a long moment, her chest heaving, her eyes still almost black with the depth of her emotion. But when she spoke, her voice was calm and tightly controlled. "I can't stop you, Gray. And at his age I can't stop him, either. If I push too hard, I'll lose him, and I couldn't bear that. He means so much to me."

She hesitated, struggling with the difficult choice she had to make, while he watched with quiet, steady compassion. "I'll let him go to these rodeos, Gray. You've really given me no choice. And I'll be terrified every second he's gone, but for his sake I'll try not to show it. I'll try to be calm and not nag at him about it or let him know how frightened I am."

Gray's eyes sparkled with surprise and pleasure. "Jo, that's great! That's just what—"

"But," she interrupted coldly, "I'm not going to forgive you for this, Gray. I think it's terrible what you've done. I'd do anything I could to change it. But I'm helpless. A parent's only real hope, at this age, is that children don't fall under the wrong kind of influence," she went on steadily. "And I've just been unlucky, I guess. Goodbye, Gray."

She turned abruptly and walked away from him, opening the gate quietly and letting herself out of the corral. Then, without looking back, she started across the field toward the ranch yard and her truck.

Gray got to his feet and moved over to lean against the upper rail, watching her slim, erect figure, gilded with sunshine as she moved rapidly away. He stroked his chin thoughtfully with his thumb, his eyes troubled, and continued to watch until she reached the truck, got in and drove out of his yard and off down the prairie trail, topping a rise and disappearing into the vast blue bowl of the sky.

Then, still silent and unhappy, he turned aside, gathered the reins and swung back up onto his horse, swaying easily in the saddle as the big rangy gelding danced back out into the center of the arena.

CHAPTER TWELVE

"CARE FOR ANOTHER egg salad sandwich? A little sip of wine? Here, let me serenade you with a tune."

Jo giggled, brushed at a fly that buzzed drowsily around her head in the noonday warmth and accepted the proffered sandwich. "This is silly," she said. "Really silly. But fun," she added, munching on the sandwich and smiling across the plaid picnic blanket at her uncle, who sat crosslegged on the other side of the blanket with his tractor cap pushed back on his bald head and his violin tucked under his chin.

"Well, Joey, we can't keep on being miserable forever, you know. It's time we put all these problems out of our minds and had some fun, and there's nothing more fun than a picnic."

Jo chuckled. "A picnic at high noon on the bald prairie amid the scenic sagebrush."

"Well," he told her, grinning, "trees and that sort of thing are kind of scarce around here, I will admit. We just have to make do with what we have. And the slough is kind of pretty, don't you think?"

"Yes, Mac, it's pretty." Jo smiled again, tossed down a pillow and lay back, finishing the sandwich and lifting her face to the sun.

Two weeks had passed since her angry confrontation with Gray, and she hadn't spoken to him since, although, true to his word, he had taken Keith to another rodeo the very next weekend, and today the two of them were off somewhere.

again. She and Keith maintained a polite, edgy silence on the topic, but each time he was gone Jo suffered through a day of worry and tension until her son was safely home.

That, she thought, was probably why Mac had suggested their picnic today, and it was a good idea. Out here in Mac's big field, by the broad slough that was dark blue and brimming from the recent rainfall, she felt more at peace, less frightened and troubled about everything.

Mac, who frequently seemed capable of reading her mind, smiled at her gently. "Is it getting any easier, Joey? Seeing him go to these rodeos, I mean?"

"A little," Jo confessed. "Not," she added hastily, "that I'm learning to approve of it or think Gray's right in what he's doing or anything like that. But it *is* starting to be a little easier to bear, especially since he doesn't seem to be getting hurt at all."

Mac nodded and drew his bow experimentally across the strings of the violin. He frowned and tightened one of the pegs.

"It's so strange, you know, raising kids," Jo mused, closing her eyes drowsily in the sunlight. "You spend all your time protecting them when they're little, putting gates on the stairs and covering the electrical outlets and teaching them to cross the street safely. And then when they're fifteen you have to send them out and risk getting their necks broken."

"Joey, he's not going to—"

"I know, I know," she said hastily. "Just a figure of speech. This really is nice out here, you know, Mac," she added, looking around her with pleasure.

Ducks and geese swam sedately about on the surface of the slough, followed by noisy, fluffy broods of new chicks. Gulls and curlews soared overhead, uttering their sharp, incessant cries, and gophers darted here and there or sat upright on their little mounds of dirt, gazing with comical surprise at these large, strange-looking intruders. The remnants of Mac's decimated cattle herd, just a few Hereford cows with glossy red calves, grazed and slept all around the slough, while the calves frisked and played and butted heads with diminutive ferocity.

"Now that's a pretty sight," Mac said wistfully. "Nice Hereford cows with calves playing all around them, grazing by a slough on a warm sunny day. That's what ranching's all about."

He fell silent, and Jo knew what he was thinking. Their hope had been that the pigs would realize enough profit to pay off the outstanding interest on the bank loan so that the sale of these calves in the fall would enable Mac to buy more heifers and start building his cow herd back up so that his ranch would become a viable operation again. But now with the setback the current group of hogs had taken, the profit wasn't going to be enough, and the bank was going to pick up this piece of property, which he had mortgaged during the worst of his financial problems, and then he wouldn't have enough land to ranch anymore.

Jo shook herself a little and reminded herself that it was just this sort of gloomy speculation that they had come here to escape from.

"Come on, maestro," she murmured, giving Mac's bony knee a gentle nudge with her foot. "Some music, if you please."

He chuckled and drew the bow across the strings of his violin, while Jo propped herself on one elbow to pour herself a cup of coffee from the thermos. He started to play "Red River Valley," and Jo sang along in a low, clear voice. "Just remember the Red River Valley, and the cowboy who loves you so true...."

But the words suddenly made her think of Gray, sitting on his big horse with careless grace and then leaning on the fence, lithe and powerful in his faded work clothes, telling her that he loved her.

Her throat tightened, and she stopped singing and lay back, letting the rippling strains of music wash over her, mingling with the sunlight and the poignancy of her memories in a caressing warmth that was at the same time both sorrowful and almost unbearably sweet.

She was sorry when, finally, Mac stopped playing. A cloud drifted across the face of the sun, casting a shadow over the prairie, and the breeze freshened.

"Well, picnic's over, I guess," Mac said. "Time to go home and water those damn pigs."

He helped Jo gather together the remnants of their lunch, shook out the blanket and walked with her to the truck, carrying his violin case carefully in one hand and the picnic hamper in the other while Jo trailed him with the blanket and the thermos.

Bumping across the rutted prairie trail to the ranch buildings, he turned to her and smiled, his craggy face creasing with affection. "Nice picnic, Jo?"

She smiled back at him. "A lovely picnic," she assured him solemnly.

He grinned and drove into the yard. "Somebody's here," he announced, and then, taking a closer look at the horse tied to the corral fence, he added, "It's one of the twins. Amazing how much the girls love those awful pigs, isn't it?"

"Pigs are lovable animals," Jo said firmly. "I've always told you that."

Mac snorted and then sobered again, turning to look at his niece. "Jo, have you noticed anything strange about those girls lately?"

Jo pondered. "Well, they seem unhappy and quiet a lot of the time, but they also seem to be visiting even more than usual. One or the other of them is here almost every day, it seems."

"Yeah, I know, but they're hardly ever together anymore. Did you notice that?"

"Come to think of it," Jo said slowly, "you're right. They seem to come alone, just about all the time. Actually," she added thoughtfully, "it's usually Libby who's been coming lately, isn't it? I asked her the other day if Peggy was mad at us or something."

Mac frowned as he parked the truck near the Quonset. "So did I just a little while ago. But I think it's more likely that they're fighting with each other. They used to do that when they were little—get mad and have a fight and then stay away from each other for a week or so until somebody decided to make up. Usually Elizabeth," he added with a grin. "Little Princess Margaret was always too stubborn and hotheaded to be much of a peacemaker."

"They were certainly fighting a couple of weeks ago when I saw them over at Gray's," Jo said thoughtfully, remembering the hushed, bitter quarrel between the twins. "The tension was so thick that day you could have scooped it up with a spoon."

"Well, I told Libby that I wanted that sister of hers to come over and see us. I'm getting worried about her. It's not like my Peggy to stay miserable for so long and ignore her old friends."

Jo nodded again. "I'm worried about her, too, Mac. I can't help feeling nervous about what she's going to do."

"Did you try to talk with Gray about it?" Mac asked, pausing with his hand on the door latch.

"Nobody can talk with Gray about anything," Jo said bitterly, staring straight ahead through the dusty windshield.

Mac knew better than to pursue *that* topic. He got out of the truck and lifted the picnic hamper from the back while Jo stepped down to greet the girl, who had heard their arrival and emerged from the pig barn.

Jo noted with relief that it was Peggy, after all, who was visiting today. As usual she looked exotic and beautiful, wearing a brilliant turquoise shirt over her jeans with a matching headband, shot through with silver sparkles, tied around her forehead.

"They're looking so much better now, aren't they?" Peggy called as she approached. "Their tails are all curly and everything. But," she added, pausing to smile a warm greeting at Jo, "they sure aren't getting very big."

"No, they aren't," Jo agreed. "They took a terrible setback with that flu. How are you today, Peg?"

"Fine," the girl said. "Just great."

But the tense, unhappy look in her green eyes belied her words. Jo gave her a quick, thoughtful glance and said, "Come on up and have a cup of coffee with me, okay? Mac and I have been on a picnic, and I'm still in a holiday mood. The garden needs to be weeded, but I don't feel like doing any work just yet."

"No kidding. A picnic?" Peggy asked wistfully, falling into step beside them as they carried the hamper and other supplies to the house. "I wish I'd known. I would have loved to come along."

Mac helped them unpack the hamper and then left to go to the east field, where he was removing a string of rotted fence posts. Jo and Peggy stayed in the kitchen, sipping their coffee and talking quietly.

Jo found she was growing really concerned about the girl. There was none of Peggy's normal ebullience or her outrageous wit and teasing high spirits. Instead, she seemed quiet, detached and terribly worried.

"Peg...would you like to talk with me about...anything? I'm not all that wise, but I *am* older, and maybe I could give a little perspective at least. Sometimes," Jo added, "it helps just to tell somebody."

Peggy shook her head and looked away, her face distant and full of pain. Jo got up silently to refill their coffee mugs, looking back over her shoulder at the girl's still profile.

Suddenly a cold chill gripped her, making her tremble with terror. There was something about the curve of the girl's cheek, the line of her mouth...

Jo set the coffeepot carefully down on the counter, turned and spoke very softly. "Libby," she said.

"Yes?" the girl asked, looking absently over her shoulder. Then, realizing what she'd done, she flushed to the roots of her hair and looked down at her hands. Her lips quivered, and she made a little choking noise, then began to sob.

Jo came swiftly across the room and put her arm around the girl's slender shoulders. "It's all right, Libby. It's all right," she murmured. "We'll work this out. But you have to tell me the truth. Where is she?"

The girl raised her tear-streaked face to Jo's, her eyes dark with fear. "I don't know," she whispered.

Jo sank slowly into a nearby chair, still holding Libby's shoulders, and stared at her. The knot of terror tightened in her stomach, making her feel weak and nauseated. "You don't know?"

Libby shook her head miserably. "She left, Jo. She said she was going to find Rob and stay with him."

"How long ago?"

"Two weeks. Remember the day you came over to our place, and Peg and I were fighting?"

Jo nodded.

"Well, that's the day she left. I drove her to the bus, and she went to Calgary, and that's the last I've heard of her."

Jo stared at the girl. "And you've been doing this... playing both parts... for two whole *weeks*?"

"I promised. She made me swear that I'd do it to keep Dad from finding out, so she'd have time to find Rob."

"But . . . but how on earth did you manage it?"

Libby dug into the pocket of her jeans for a tissue and wiped her eyes. "It's surprising how easy it is. We've been doing it all our lives just for fun."

"I know," Jo said dryly. "Mac told me about your 'twin games.' But surely it must be harder now that you're older."

"Not really. You see, we dress so differently, and when the hair and the headband is like this—" she gestured to her own hair "—everybody just assumes it's Peggy. Dad would have known right away, of course, if I'd talked to him much, but then he and Peg haven't been speaking for weeks, so when I'm being Peggy, I just stay away from him. But I've been wishing that I hadn't ever promised her I'd do this. I'm so glad you found out," she said, her words coming in a tumbling rush now that her lonely, terrifying ordeal was over and she was finally able to talk about it. "It's awful, Jo," she whispered, staring up at the older woman, her face white beneath her tan. "I'm so scared."

"Why, Libby? Why are you scared? Because of what your father will do when he finds out?"

Libby shook her head, and her brilliant hair flew about her face, sparkling like fire in the sunny kitchen.

"Then why?" Jo persisted.

"Because," Libby whispered, "she doesn't even know where Rob is. She's all alone in the city, looking for him, and she doesn't have a clue where to find him. And I haven't heard from her since she left. She could be dead, Jo! She could be lying in an alley somewhere, and nobody would even know who she is!"

Libby began to cry in earnest, and Jo took the girl in her arms, murmuring and soothing her like a little child. "It's all right," she whispered, stroking Libby's silken hair and her hot forehead. "It's all right, dear. We'll find her. It's all right."

When the storm of tears finally subsided, and Libby began to compose herself again, Jo returned to her urgent questions. "Libby, you said she doesn't know where Rob is. What do you mean?"

Libby sniffled and looked bleakly at Jo. "After Rob came to the ranch that last time and Dad kicked him out—do you know about that?"

Jo nodded tensely. "Yes, I know. Go on."

"Well, Rob called Peg after that and told her that it would be best for her if he just split, dropped out of her life. He didn't want to cause that kind of trouble for her, he said."

"That seems like a fairly unselfish thing for him to do."

"It was. He really loves her, Jo. He's crazy about her. He'd do anything to keep from hurting her, and I guess he thought that was the best thing to do, considering the way Dad feels about him."

Libby sobbed again quietly, and Jo waited.

"Right afterward, Peg tried to call him, but his landlady said he'd moved. So then she called the store where he works, and he'd quit his job, too. Then Peg just flipped out. She was so scared he was going to leave . . . go down east or something, and she'd never be able to find him, so she went to Calgary to look for him."

"But . . ." Jo considered this, appalled. "Where's she staying? Will she be able to find him?"

"I don't know," Libby whispered. "I just don't know. She cleaned out her bank account and took a few clothes, and that's all I know."

"Oh, my God!"

Jo sat silently, thinking, and Libby peeped up at her with the relief of a child who has, at last, confided her troubles to someone who will be able to help. "Jo, what are you going to do?"

"Well," Jo said briskly, "first, I'm going to tell your dad. And then we're going to Calgary to find her and bring her home."

"Jo," Libby said in panic, "don't do that! You can't tell Dad about this!"

"Of course I can. I have to tell him. He needs to know this, Libby. It isn't just some kind of harmless adolescent prank. This is really serious."

"But he'll kill her, Jo. He'll be so mad. It'll be just awful."

"What do you mean, 'kill her'?" Jo asked sharply.

"Oh, I don't mean it literally," Libby said. "He's never been that kind of father. I can't remember either of us even getting a spanking. Although," she added with a wan, reminiscent smile, "when we were little, we certainly deserved a few. But he gets so furious, Jo, and he lets you know that he's so terribly disappointed in you, and it hurts so much."

"Well, that's beside the point. Mad or not, he has to know about this, Libby. We have to find her." Jo got up and rinsed their cups out, smiling at the girl in an attempt to reassure her. "It's going to be all right, Libby," she added gently with considerably more confidence than she actually felt. "If something terrible had happened, we'd have heard about it. And we're going to find her. I promise."

For the first time the tense, terrified look began to fade from the girl's eyes, and she smiled faintly. "Thanks, Jo," she said shyly. "You're just wonderful." She hesitated. "Could I . . . do you think I could stay and . . . and help you weed the garden or whatever? It's so lonely at home, and Dad and Keith won't be back from the rodeo until late."

Jo grinned. "Now *that's* what I like to hear! Wait'll you see those weeds. We need machete knives just to get in there!"

She continued talking nonsense in a bright, cheerful voice while she collected the gardening tools from the porch. Libby relaxed visibly and followed her outside into the sunlight, looking as if a mighty burden had been lifted from her slender shoulders.

MAC STUDIED the checkerboard thoughtfully and then looked up at his niece. "Jo, are you *sure* you want to make that particular move?"

Jo tore her gaze away from the dark square of window framing a nearly full moon and a few stars. "Why not?" she asked in a distracted voice, and looked down at the board, where her uncle was pointing a long, knobby finger. "Oh, I see. Well, maybe not. Thanks, Mac," she added, giving him a weak smile and returning her checker to its original position, out of the danger she had carelessly placed it in.

He tilted back in his chair and studied her bent head, his gentle, weathered face quiet and concerned. "It's going to be all right, you know, Jo," he said firmly. "Just as soon as Gray gets here and you tell him, he'll make plans to go and find her. She'll be fine. She's with Rob right now, I'm sure, and safe and well. If she was hurt or something, just like you told Libby, Gray would have heard about it before now."

Jo met his eyes miserably. "I know you're probably right, Mac. But I just can't help..." She paused, listening intently. "Mac, do you hear something?"

He nodded. "That's probably them. Wouldn't likely be anybody else this time of night. You'd better go out and watch for him, Jo. He usually just drops Keith off and leaves without coming in, doesn't he?"

Jo nodded grimly. "Gray never seems all that anxious to visit with me after these rodeos."

She ran through the kitchen, grabbed her denim jacket from its hook in the porch and went outside to sit on the step, watching for Gray's truck. He pulled into the yard and parked by the gate, and Keith hopped out the passenger door, saying something cheerfully to the man in the truck.

"Keith," Jo called, standing up quickly in the pool of light from the lamp above the steps. "Tell Gray I need to talk with him for a minute, would you, please?"

As soon as Keith saw his mother and heard her words, his shoulders tightened and his smile faded into a firm, stubborn, despairing line.

"Aw, *Mom*," he said, letting himself through the gate and starting up the walk toward her, "can't you just let it *go* just this once? Please? I'm fine, Mom. Look at me. Not a mark on me."

Jo looked him over with one, quick, anxious glance and saw that what he said was true. But she shook her head, trying to smile at him. "You're so conceited that you think you're the only thing that's ever on my mind. It just so happens, my boy, that I want to talk with Gray about something entirely different, something that has nothing to do with you. Nothing at all."

"Honest?" he asked, hesitating by the door.

"Honest. Now go to bed." She paused. "No trophies today?" she asked, forcing herself to keep her voice light and cheerful, as if they were discussing a school play or a math exam.

He looked at her in amazement and then shook his head. "I rode to the whistle, but my steer hardly bucked at all, and I marked too low to win anything."

"Well, at least you didn't get bucked off," she observed in that same tone of casual interest. "That's good, isn't it?"

Keith stared at her and finally gave her a slow, wondering smile. "Mom, you just freak me out. You really do."

Jo smiled back at him and reached out to ruffle his hair fondly, noticing that, for once, he didn't dodge away from her hand. "Go to bed," she said firmly. "After all, athletes in training need their sleep. Right?"

Keith grinned, still shaking his head in wonder, and disappeared inside the house.

Jo turned and walked slowly down the walk to where Gray waited by his truck, wary and silent. "I need to talk to you, Gray," she said without preliminaries.

He tensed and leaned against the fender of the truck. His face was silent, its strong planes etched with silver in the moonlight, and he looked down at her steadily. "I'm listening," he said in a careful, expressionless tone.

"Gray, it's not what you think. It's... it's about Peggy."

Impulsively she reached out and took his hard brown hand, holding it in both of her own while she told him about her day's discovery, about Libby's incredible masquerade and her fears for her sister's safety.

Gray listened, staring out at the moonlit yard and saying nothing, but his grip tightened convulsively on Jo's fingers until she almost cried aloud with pain. Finally he dropped her hand and turned around, resting his elbows wearily on the fender of his truck and burying his face in his hands. "Damn," he muttered. "What a fool I've been."

"Gray..." Helplessly, her heart aching for him, Jo slipped an arm around his shoulders and held him briefly. "Gray, you couldn't have known she was going to do something like this."

He lifted his head and looked at her, his eyes dark and bleak in the moonlight. "Maybe not. But I've raised that girl since she was a baby. I should have known how far I could push her without forcing her into something desperate." He paused and stared down at the woman beside him. "Why don't you go ahead and say it?"

"Say what?"

"Say that you told me so. Tell me I was wrong and stubborn and a damn fool and that you were right all along."

Jo looked at him in sorrow. "None of that matters now, Gray. It doesn't matter a bit who was right and who was